"I'VE GO
IT'S AN

"Get us on the ground, _____ Dolan said tersely.

While the pilot desperately tried to duck under the radar-directed gun, McCarter searched for the threat with his infrared target seeker. When his helmet visor pip blinked to indicate that he had a lock on, he squeezed the trigger.

The chain gun growled as a string of 20 mm tracers reached out from the Osprey's nose turret and connected with the ground. A twitch of the turret-control joystick walked the fire to the left and raised a bright secondary explosion that put the 23 mm gun out of action.

Turbines screaming on full-reverse pitch, Grimaldi dropped the rest of the way onto the sand. "Go, go, go," he yelled, hitting the rear-ramp release.

Even with the advance warning from the antiaircraft gun, the defenders were still running for their posts when the Stony Man force hit the sand. James and Encizo dropped their initial targets, then raced for the perimeter trenches, trying to get there before the Libyans. If they could take out all the heavy firepower in the bunkers, they just might be able to get out of there alive.

Other titles available in this series:

STONY MAN II
STONY MAN III
STONY MAN IV
STONY MAN V
STONY MAN VI
STONY MAN VII
STONY MAN VIII
#9 STRIKEPOINT
#10 SECRET ARSENAL
#11 TARGET AMERICA
#12 BLIND EAGLE
#13 WARHEAD
#14 DEADLY AGENT
#15 BLOOD DEBT

DON PENDLETON'S

MACK BOLAN.

STONY MAN™

DEEP ALERT

A GOLD EAGLE BOOK FROM

WORLDWIDE.

TORONTO • NEW YORK • LONDON
AMSTERDAM • PARIS • SYDNEY • HAMBURG
STOCKHOLM • ATHENS • TOKYO • MILAN
MADRID • WARSAW • BUDAPEST • AUCKLAND

First edition May 1995

ISBN 0-373-61900-6

Special thanks and acknowledgment to
Michael Kasner for his contribution to this work.

DEEP ALERT

DEEP ALERT

PROLOGUE

Republic of the Ukraine

The gentle lapping of the Black Sea against the docks and the hulls of the ships and the creaking of hawsers were the only sounds that could be heard in the massive Russian naval shipyard south of the Ukrainian city of Sevastopol. It was past midnight on a moonless night, and, except for a single light at the guardhouse at the entrance to the yard, all was dark. Electricity was too precious in the new Ukrainian Republic to waste it on ships that would never go to sea.

The fledgling government of the Ukraine had signed a treaty with the Russians that would divide up the old Soviet Black Sea Fleet between the two nations. In another treaty, the Ukraine had agreed to surrender the Soviet nuclear missiles that had been stored on its soil.

The Nikolayev Shipyard Number 444 was where the now-defunct Soviet Union had built its aircraft carriers. Now that the yard was in Ukrainian hands, the fate of the partially completed hulls moored at the docks was in question. The full-deck, nuclear carrier *Varyag* was seventy percent complete, and there was talk of the Ukrainians finishing the ship for sale to a foreign customer. China and India both had been mentioned. Most of the uncompleted vessels, however, were destined for the breaker's yard and conversion into industrial materials and consumer goods.

Almost hidden among the hulls of the larger ships was the small, sleek shape of a submarine. Most Soviet submarines had been built at the massive Severodvinsk Shipyard Number 402 on the northern Baltic coast. This particular submarine, however, had been constructed in this Black Sea yard to hide it from the American and NATO spy satellites that kept such a close watch on the Number 402 yard on the Baltic. It had been the simple matter of hiding a small needle among much larger nails, but it had worked. No one in the Defense Department or any of the American intelligence services had any idea of this sub's existence.

Based on the design of the Soviet Alfa-class nuclear attack sub, this ship looked like an Alfa's big brother until under closer scrutiny. The sails of the Alfas were sleek and streamlined to better slice through the water, but this sub's sail was sharply faceted like a flattened diamond.

The Alfa's titanium hull was a sleek, unbroken curve from her rounded nose to the single prop at her stern, and she looked like a science-fiction space-ship. This sub's hull, however, while still showing its Alfa parentage, was decidedly different. For one thing, it was longer by roughly thirty meters and the nose was more sharply pointed. The biggest difference, however, was that the sub's hull wasn't sleek and round like an Alfa's. Sharp-edged chines that ran most of the length of the hull on each side made the hull's cross section an ovoid. It looked as if someone had put an Alfa boat's hull into a vise and squeezed it.

The four rectangular, cruciform tail fins that served to "fly" the Alfa through the water were also absent. They had been replaced by three triangular fins set at the 0-, 120- and 240-degree positions directly in front of the single nine-bladed screw that would drive the submarine through the water at well over fifty knots.

The Russians called their Alfa boats the "submarine interceptor submarines" because of their speed, maneuverability and deep-diving capabilities. The new sub could be termed the "stealth fighter submarine interceptor." The changes to the hull, sail and fin had been designed to deflect sonar pulses the way the airframes of the American stealth aircraft had been designed to deflect radar pulses.

The Alfa boat had been fast and deep diving, but it had been very noisy. Its reactor had been cooled by a liquid-metal mix of lead and bithnium, and the pumps needed to drive the coolant had been massive. Also, her single-screw design, though fast, had produced serious low-pressure cavitation at speeds above forty knots.

To date, the state of the art in underwater silent weapons systems had been the U.S. Navy's Seawolf-class attack submarines. Billions of American tax dollars had been spent redesigning the mechanical components of the Seawolf to reduce noise levels far beyond anything known before. More of those dollars, however, should have been spent on background security checks for the men and women working on the Seawolf project.

During the design and prototype phase, two engineers had fed the Soviets a steady stream of information relating to the new sub. In particular, they had given them material about the Seawolf's silent-running mechanical systems and a new design for a screw that didn't cavitate at high revolutions.

With the results of the Seawolf research to work with, the Russian engineers had been able to duplicate the American sub's silent-running systems. In fact, they had even made a small improvement or two. The old liquid-cooled reactor of the Alfas had been replaced by a silent-running, American high-pressure type. The screw cavitation noises had also been silenced by a complete redesign.

With her stealth hull and Seawolf-style mechanical systems, this lone ex-Soviet sub in the Nikolayev

Shipyard Number 444 was the world's first stealth submarine. If she were to set to sea, it would be difficult, if not impossible, to detect her when she was operating under the surface. Particularly if no one even knew of her existence.

Unlike with the unfinished aircraft carrier *Varyag,* however, the fate of the prototype stealth sub was no longer in question.

A group of half a dozen men quickly made their way past the silent hulls tied up to the docks of the shipyard. As well as not wanting to waste electrical power, the Ukrainians didn't want to waste manpower guarding ships that were destined to be turned into scrap metal. When the men reached the submarine, known only by her hull number, 3865, they silently opened a hatch in her hull and disappeared inside.

Once the hatch closed behind them, Hull Number 3865 became the *Simon Petlyura,* a ship of the fledgling Ukrainian navy named after the first Ukrainian minister of defense in 1917.

Fifteen minutes later, there was a soft sigh of escaping air from pressure tanks as the sub started to settle in the water. She sank lower until her deck was awash and the single nine-bladed screw at her stern was completely submerged. A few moments later, the large screw began to turn slowly and the stealth sub inched away from her mooring.

Once clear of the harbor mouth, the *Petlyura* silently slipped beneath the waves and turned her pointed nose to the Black Sea and the west.

HOURS LATER, Captain Oleg Yatkin rested the *Petlyura* on the bottom of the Black Sea at the entrance of the Bosporus, the start of the two-hundred-mile passage that connected the landlocked Black Sea to the Mediterranean. The Bosporus had always presented a challenge to mariners. From the time men first put to sea in the Old World, they had told stories and had made up myths about the perils of its passage.

The Bosporus is eighteen miles long and roughly seven hundred yards wide at its narrowest. The surface current runs to the southwest at an astonishing four to five nautical miles per hour. Deep down, however, a countercurrent runs in the opposite direction. These turbulent currents and coutercurrents make the passage tricky even for modern ships.

The wild waters rushing through the narrow channel also created so much noise that it was difficult for even the most skilled sonar man to detect a submarine passing through it. And since the end of the cold war, though the sonar watch was still being kept, it wasn't being kept well. Russian subs still came through the Bosporus, but they came announced in advance and on the surface.

Since Yatkin didn't want to announce the passage of his stolen sub, he kept the *Petlyura* on the bottom as he waited for a particular ship that was scheduled to make the passage from the Black Sea to the Mediterranean. The ship in question was an American-owned oil supertanker flying the Liberian flag of convenience. She had been chosen because of her size and the corresponding size of her wake as she drove through the water. The big ship would clear a path for them, and her wake was the perfect place to hide a submarine.

"That should be her," the first officer announced, taking the sonar earphones from his head.

"Bring us up to periscope depth," Yatkin told the helmsman.

A few minutes later, the tip of the periscope broke through the waves. Though it was night, the steel cutout letters welded to the ship's stern were lighted and Yatkin could make out the name *AMOCO—Georgia*.

"That's her," he said. "Get ready to follow in her wake."

Yatkin brought his sub in a circle to move in behind the supertanker within three hundred meters of her stern. Even though the sub displaced four thousand tons when submerged, tucked in so close behind the larger ship, the pounding of the tanker's huge screws churning the water hammered the *Petlyura* as though she were a tin drum. The swirls and crosscurrents buffeted her, as well. Yatkin and the two dozen men of his makeshift crew hung on to anything they could to keep their feet.

With the Turkish sonar men on duty, Yatkin couldn't use his depth-ranging sonar to see how close he was to the rocky bottom of the passage. He had to rely on his charts and pray that they were as accurate as man could make them. Even with her titanium hull, the *Petlyura* couldn't afford to scrape against the rocks.

The supertanker made the passage in a little more than an hour with the submarine right behind her. At the southern exit of the Bosporus, she entered the Sea of Marmara, a widening of the waterway. This sea is more like a landlocked lake leading to the Dardanelles, the last narrow passage before the open waters of the Mediterranean.

Once in the calmer water, Yatkin slowed the sub temporarily to give the tanker a greater lead and lessen the pounding his crew was taking. He kept his new distance when the tanker entered the Dardanelles. Though longer than the Bosporus, this passage wasn't as rigorous, and Yatkin was able to use his depth-ranging sonar.

Right on time, the supertanker's screws took on a different sound as her captain reached the open sea of the Mediterranean and increased his engine revolutions to full speed. Slowly the hammering lessened as she pulled away from the slow-moving submarine.

A faint smile formed on Yatkin's face as he turned to his helmsman. They had escaped from the Black Sea without being detected. "Take us down to a hundred meters and steer a course of one-nine-eight," he ordered.

"Depth one hundred, course one-nine-eight, aye, Captain."

That course would take the sub to the south of the Greek island of Lemnos and into the international waters of the Aegean Sea. There, the *Petlyura* would have to stay clear of the U.S. 6th Fleet until they were in position to make the run north to the coast of Yugoslavia.

Yatkin laid his hand on his first officer's shoulder. "I'm going to my cabin. Give the crew as much rest as you can and call me when we pass Lemnos."

"Aye, Captain," the first officer answered.

OLEG YATKIN LAY on the bare mattress of the bunk in his cabin. As with most of the rest of the nonessential furnishings, bedding hadn't been on board when he and his small crew had spirited the submarine away from the Nikolayev shipyard. But even though it had been days since he had had a full night's rest, the Ukrainian captain didn't go right to sleep. He was still running on adrenaline and would be until the sub was safely tied up to the dock in Split.

He had come a long way from his days as a lowly cadet in the Soviet naval academy to being the captain of the most powerful ship of any independent navy and one of the most powerful in the world. Not even the Americans had a submarine like the *Petlyura*. They had their Boomers, as they called their ballistic missile launching subs, and they had their Seawolf and Los Angeles–class attack subs. But they didn't have a single ship that could carry out both missions, as well as being a submarine that couldn't be detected by any known means. It was the last part of that equation, though, that was the most important for the future of the new Ukrainian Republic.

Even though the Ukraine was now free and independent of Russian domination, she hadn't always been. The Ukrainians had suffered under the Russians for centuries. The worst, though, had been when the Communists triumphed in Mother Russia and brought their harsh rule to the fertile farmlands of the Ukraine. The collectivism of farms and poorly thought out five-year plans almost destroyed the Ukrainians as a people. Tens of thousands more died when Stalin tightened his grip on them in the 1930s.

It wasn't surprising that when the German army blitzed into the Ukraine in 1941, the Ukrainians welcomed them as liberators from Communist Russian domination. Many Ukrainians joined the German army and fought all the way to Stalingrad before the huge Red Army overwhelmed the Germans by sheer numbers and handed them a disastrous defeat. Then came Hitler's long retreat.

When the Germans were pushed out of the Ukraine in the waning days of WWII, the Soviet Russians moved back in with a vengeance. After their troops ended all armed resistance, the NKVD, the secret police, followed close behind them. Any Ukrainian who was suspected of having cooperated with the Germans in any way disappeared. Some of them disappeared permanently; some disappeared to the infamous gulags of Siberia.

Yet Ukrainian partisans fighting for their nation's independence continued the struggle against the Soviet occupation forces until 1952. The desire of the Ukrainians to live free didn't die with the last of the partisans, however. It just went into hibernation. Then came the breakup of the Soviet Union in 1990 and freedom again for the Ukrainian people.

Even though the Ukraine was free to pursue her own destiny now, the shadow of the Russian bear was still heavy on the land. The Ukrainian army, while sizable and fairly well armed, wouldn't be a match for the full power of the Russian military machine if it tried to take back what had once been called the "Breadbasket of the Soviet Union."

The only thing that kept the new Russians at bay was the fact that the withdrawal of the old Red Army had left enough ex-Soviet ballistic nuclear missiles behind to make the Ukraine the world's third largest nuclear power. The missiles had been retargeted, and now were aimed at the heart of Russia. The problem was that the Ukrainian president had been forced into signing a treaty to give back all the ex-Soviet nuclear missiles on Ukrainian soil to the Russians. Without the threat of a nuclear weapon defense, it would be all too easy for the Russians to overwhelm them again.

This threat was behind the nationalists' plan to steal the *Petlyura* from the Nikolayev Shipyard. The nuclear missiles she carried would ensure that the Russian bear wouldn't threaten the Ukraine until the fledgling republic could take her rightful place in the world.

That this critical task of guarding his homeland had fallen to Oleg Yatkin was a fine irony. His grandfather had fallen victim to the NKVD right after WWII ended. Because of that, Yatkin's father had been put on the politically unreliable list and had spent his life working as a janitor. Oleg himself had been able to overcome his family background only by joining the Young Communists as soon as he was old enough. It had been done, though, at his father's urging. As his father had said, if Ukrainians were ever to control their own destiny, they needed to be trained and ready. And since the Communists controlled the military, he would have to become one of them so he could be trained.

It had been difficult being a Ukrainian in the Soviet naval academy, but he had persevered and had volunteered for the elite submarine fleet upon graduation and commissioning. He had done well in the all-volunteer force, rising to the position of first officer on an Alfa-class attack boat before the Soviet collapse. Now he commanded the most dangerous submarine that had ever gone to sea.

CHAPTER ONE

Stony Man Farm, Virginia

Fall colors had come to the densely forested Blue Ridge Mountains of Virginia. Though spring was always a nice time of year in the Shenandoah Valley, the autumn was truly spectacular. During the bloody Civil War this had been the "Valley of Humiliation" for the Union forces, as Confederate General Thomas "Stonewall" Jackson waged his campaigns against the Union. Now, more than 125 years later, much of the region was a national park only eighty miles from Washington, D.C.

Carved into the foothills was a small farm. Named after Stony Man Mountain, one of the highest peaks in the area, this farm didn't look much different than the other small farms in the valley. In the center of the grounds was a three-story main farmhouse, with two outbuildings flanking it and a tractor barn in the back. On the surface, it looked like a legitimate agricultural enterprise, complete with farmhands and the well-used machinery necessary for making a living from the fertile earth of the valley. The land closest to the house was planted in row crops, while apple and peach orchards formed a wall around the outer perimeter.

But along with the agricultural enterprise, Stony Man Farm also served as the operational base for the most covert arm of the United States government, the Sensitive Operations Group. As the command center for the elite antiterrorist and antiorganized-crime operations, the innocent-looking buildings of the Farm concealed the equipment and personnel needed to track data, gather intelligence and make war on the nation's most elusive enemies, domestic and foreign.

The men who saw to the Farm's day-to-day agricultural operations were more than your run-of-the-mill hands. Though they were clandestinely armed during the day, at night they traded their work-worn blue jeans and faded shirts for combat blacksuits, face paint, night-vision goggles and high-tech fire-power. They patrolled the grounds during the hours of darkness, adding their trained eyes to the mechanical and electronic security systems.

Inside the farmhouse, a big man sat in a wheelchair in front of a bank of computer terminals and monitors. Aaron "The Bear" Kurtzman, the Farm's resident computer genius, was intently reading the information scrolling across his monitor when Barbara Price, the Farm's mission controller, walked up behind him.

"We just got a flash message from the Russian SVR," she announced to Kurtzman. "It seems that someone stole their prototype stealth submarine from one of the Ukrainian Black Sea shipyards."

"Say again?" Kurtzman wheeled his chair around to face her. "I know about the B-2 stealth bombers, the F-117 stealth fighters and even the still-classified Aurora stealth spy plane, but a stealth sub?"

"According to this—" she handed him a long printout "—before the collapse occurred, the Soviets were working on a prototype attack sub that would be invisible to sonar. It was supposed to be similar to the Seawolf class we're building and had the same mission, a sub-killing sub. Apparently it was complete except for final outfitting and was ready for testing when they stopped working on it."

Kurtzman sighed. "I suppose they want us to find their missing sub and send it back to them? Just another routine job. Funny how it all worked out, that the SVR, the inheritors of the former KGB, should be looking to us for assistance."

One of the drawbacks to the collapse of the old Soviet Union was that the United States was now the sole superpower in the world. When something went wrong, it was the United States that had to sort it out. The Russians were more than willing to help in any way they could, particularly when the trouble was in one of their old territories. But, with the new Russian republic's budget and political restraints, their out-of-country operations had been cut to almost zero.

"Actually not," she replied. "This was just an FYI, for your information. Apparently, in the name of glasnost, this submarine was one of the things they promised not to work on anymore and it was scheduled to be dismantled. Now that it's missing, they wanted us to know that it's no longer under their control."

Kurtzman shook his head slowly. "Did this sub by any chance happen to disappear with a full weapons load?"

Price frowned. "They're working on that part of it right now. Apparently there's been something going on at the naval arsenal in that yard, involving falsified inventories. You know how the Russians are about admitting to a screwup."

"When did this happen?"

"That's the problem—the Russians aren't sure. They just discovered the sub was missing yesterday, and they don't know when anyone saw it last."

"Is Hal aware of this yet?"

"I don't think so."

On paper, Hal Brognola was a high-ranking agent in the Justice Department and a liaison officer to the White House. He was also director of the Sensitive Operations Group, and the man who passed the President's orders to the people who would do the work in the field. As well, the big Fed briefed the

President on intelligence that originated at Stony Man Farm, and the Man in the Oval Office would want to know about the missing stealth submarine ASAP.

"Better flash it to him. And we'd better keep on the Russians about the weapons issue. We need to know what got shipped out in that sub."

"What's the latest from Mack?" Price changed the subject to their current operation in progress, a clandestine counterterrorist hit in the Middle East.

Kurtzman turned back to the keyboard, punched in a code word and read from the timetable that appeared on his monitor. "They're supposed to be kicking off before long. We should hear from them in a couple of hours."

The long-sought lead on Abu Askari's hideout in the Bekaa Valley of Lebanon had been a very welcome piece of intelligence at Stony Man Farm. Even though his band of murderers was small as far as terrorist groups went, their methods were particularly brutal, and their chosen victims were usually women and children.

"I hope he zeros that bastard this time." Price's voice was tight. She would never become accustomed to seeing the shattered bodies of innocents. To celebrate, as it were, the signing of the newest peace accord between the Israeli government and the Palestinians, Abu Askari had set his pack of killers on a small school. Almost two dozen small bodies had been butchered this time, along with their teachers.

"This is the best lead we've ever had on him," Kurtzman said. Several times previously, missions targeted against Abu Askari and his Soldiers of God had been aborted at the last moment when he had slipped away.

"He'll get him this time," Kurtzman predicted. "We have the Palestinian leaders' fullest coopera- tion. Now that Arafat has gone legit, he's trying hard to look like a real member of the world community. Having a man like Askari killing women and chil- dren in the name of the Palestinian people isn't the way to polish your image."

The Palestinians had leaked the information about Askari's hiding place that was making Bolan's strike possible. Not only had the Soldiers of God's recent attack threatened the latest peace accord, Abu As- kari had announced that he personally was going to kill Arafat for "crimes" against the Palestinian peo- ple. The PLO chairman was having a difficult enough time smoothing the political waters. He didn't need to have a madman gunning for him as well.

"While we're waiting to hear from Mack, I'll get the SVR report to Hal and see what he wants us to do about the stealth sub."

"Considering that we don't have much in the line of attack submarines or antisubmarine aircraft lying around here," Kurtzman stated, "I'd say this one will have to go to the Navy to take care of."

"You've got a point. But knowing Hal, he'll get us involved if he thinks we can help."

The "sensitive operations group" title of the organization she headed meant exactly that—when the problem was too sensitive to be handled through normal channels, the Stony Man Farm teams were given the job. A missing stealth sub, while out of their normal realm of activity, could well fall into that category.

Two hours after Barbara Price sent the Russian report to Brognola, he was back to them with a priority message from the President. Not only was Stony Man to get involved in the hunt for the stealth sub, they would lead the search and do the coordination between all the Intelligence services and armed forces looking for it, as well.

She handed Kurtzman the printout from Brognola. "The Man says that it's our turn in the barrel again."

"It's always our turn." The Bear shook his head slowly as he read the hard copy. "How in the hell are we going to find a stolen submarine?"

CHAPTER TWO

On the Israeli-Lebanese Border

Mack Bolan scanned the rocks and scrub brush on the barren Lebanese hills in front of him with his night-vision goggles one last time before clicking in his throat mike. "Three Zero," he said softly.

A voice from the small earphone in his left ear gave him the countersign, "Four Six."

Motioning for his team to follow him, Bolan moved forward to link up with the small Israeli recon team inside the Israeli "security zone," which separated the Jewish state from the terrorist camps in southern Lebanon.

A single shadow detached itself from the other shadows and Bolan saw that it was a man wearing a combat blacksuit.

"Belasko?" the man whispered, using Bolan's cover name for the operation.

"Right," Bolan said, extending his gloved hand.

"Captain Yacob Hod, sir." The Israeli shook his hand. "Glad to meet you."

He'd noted that the tall man in front of him had come prepared to fight. He wore an Israeli-made .44 Magnum Desert Eagle semiauto pistol on his hip, and a Beretta 93-R autoloader in a shoulder rig. A 9 mm Heckler & Koch MP-5 SD-3 with the folding stock and built-in silencer was slung over his shoulder, and his assault harness was loaded with grenades. It was quite a combat load for a stealthy night raid, but the big man wore the weight as if he had been born bearing it.

The Israeli recon officer looked around. "Where is the rest of your team?"

Bolan made a small motion with his right hand and five silent shadows moved up to join him. "We're all here."

Hod was mildly surprised to see that the rest of this mysterious team was as heavily armed as its leader. Whoever these men were, they weren't playing around.

Each member of Phoenix Force was an experienced warrior and brought a combat specialty to the team as well as their own personal reason for joining Bolan's covert war.

Calvin James was an ex-Navy SEAL by way of the mean streets of Chicago. An expert knife fighter, parachutist, scuba diver, martial-arts and small-arms expert, James also put his medical training to good use as the team's medic.

David McCarter, a former officer with the British SAS, was a man whose easygoing, casual manner concealed a short-fused temper and a love of danger. As far as he was concerned, a life untested by constant brushes with death was hardly worth living.

Gary Manning, on the other hand, was a mild-natured Canadian citizen with the build of a lumberjack. His background with explosives made him an invaluable member of the team.

Rafael Encizo was a Cuban patriot who had been captured at the ill-fated Bay of Pigs invasion of Castro's Cuba. He had survived the infamous Communist prison on the Isle of Pines to be repatriated to the United States. His experiences at the Bay of Pigs had left him with a deep-seated distrust of authority, yet Bolan had convinced him to join the team.

Yakov Katzenelenbogen was the senior member of the team, and its usual leader. The French-born warrior had emigrated to Israel as a young man and had fought in many of her wars while in the army. He continued in the Israeli army until the Six-Day War when he lost his right arm. When Bolan approached him, he was working counterterrorist operations for the Mossad, the Israeli Intelligence service. Having fought against terrorists all of his life, he had jumped at the chance to work for an organization that wasn't hampered by politics, or by the law.

Blooded on too many missions to count, Phoenix Force was once again doing what it did best—striking hard at those who shed the blood of innocents.

THE NEWEST VERSION of a peace plan that had been negotiated between the Israelis and the Palestinians looked like business as usual to most longtime observers of the decades-old Middle East conflict. Regardless of Yassir Arafat's promise to keep the PLO in check, not all Palestinians belonged to the PLO. Since the beginning in the Intifada in the previously Israeli-occupied zones, the PLO had been shown to have little influence over those who wanted to drive the Jews into the sea. In fact, by many Palestinians Arafat was considered a traitor who had sold out to the Jews so he could hold on to his political power.

One of those Palestinians who most wanted to see every last Israeli dead was a man known as the Ghost of the Bekaa, Gemel Abu Askari. Now in his late fifties, Abu Askari had left the PLO in the mid-1970s because he felt they weren't serious enough about cleansing the earth of the infestation of Jews. In fact, his resignation had been delivered in the form of a bomb that had failed to kill its intended target, PLO Chairman Yassir Arafat.

He later broke with the Black September, the Islamic Jihad and Hamas terrorist organizations for much the same reason—they weren't killing enough Jews for his taste. Now he headed a very select group of fanatics, known as the Soldiers of God. It was a small enough organization, but its body count was very high.

Askari had never received financial support from any of the Islamic states that routinely funded terrorist groups. His form of Islamic insanity had been too extreme for even Iran to support. As a result, Askari had been forced to live off "donations" from the locals, wherever he and his band of killers were camping out.

The farmers and herdsmen whom the Soldiers of God hid out with saw him as an Islamic Robin Hood, as their champion against their oppressors, both Israeli and Arab. They willingly made donations to support his operations. Sometimes the donations were food and shelter, other times they were the temporary use of vehicles and fuel. Rarely were they in the form of cash because Askari's men didn't go into urban areas and had little need of money.

Living with the pious and poor was the reason Askari hadn't been tracked down earlier and killed by Israeli counterterrorist teams. They protected him and his men not only from the Jews, but from the other Palestinians, as well. He might have continued that existence had he not made a mistake on his last raid.

Askari's latest outrage had been committed against a grade school in a village a few kilometers from the security zone.

Coming as it did while the Palestinian leadership was desperately trying its best to show the Israelis that the days of terrorism were over, Askari's raid was more than a mere embarrassment. Arafat saw it as treason against him and acted accordingly. Within a week, his agents had located Askari's new hiding place, and Arafat passed the information on to his old archenemy, the Israeli Mossad.

Even though they knew where the terrorist was, the constraints of the fledgling peace plan meant that the Israelis couldn't strike back themselves at this latest outrage. An Israeli retaliatory raid into the Bekaa Valley would torpedo the uneasy agreement and could plunge the region back into full-scale war—which was exactly what Askari was counting on. He knew that the Israelis couldn't allow attacks on their women and children to go unanswered. If they did, their own people would turn their backs on the peace plan and the war could continue. Either way, Askari would win.

Mack Bolan, however, was not under any such constraints, nor was Phoenix Force. Askari had been on Stony Man Farm's hit list for a long time. And now that he had finally been located, it was time to draw a line through his blood-soaked name.

The fact that it was the PLO that had fingered Askari was in a way poetic justice. It wasn't the first time that a terrorist organization had leaked information about one of its enemies. But it was the first time that it had been done in the name of forging peace.

"HAS THERE BEEN any change in the target?" Bolan asked Captain Hod.

"The butcher is still there, sir." The Israeli's voice shook with seething anger. "We've seen him."

A cousin of his, a young girl not yet even into puberty, had been slaughtered in one of Askari's attacks a few years earlier. Since then, he had made finding the terrorist leader the focus of his life in the army.

Were it not for the fact that he had been threatened with immediate trial and imprisonment if he so much as stepped across the border, he would have led his own troops against Askari in a flash. Instead, he was pointing out the target to these foreigners. He only hoped that these men were as good as they were said to be. If they weren't, and Askari escaped again, it might be years before the man could be tracked down again. A great deal was riding on this team.

"Are the sentries and manned weapons still in the same places you reported earlier?" Bolan asked.

"As near as we can tell, sir."

"Has there been any sign of reinforcement?"

"There's been a little traffic in and out," the Israeli replied. "But it's all been civilians, no armed men. I think they've just been laying in supplies."

Bolan glanced at the luminous face on his watch. It was time to pay a long-overdue visit to the Ghost of the Bekaa. "Pull back into your positions, Captain, and wait for us to return. Under no circumstances are you or your men to cross the line into the valley."

"I understand, sir," the Israeli answered. "Good luck, Colonel."

THE SMALL, STONE farmhouse glowed in muted green tones through Mack Bolan's night-vision goggles. The warrior scanned the approach carefully, looking for anything that he might have missed earlier when he studied the recon photos of the target area.

Yakov Katzenelenbogen lay beside him, also scanning the open ground in front of them. Of all the men of Phoenix Force, Katz knew this area best. He had been in the Bekaa Valley more times than he liked to remember and, each time he had been here, blood had been shed. Usually it had been the blood of Palestinian terrorists, but Israeli blood had flowed, too.

Katzenelenbogen had fought for the Jewish state of Israel a good portion of his life so his people could live in peace. That goal, however, had always eluded the embattled Israelis, until now. He wasn't one of those who distrusted this revamped peace plan with the Palestinians. As an old soldier, he knew only too well that a bad peace was eminently better than even the best war. But for this initiative to have a chance to succeed, it was necessary that still more blood be shed. Yet this time it would be the blood of those who wanted to see the peace plan fail.

It was ironic that more killing was necessary for peace to thrive. But this was the Middle East, and the Middle East was rich in ironies—particularly those ironies related to the shedding of blood. It was a tale that went far beyond the histories of the states involved this time. It was a tradition even older than the religions that were now involved and it was time to put a halt to it.

"It looks good to me," Bolan whispered to his companion. "Let's do it."

Katz raised himself to a kneeling position with his good arm and swung his Uzi into a firing position resting on his stainless steel prosthesis. "I'm actually looking forward to this one."

"So am I," Bolan replied.

CHAPTER THREE

Bekaa Valley

The Koran, the holy book of the Prophet Mohammed, strictly forbade Muslims to drink alcohol. While many modern followers of Islam thought the prohibition was old-fashioned and ignored it, Askari required that his Soldiers of God strictly observe the teachings of the holy book. Being found with even as much as a bottle of beer was enough for one of his men to be brought before him for punishment. And Askari had only one punishment for those who wouldn't live the pure life of a holy Islamic warrior—a 9 mm bullet in the back of the head.

In most instances, however, the absence of alcohol wasn't the problem for Islamic troops that it would have been for any modern Western army. The Koran didn't prohibit the use of hashish, and the Bekaa Valley of Lebanon produced some of the world's finest hash. Whether alcohol befuddled the mind more or less than hash had been debated for a long time, and wasn't going to be concluded tonight. But the Soldier of God who was supposed to be standing guard at the listening post on the approach to the farmhouse had chosen to get stoned instead.

Even if Encizo hadn't known where the sentry was standing, the pungent, sweet odor of burning hash would have marked him as well as if he had been wearing a rotating searchlight on top of his head. The Cuban had no way of knowing how stoned the terrorist was, but he knew that hash could heighten the senses even while slowing the smoker's reaction time.

Clicking his throat mike to let the others know that he was going for his target, the Cuban started to inch forward. When he was only a few feet away from the sentry, he slowly gathered his feet under him to make his lunge.

Encizo leaped, his left hand clamping over the Palestinian's mouth and jerking his head to one side. At the same time, his right hand punched his Cold Steel Tanto combat knife into the man's neck. The razor-sharp, chisel-pointed blade entered the side of the guard's throat and ripped through to the other side, severing his windpipe, jugular vein and carotid artery with one swipe.

The hot, metallic smell of fresh blood momentarily covered the rank stench of the guard's body and sweetish odor of his hash cigarette. It was followed by the stench of his bowels and bladder voiding in death.

Holding the dying man upright with one arm, Encizo snatched his AK from the air as it fell before easing the corpse to the ground. Leaving the sentry in a sitting position, he put the AK across his lap so it would look as though he were sleeping.

Two clicks on Encizo's throat mike brought the others to his side.

Bolan signaled David McCarter to take the right side of the house and the Cuban to continue around to the left. He, Katz, Calvin James and Gary Manning would storm the house. According to the Israeli Intelligence, Askari had fourteen or fifteen of his men with him. However, they had little in the way of heavy weapons beyond a couple of RPG rocket launchers and RPD light machine guns.

Though the raw numbers were against Bolan and Phoenix Force, the odds weren't all that bad. The Stony Man forces had gone up against worse odds many times before. They had a job to do, and achieving their goal was what they focused on.

ABU ASKARI SAT across from his second in command at the low wooden table in the main room of the house, planning his next strike. Since the Israelis hadn't responded as he'd wanted after the attack on the school, they obviously needed more encouragement. He knew of an exclusive boarding school for daughters of strictly Orthodox families that would do nicely for a second act.

The only problem was that it was several kilometers inside the border and the logistics would be difficult. But wasn't it said that nothing comes without its difficulties?

The terrorist leader slowly raised his eyes from the map in front of him. "Did you hear that?"

"Hear what, Father?" the younger man asked.

Abu Askari's name meant "father of soldiers" in Arabic, and he demanded that his men call him Father.

"I heard something that shouldn't be out there."

"What?"

Askari's eyes glittered in the kerosene lantern light as he slowly rose from the low stool. "A Jew."

The second in command jumped to his feet and started for the door. "Don't!" Askari held out his hand to stop him. "Let them come."

The younger man looked at his leader with disbelief, his thumb automatically going for the selector switch on the AK-47 assault rifle in his hand. "But Father," he said. "I must warn the men."

"God will warn them," Askari's dark eyes flashed. "We are doing his work and he will protect us from the infidel dogs."

The terrorist leader reached down to the holster belted at his side, drew the Egyptian 9 mm Model 58 Tokagypt pistol and thumbed off the safety. "But, even with his protection, we still have to do our part. Wait for them to come to us, then we will kill them."

"Yes, Father."

DAVID MCCARTER SLIPPED around the right side of the waist-high stone fence that surrounded the farmhouse like a perimeter wall. The recon photos showed a machine-gun nest a few meters distant that could be a problem if it wasn't taken out before the strike went down.

Through his night-vision goggles, he could make out the figure of only one man standing next to what looked like an RPD machine gun resting on top of the wall. He would have expected two men at the post, a gunner and a loader, but these were terrorists, not trained troops.

Taking his silenced Beretta in a two-handed Weaver combat stance, the Briton centered his sights and triggered a short burst. The trio of subsonic, silenced 9 mm slugs punched into the gunman's chest, forming a triangle over his heart and spinning him. He collapsed over the RPD, down and dead.

Before McCarter could move out and check his kill, he heard a harsh cry and a single pistol shot from the other side of the compound.

The clatter of a Kalashnikov on full autofire shattered the night on the other side of the wall close to McCarter's head. Even though it wasn't aimed at him, he ducked lower behind the stone wall in reflex. Snatching a minifragmentation grenade from his assault harness, he pulled the pin and tossed the bomb over the wall. By the count of three, it detonated and the Phoenix Force warrior came up from behind the wall, the H&K in his hand blazing silenced fire.

Shrapnel from the grenade had wounded the terrorist, but his AK-47 was still in his hands. A burst from McCarter's weapon raked across his chest, finishing the job. Now the Briton had to get to that RPD to disable it before someone else used it against his teammates.

NOW THAT THE ENEMY was on to them, Bolan's group had no choice but to rush the house. With Manning and James providing supportive fire, Katzenelenbogen raced for the house. Given the chance, he'd like to be the one who took out Abu Askari.

Bolan followed close behind him without trying to catch up. He knew how his old friend felt about this particular mission and was willing to back his play.

When a lone gunman appeared in the window, an AK-47 in his hand, the Executioner sensed, more than saw, the danger. Without breaking stride, the warrior drew the big Desert Eagle autoloader and fired a single shot.

The 240-grain .44-caliber round caught the hardman in the center of his chest and tore through his body to sever his spine on the way out. A gout of blood and lung tissue splattered the stone wall behind him as he was slammed off his feet.

When Katz reached the door, he slipped a grenade from his harness, kicked the door open, tossed the bomb inside and pressed against the wall as it went off. A heartbeat later he was across the threshold and charging into the dimly lit house, his Uzi blazing a 9 mm trail for him to follow.

Only one man appeared to contest Katz's uninvited visit, and the Phoenix Force warrior emptied the rest of his Uzi's magazine into him with one long burst. He had paused against the wall right inside the door to change magazines, when an older man with a pistol in his hand stepped out from behind a partition wall at the rear of the large room.

The Israeli instantly recognized Askari. The self-proclaimed Father of Soldiers looked exactly like the only two photos of the terrorist known to exist—the mane of white hair, the piercing black eyes and the long, patriarchal beard flowing around the wide, thin-lipped jaw. This was his man, and it was time for payback.

As Katz slammed the fresh magazine into place and snapped up the subgun, a young man suddenly dashed forward, pushed Askari aside, took the burst full in the chest himself and slumped to the floor.

Recovering his footing, Askari brought his Toka-gypt into play, triggering off two snap shots. As Katz dropped to the floor, the 9 mm slugs sang over his head before eating into the stone wall behind him. Rolling to the left, the Israeli came up with the Uzi resting across his prosthesis.

When he saw the terrorist's head turn to one side, Katz yelled, "Don't shoot! I've got him!" and triggered a long burst.

The storm of lead drilled into the terrorist, driving him back against the wall. His dark eyes glared briefly before they dimmed. Askari slid down the wall, dead before he reached the floor.

"Target down!" Katzenelenbogen transmitted.

"Finish clearing the house," Bolan radioed back.

OUTSIDE, McCarter's grenade had drawn more attention than he liked. A pair of half-dressed Palestinians with AKs blazing in their hands rushed around the far corner of the house. Through his night-vision goggles, McCarter saw them clearly and had time to take careful aim. A long figure-eight burst swept both men off their feet.

Sounds of firing to the rear sent him racing for cover behind the trunk of the olive tree to his right. Three men were facing the way he had come and had their backs to him.

Before he could shoot, gunfire from their right front sent two of the terrorists to the ground. The third gunner broke away and raced for the tree McCarter was hiding behind. In his panic, the Palestinian didn't see the shadow step out in front of him, a matte-finished, broad-bladed combat knife in his right hand.

The hardman's rush brought him up against McCarter's blade. The Tanto's point entered the pit of his stomach, and the Briton ripped the razor-honed edge toward his chest. With the knife angled upward, the point touched the gunner's heart before the resistance of his ribs halted its travel.

Twisting the blade to free it, the Phoenix Force commando stepped aside to let the man fall. The terrorist went down to his knees, his hands vainly trying to hold his guts in place before the loss of blood made it unnecessary.

Suddenly silence reigned again and Bolan's voice came over his earphone. "Report."

"McCarter, clear."

When the other four called in that their areas were clear as well, Bolan told him and Encizo to secure the grounds while they searched the house.

SNAPPING ON HIS RED LENS flashlight, Bolan shone the beam into the dead terrorist's face. "Is that Askari?" he asked Katzenelenbogen.

"That's him all right."

"You want me to take his head back to the Mossad for a positive ID?" James grinned.

"I think a picture will do just as well."

Manning reached into his assault pack, took out a small Polaroid camera and snapped a picture. Changing his position, he took another and checked them both to make sure the man's face could be clearly seen.

"Make sure you get the bodies outside as well," Bolan told him. "The Mossad is going to want proof on them as well before they'll close the book on this bunch."

"Hold your fire," Manning radioed to the two men on guard outside. "I'm coming out."

While Manning was taking the mug shots, Katzenelenbogen and Bolan went over the few papers and documents in the room. Since Askari was an outlaw, even by terrorist standards, he didn't need paperwork to keep track of his Islamic benefactors. What maps and scribbled notes there were, however, might be of some use to the Mossad.

"I got all fourteen of them," the Canadian reported as he came back into the room and handed Bolan a stack of photos.

Tucking the photos into his breast pocket for safekeeping, Bolan glanced at his watch. They'd have to get started back if they didn't want to have the dawn catch them in the open tracts of the Bekaa.

"Let's go," he said. "We're done here."

Outside, the six commandos took up a diamond formation and moved out. None of them bothered to look back.

CHAPTER FOUR

Split Harbor, Republic of Serbia

Captain Oleg Yatkin smiled in satisfaction as he took one last look around the control room of his submarine. The final outfitting and stockpiling of supplies had gone much faster than he had expected. The Serbs had put dozens of men to the task, and, under the supervision of the Ukrainian crewmen, the job had gone smoothly. The sub's major systems were up and running, and he had supplies on board for a month's cruise.

Just as important as the outfitting was the fact that the Libyan submariners were now on board and he finally had a full crew. He had run them through several hours of drills while the boat was tied up to the dock, and the men had done fairly well. He knew from experience, however, that dry runs were a lot different from the real thing. The Libyans had never served in a nuclear submarine, and their navy's diesel-powered boats were a far cry from the high-tech *Petlyura*. Nonetheless, he had to put to sea now, so they were going to have to do. Later, he hoped he would be able to replace them with more Ukrainian navy submarine veterans.

"Prepare to get under way," Yatkin commanded.

There was a flurry of activity in the control room as the nuclear reactor, the "teapot" as it had been called in the old Soviet navy, was brought up to full pressure. When the propulsion system was all green, he radioed for the two Serbian hydrofoil patrol boats to take their positions again. As soon as they were alongside in their screening positions, the crane lifted the wooden dockside "shack" high enough in the air to allow the sub's sail to clear it.

"Release the lines," Yatkin commanded.

"Lines released, Captain," the boatswain replied.

"Back one-quarter."

"Back one-quarter, aye," the helmsman repeated.

The nine-bladed prop at the sub's stern began to churn the water, and the stealth submarine slowly slipped backward from the pier. As soon as she was four hull lengths away from the dock, Yatkin ordered, "Left full rudder. All ahead one-quarter."

"Left full rudder, ahead one-quarter, aye," the helmsman answered.

The hydrofoils easily kept pace with the sub as she completed her slow turn and pointed her bow toward the open water of the Adriatic Sea. "Ahead one-half," Yatkin ordered, "and come down to sail depth."

As soon as the sub cleared the shallow waters of Split's harbor, Yatkin asked the Libyan sonar man for the depth reading.

"Thirty meters under the keel, sir."

"Very good. Helm, take her down to periscope depth."

"Periscope depth, aye," the helmsman answered.

As the sub's sail disappeared under the water, the Serbian patrol boats broke off and continued on their way as if they were on a regular patrol of the harbor area.

"Up periscope," Yatkin commanded as he turned his visor cap around backward on his head to clear the eyepieces.

When the metal shaft slid up into position in front of him, he took the control handles in each hand and leaned forward to bring his eyes to the optics. Even at full magnification, he couldn't see any of the NATO ships of the UN blockade force off the former Yugoslavian coastline.

There were several vessels in the blockade fleet that were capable of tracking, and killing, his submarine, and he had to get past them to reach the Mediterranean. It was a risk, but it would be a good test of the stealth capabilities of the *Petlyura*. If the boat didn't perform as advertised, he could still turn her around and go back to Split.

"Course one-eighty-nine," he said. "Make revolutions for thirty-five knots."

"Course one-eighty-nine, aye. Revolutions for thirty-five knots."

There was a small risk of going so fast in relatively shallow waters, but Yatkin wanted to pass through the Adriatic and reach the Mediterranean as quickly as possible. His charts were up-to-date and would let him navigate the deepest channel without using his depth-ranging sonar.

"Down scope and rig for silent running."

"Silent running, aye."

The cacophony of sounds that made up the normal background noise of every sub he had ever served in lessened to a mere whisper. It was so quiet, he thought that he could hear the water rushing past the sub's titanium hull, but that couldn't be.

A half hour later, the Libyan sonar man turned to Yatkin. "Captain, I'm getting sonar pulses from an American warship."

"Ignore it," the Ukrainian responded confidently. "They'll never spot us."

"Aye, Captain."

ENSIGN JASON RATCLIFF had the watch in the sonar room of the destroyer USS *Balmoral*. His ship was taking part in the NATO fleet blockading the coast of the former Yugoslavia, but so far it had been a very boring operation. The only break in the routine had come when the *Balmoral* had stopped a refugee ship trying to break through to Italy. Ratcliff had joined the Navy for adventure and was finding the endless blockade routine boring.

Of all the routine tasks that the newly commissioned officer was required to do on this first ship assignment, standing watch in the sonar room was his least favorite. Since none of the new republics had a submarine force worth squat, he didn't see much reason for him to waste his time looking for something that wasn't there and wasn't going to be there.

Since he had vocalized his discontent more than once, the young officer's attitude had rubbed off on the *Balmoral*'s sonar crew. The ensign was right, they thought. It wasn't as if they were back in the good old days when the Soviet Akula and Alfa attack boats had shadowed the 6th Fleet day in and day out. The Serbs and Croats didn't even have a sub fleet. Sure, they had some old Russian diesel boats, but most of them were tied up at dock for lack of crews. Even if they did put one of them to sea, they were such noisy crates that they could be detected twenty miles away.

Petty Officer Third Class Jim Boyd frowned as he stared at his sonar scope. He finally had something other than a bottom return, but it certainly wasn't a hostile sub. It looked like it was a thermocline return, and he had seen enough of them in the Atlantic to know better than call the chief over. CPO

Williams had been on the rag about something lately, probably his old lady or his kids again, and Boyd didn't feel like getting yelled at right now. Usually the waters of the Adriatic were too warm to form the kind of thermoclines found in the Atlantic, but what the hell, there it was.

He turned the sonar to another sector and his mind back to the scheduled liberty he had coming in a little more than a week.

"What was that last return, Boyd?" he heard the ensign ask from behind him.

"Just a thermocline, sir," he answered.

"Let's see it again."

"Aye, sir."

Petty Officer Boyd rewound the tape that recorded all the sonar returns.

"Put it up on the scope."

"It's just a thermocline, sir," Boyd offered, pointing to the spikes on the return. "See where the sonar pulses break up and scatter? We get that all the time in the Atlantic."

Ratcliff didn't remember seeing that kind of return before in the short sonar school he had attended. But, like almost all ensigns, he felt that he was a bit of a fraud. He had an officer's rank, but he knew less about his job than the lowliest seaman on the ship. To call the chief over to look at the return would only make him look even more foolish. Boyd was a third class petty officer and an experienced sonar man on his second enlistment. If he said it was a thermocline, then it was a thermocline.

"Make sure you log it," Ratcliff said before turning away and going back to his station.

"Aye, sir."

YATKIN HEARD the destroyer's sonar pings fade away and he smiled. So far, so good. The boat's designers had done their work well. The sub had been right in the middle of the ship's sonar search pattern and had obviously escaped undetected. He was glad he'd had this chance to test the stealth design before someone was seriously searching for them. Now he had one less worry on his mind.

"Helm," he said, "make full-speed ahead."

"Full speed, aye, Captain."

At her flank speed of fifty-two knots, it wouldn't be long before the *Petlyura* was completely past the NATO blockade fleet and in open water at the mouth of the Adriatic. Once there, Yatkin would turn the bow of the stealth sub west past the toe of Italy and enter the Mediterranean. And, once they were in the Med, he wouldn't have to worry much about dodging antisubmarine ships until they ran the Strait of Gibraltar.

"AARON," Barbara Price said, her voice tense, "we just got another flash from the Russians through Hal."

"Don't tell me," he replied wearily. "They lost some more of their nukes, didn't they?"

"That missing sub took six nuclear-tipped torpedoes and four SS-N-19 sea-to-ground attack missiles with her."

"What is it with those people?" Kurtzman asked rhetorically. "Why can't they keep their nuclear weapons under tighter control?"

A smile tugged at a corner of Price's mouth. There was nothing that could get Kurtzman riled quicker than a Russian screwup, particularly one that involved nuclear weapons. The last one they had gotten involved with had been the hijacking of ten tactical nuclear warheads from a convoy in central Asia. Before they were done, they had tracked the warheads to a Vietnamese, North Korean and hard-line Chinese cartel bent on starting a nuclear war. It had required an assault on Cam Ranh Bay, Vietnam, to destroy them and end the threat.

"What are Hal's orders this time?"

"The usual. The Man wants us to help the Russians locate and recover them as soon as possible," Price stated.

"From a submarine submerged several hundred feet under the sea that no one can locate. Piece of cake, nothing to it."

"The Russians are sending a nuclear-submarine expert to assist us and to act as technical liaison on the submarine part of it."

"When's he due in?"

"Grimaldi will fly him down tomorrow morning. Oh, yeah. There's one other thing. Hal hasn't asked for them yet, but you'd better alert Carl that we have another nuke hunt under way. With so much ground to cover, there's a good chance that we'll have to get Able Team involved before this is over."

Kurtzman called up a menu on his monitor. "They're closing in on their quarry and should be available tomorrow."

"Good. Let me know as soon as they're free."

CHAPTER FIVE

Benton, Oregon

"Here comes the brown van, Ironman," a lean man with salt-and-pepper hair cut short in military fashion announced as he took the field glasses from his eyes. "It just left the main road and is headed this way."

"It's about time," growled the bulky blond man lying on the ground next to him. His own field glasses were trained in the other direction, keeping watch on a house in the small clearing below their hillside position in the scrub brush.

The blond man was Carl Lyons, leader of Able Team, an ex-LAPD cop whose path had crossed that of the Executioner several times during Mack Bolan's Mafia Wars, as they had come to be known. The big man's nickname, Ironman, reflected his mental attributes more than his physical. But he had the physical to go along with the never-say-die mental style of dealing with the obstacles life threw in his path.

The man keeping watch with him under the towering fir trees of southern Oregon was Hermann Schwarz. Known as Gadgets because of his uncanny skill with anything mechanical or electronic, he had picked up the nickname in Vietnam because of his work with booby traps and surveillance devices.

The third man on the team, Rosario Blancanales, was in position on the other side of the clearing. Blancanales was a Puerto Rican known as The Politician because of his unique ability to work people and situations to his decided advantage. On this mission, however, he hadn't been able to make many inroads with the locals because he was Hispanic. This wasn't to say that Oregon didn't have a sizable Hispanic population. But they were mostly found in the agricultural areas of the state, not up in the mountains of the Cascade Range and specifically not in this particular part of the southern Oregon Cascades.

The little logging community of Benton was deep in America's hinterland, where every pickup truck had a full rifle rack in the rear window of the cab. Country bands played in the local tavern every Friday and Saturday night to a loudly appreciative audience of ranch hands and out-of-work loggers. The footgear of choice was either well-worn cowboy boots or work boots. Nike might have been an Oregon company, but trendy, urban pretentious Portland was a long way from Benton. Wearing an expensive pair of Nike running shoes around there was a good way to be branded an outsider.

This was also a part of Oregon where wearing an earth-hugger bumper sticker on the back of a Volvo station wagon with a Baby On Board sign was likely to get a family run off the road into a federally protected fir tree. The region had been completely decimated by the environmental lockup of the federal forest land supposedly to protect the endangered spotted owl. Benton had once been a vibrant, prosperous timber town. Several wood products mills had provided good jobs for the sons, fathers and brothers of the community. Now, with the federal timberland tied up in court by environmental battles, the town was dying. When the last of the extended unemployment benefits were exhausted, it would be dead.

But it was neither the endangered owls nor the even more endangered loggers who had drawn Able Team to the hills of southern Oregon.

Another trait of this part of the Northwest was that many of the inhabitants felt that American society was headed for a big fall, and they wanted to be ready when it happened. Rugged survivalists had been living in the hills of southern Oregon for as many years as they had been in northern Idaho. The difference was that there were not as many outwardly vocal white supremacists in Oregon.

Needless to say, though, liberals weren't appreciated in Benton. Neither were the ever-encroaching liberal-backed laws restricting firearm ownership. Most citizens of southern Oregon believed in the right to bear arms the way Catholics believed in the Blessed Virgin Mary. Everyone owned at least a deer rifle and a shotgun, and the majority owned several such weapons. Handguns were as popular as popcorn, and it wasn't unknown for the locals to have illegal fully automatic weapons hidden on their property.

Automatic weapons in the hands of the locals weren't a real problem in Benton, though. These people had been born with guns in their hands and, regardless of their politics, rarely committed crimes with them. Someone in the area, however, was feeding the gang wars in the West Coast cities with converted automatic weapons.

Regardless of all the liberal antigun hysteria in the media about the dangers of semiautomatic assault rifles, it was difficult to convert a semiautomatic rifle into a fully automatic weapon. To make the conversion required an expert gunsmith, a well-equipped machine shop and several hours of highly skilled labor. Anyone could buy a brand-new Chinese-made semiautomatic AK-47 copy, but few had the skill, the know-how or the machinery necessary to convert it into a real AK.

Even so, someone was selling fully automatic Chinese AK-47 conversions in the major West Coast cities for a flat thousand dollars apiece. For that price, the weapons came complete with a cut-down buttstock, two extra magazines and 120 rounds of Chinese military-issue ammunition.

In the hands of warring gangbangers, these full-auto blasters were extracting a fearful toll. So far, most of the dead had been other gang bangers and drug scum, but a couple of police officers had been hit and several civilians had been killed in gang cross fires.

The AKs had been traced back to southern Oregon, which was why Able Team was keeping watch in the clearing in the woods well outside of Benton.

Considering the recent history of botched ATF and FBI raids, it wasn't surprising that this particular mission had been given to Able Team to handle. No one would ever mistake Carl Lyons, Hermann Schwarz and Rosario Blancanales for federal officers. There was nothing of the short-hair, polished-shoes mentality about them. They were bona fide hard cases and looked the part, which was the only way they had been able to make inroads on the situation in this particular part of Oregon.

"Man, this place looks like *Northern Exposure* meets East L.A. after the riot," Blancanales commented as Lyons drove their Blazer four-wheel drive past boarded-up shop windows along Benton's main street.

"Nah," Schwarz disagreed, shaking his head. "Not enough graffiti."

"Where the hell's that motel Aaron told us about?" Lyons growled. "If it's closed, too, we'll be camping in the woods."

"There it is." Schwarz pointed to an unlit neon sign at the far end of the street.

After checking into the motel, the three men headed for the Stewed Owl Tavern to start the process they hoped would lead them to whoever was converting the legal AK semiautomatics into deadly, full-auto street sweepers.

The Stewed Owl was a typical Northwest local hangout. The country music, however, came via a fairly modern sound set rather than a Rockola jukebox. That helped cut down on the fights about the selection because the barkeep controlled the tapes. Other than that, the battered tables, dirty windows and beer sign decor could be found anywhere from Canada to San Francisco.

As was only to be expected in a place like the Stewed Owl, some drunk made a nasty crack about Schwarz's fancy ostrich-skin cowboy boots. The comment had been loud and made while the barkeep was changing the tape on the sound set, so that everyone in the tavern heard it.

Schwarz calmly drained the last of his beer, stood and walked over to the loudmouth. "I heard you admiring my boots. Maybe you'd like a little closer look at them."

"You need to dig the crap out of your ears," the drunk snarled. "I said that only chicken-shit faggots wear chicken-skin boots."

"That's what I thought you said."

The drunk never saw the hand that hauled him out of his chair and put him on his feet. Nor did he see the other hand before it slapped him on the cheek with stunning force. When he could see again, he launched a furious roundhouse blow at his smaller opponent.

Schwarz batted the attack away with his left forearm and sunk his right fist almost to the wrist in the drunk's beer gut. He stepped aside when the man folded at the middle and went down.

The drunk's buddy decided to deal himself a hand and made the mistake of standing. When Schwarz lined up on him, the bartender reached under the counter. Lyons kicked his chair back and stood, getting the bartender's attention. Swinging the tail of his coat aside to reveal the .357 Magnum Colt Python resting in shoulder holster, he shook his head. The barkeep brought both of his hands up empty and stood against the back of the bar.

Lyons remained standing while Schwarz took care of his adversary. Leaving the bodies where they lay on the not-too-clean floor, he walked back to his table and sat again.

"Are you through screwing around?" Lyons asked.

"Yeah," Schwarz said with a grin, "but I need another beer. That's thirsty work."

FROM THAT EVENING ON, Able Team had had no more problems in Benton. They returned to the tavern every night, but there were no more comments about Schwarz's boots. They had been accepted as "good ol' boys" who didn't take guff from anyone. Getting a line on the elusive outlaw gunsmith, however, proved to be more difficult.

Their cover story was that they were looking to buy a tract of land outside town. They didn't say what they wanted the land for, but the brand-new four-wheel-drive Chevy Blazer they drove and the wads of cash in their pockets told the locals that they were drug growers. The towering fir forests of southern Oregon had their fair share of pot farms and the problems that went with them. But with the economic strangulation of Benton, the hope of money, even drug money, was welcomed.

Since they were already considered to be on the wrong side of the law, the locals didn't mind telling Lyons and his companions about the town's other source of illegal dollars, Red Granger the gunsmith.

Apparently Granger did a landslide business selling weapons to city people.

Having their suspicions confirmed, however, wasn't enough for them to go into action. Before the men of Able Team could make their play, they had to have the guy cold—and that meant buying a converted AK from him.

The hardware store in town did double duty as the local gun store. When Lyons walked in, he made his way past the dusty chain saw display and bins of nails to the counter at the rear of the store. The few guns in the racks were various hunting and varmint guns, and there was nothing more high-tech than a lever-action Winchester.

After examining a couple of scoped hunting rifles, Lyons looked around the store. "Don't you have anything with a little more firepower? An AK or an M-16?"

The shopkeeper eyed him carefully. "We don't get too much call for that kind of thing around here."

"That's too bad," Lyons said. "I was hoping to buy a couple of pieces for the coyotes."

He pulled his wad of flash money out of his pocket and peeled off two hundred-dollar bills. "You don't happen to know of anyone around here who might be able to help me, do you?"

The shopkeeper licked his lips. That two hundred this month would make all the difference in his staying open or finally having to give in to the new economic realities of life in rural Oregon and close his store. "I know a guy who might be able to help you."

Lyons laid the bills on the counter. "How do I get in touch with your friend?"

"I'll give him a call and see if he wants to talk to you."

Granger was willing to meet Lyons, but he wasn't as trusting as the rest of the locals. With his line of work, he wasn't hurting for money and wasn't swayed by a lot of money. Feds showed flash money, too.

Finally Blancanales could go into action and do what he did best. Putting on a convincing Hispanic accent, he posed as the Colombian moneyman behind Lyons and Schwarz's plan to buy a plot of land and grow pot. A dummy Mexican passport prepared by the Farm was the clincher, and the gunsmith sold them five AKs, all the stock he had on hand.

After checking to ensure that the weapons had been illegally converted to full-auto, Blancanales placed an order for five more and was told that he would have to wait until the next shipment of semiautos came in at the end of the week. Pol said that he would wait.

Now they were in position overlooking Red Granger's house, waiting for the van with the new guns to pull up so they could get the entire gang at one time. The last thing they wanted was to leave loose ends for someone else to have to clean up.

And Able Team wasn't known for loose ends.

"IS POL READY?" Lyons asked when he heard the sound of the approaching van.

Schwarz quietly spoke into his throat mike, then nodded. "He's still in place, just like he was the last time you asked."

Lyons ignored Gadgets's crack and went back to watching the two story farmhouse. Even though this was going down as planned, he was still concerned. They had the high ground, as well as the element of surprise, but they didn't have the military advantage. The clapboard structure in the clearing below didn't look like a fortress, but it was—at least according to the information they had about it. If the building itself was half the problem the approaches leading down to the clearing had been, they would have their work cut out for them.

The tall fir trees and tangled brush on the hills surrounding the house had been turned into a killing zone that would have done an old-time VC sapper squad proud. Booby traps, land mines and electronic surveillance systems had been laid out in a five-hundred-yard radius all the way around the house. Schwarz and Lyons had spent the better part of two days carefully deactivating enough of the devices to clear two paths for their attack.

The only good thing about this situation was that the heavily defended perimeter also kept the people they were after somewhat corralled inside. Nonetheless, Lyons knew that only a total idiot would barricade himself without having an escape hatch. This Granger guy had made a mistake in situating his workshop in a valley rather than on top of a hill, but he was anything but an idiot.

During their recon of the site, Schwarz had discovered two semicleared paths that led away from the house into the deep woods. Taking some of the mines and booby traps they had cleared from their attack routes, they put them in place covering both of Granger's escape routes. If the bust went bad and the gunrunners tried to flee, they would run into their own deadly devices.

EIGHT MINUTES LATER, the battered brown van drove into view at the edge of the clearing. Lyons and Schwarz put down their field glasses and took up their weapons. Show time.

Schwarz's weapon for the mission was an M-16 with an attached M-203 grenade launcher mounted under the barrel. Unlike the military version of this weapon, he had an 8-power Redfield ranging scope on top of the receiver and a custom silencer fitted to the muzzle of the assault rifle.

Ironman lived up to his nickname when he assumed a prone position and snugged his shoulder into the buttstock of a .50-caliber Model 82 A-1 Barrett semiautomatic sniper's rifle. It took a real man to fire that gun, particularly when the magazine was loaded with high-velocity armor-piercing and high-explosive ammunition.

On the other side of the clearing, Blancanales shouldered a 4-shot LAW antitank rocket launcher and flipped up the sight. The 66 mm shaped-charge rockets the weapon fired could penetrate more than six inches of armor plate or twelve inches of reinforced concrete. If they needed to make a hole in the house below, he should be able to handle it.

First, though, they had to take care of the van that should be bringing another four men to the house along with the load of weapons to be converted. That honor had been given to Schwarz and his grenade launcher. The range to the parking area was a little more than two hundred yards, and he carefully set his sights before centering them on the front of the van.

"Do it!" Lyons growled.

Schwarz pulled the trigger and the characteristic "thump" of the grenade launcher sent the 40 mm HE round flying through the air to hit dead center in the van's grille. The detonation sent razor-sharp shrapnel slicing into the radiator, and a cloud of steam immediately shot out in the cool mountain air.

He quickly reloaded and, shifting his aim, triggered the launcher again. The second grenade purposefully landed under the rear of the powerful Chevy El Camino pickup parked in front of the shed. The detonation set off the gas tank, engulfing the vehicle in a ball of flame.

Now the hardmen were on foot and would have to either run or stand and fight. And fight they did.

Two gunmen erupted from the cab, firing. Since they didn't have specific targets, they were wasting their ammunition.

Carl Lyons's scoped Barrett 50 spoke once, and one of the gunners was knocked completely off his feet. The heavy slug blew his chest apart, and he collapsed to the ground in a heap.

His partner dived for cover before Lyons could shift his sight, so Schwarz fired a quick burst of 5.56 mm rounds from his M-16 to make sure he stayed down.

The rear doors of the van flew open and two more hardmen charged out, fisting AKs. They immediately went to ground behind the burning El Camino and started firing up the hill at Lyons and Schwarz.

The Able Team leader responded with the Barrett. The steel-core .50-caliber rounds had no trouble punching all the way through the burning pickup. The problem was that the smoke was blurring Lyons's sight picture, and his first two shots didn't connect.

Before he could fire a third round, the authoritative sound of a .50-caliber M-2 Heavy Barrel Machine Gun roared through the clearing.

Granger had sited the heavy-duty blaster behind fake curtains in one of the house's second-story windows. From his high vantage point, he had good fields of fire and knew how to take advantage of them.

A ranging burst of tracer cut into the fir tree over Lyons's head. Bark chips and fir needles rained on him as he scrambled to get behind the trunk. "Tell Pol to take him out!" he yelled to Schwarz.

On the other side of the clearing, Blancanales was having his own problems. One of the two gunners from the back of the van was proving that he had had weapons training and was firing on Pol with grim determination. The other one had taken a round and was down and out.

Blancanales ducked a long burst from the gunner's full-auto AK. He'd been forced to put his LAW launcher aside and pick up his Heckler & Koch assault rifle to dispose of his adversary. And until he could, Ironman and Gadgets were going to have to deal with that .50-caliber themselves.

"He's busy!" Schwarz yelled. "I'll try the Thumper!" Though the over-and-under combination he was carrying was a far cry from the original M-79 grenade launcher, it still went by its old Vietnam War nickname.

Loading a fat 40 mm HE round into the breech, Schwarz snapped it shut and cautiously peered out from around his tree trunk.

Granger had to have had a scope on that fifty because the instant Schwarz moved, the weapon boomed again. The inch-long slugs tore into the tree right above his head, sending a shower of wood and bark splinters into his face.

"He's got me pinned down!"

With a curse, Lyons grabbed the carrying handle on his big sniper's rifle and jumped to his feet. A quick dash took him fifty feet down the hill, and he dived for cover behind a tree just as the machine gun opened up again.

"Try it again," he radioed back to Schwarz. "He can't sight in on both of us at the same time."

Lyons had a point. No matter what kind of scope Granger had on his rifle, it didn't have a field of vision wide enough to cover both men—no telescopic sight did. He would have to resight the gun each time he shifted fire from one to the other. Now he and Lyons could swap off drawing his fire while the other one tried to take him out.

It would be a dangerous game. But if either man wanted to get out of the situation alive, it was the only game in town. Staying where they were would get both of them killed sooner or later.

"I'll go first," Schwarz radioed to his partner.

"Got you covered."

Lyons triggered the Barrett twice to draw the M-2's fire. When Granger sent a burst his way, Schwarz triggered the 40 mm launcher, sending the grenade arching into the air. Before it landed, though, Granger was back to hammering at him with the M-2.

ON THE OTHER SIDE of the clearing, Blancanales had gone completely into termination mode. If this guy wanted to play games, he'd be glad to oblige him. The problem was that he was the hunted and needed to become the hunter. But, often even the prey had a trick or two.

One of the Claymore directional mines that had been set around the perimeter had been replaced so it protected Blancanales's position. Gadgets had also given him a clacker to fire the mine instead of the trip wire. Grabbing the Claymore, he retreated up the hill a few yards, before replanting the mine in a clump of fern. Playing out the firing wire, he moved off to the right and ten yards higher up before finding a position behind a tree above a cut bank.

As soon as he was in place, the Able Team warrior triggered off a short burst from his H & K to let his opponent know where he was. The gunman took the bait. From his vantage point, Blancanales was able to watch the man's progress as he worked his way up the hill. The faintest movement of a fern or snap of a dry stick was all he needed. When it looked as if his man was going to get lost, he fired another burst, purposely off target.

The man responded by charging uphill, his AK blazing as he ran. Ducking from the barrage, Blancanales pressed hard on the handle of the firing device, and the Claymore detonated.

The explosion sent seven hundred .25-caliber steel balls cutting across the hillside like a chest-high scythe. The gunman wasn't directly in front of the mine when it went off, but it didn't matter. The balls flew out in a sixty-degree fan from the point of the blast, and he was caught up in the steel storm anyway.

More than half a dozen of the balls slammed into him. The gunner looked rather puzzled as he watched his lifeblood pump out onto the fir needles under the tree. His eyes went blank, and he crumpled to the ground.

Blancanales scrambled back down to where he had left his LAW launcher. It was time to put an end to this.

Lining up the sight for the windowsill under the machine gun's barrel, he triggered the first 66 mm armor-piercing rocket. Before it had even reached the house, he shifted his point of aim to the center of the window and fired a second round.

The first rocket was a little off course. It struck the corner of the sill and detonated with a flash and a puff of dirty black smoke. Through the smoke, he saw the second round fly right through the window and detonate inside the room. When the smoke cleared, he fired a third rocket for insurance.

He was reserving the fourth and final rocket in the launcher when he saw a gunman step out and aim his AK up the hill at him.

He lined up the launcher's sights on his adversary and triggered the weapon.

When the rocket left the launcher with a whoosh, the gunman dropped his weapon and turned to run. He made the mistake of not dodging to one side or the other, but simply spun and ran in a straight line. The rocket hit a few yards behind him, but the detonation of the warhead sent a spray of gravel after him like a burst of machine-gun fire. He staggered and went down, a dozen rock holes in his back.

By the time Lyons and Schwarz had picked their way down the hill into the clearing, Blancanales was waiting for them. Weapons at the ready, they swept the grounds and checked the bodies. Only one of the gunmen from the van was still alive. He had taken a round in the thigh and was holding both hands over the wound to try to stop the bleeding.

Blancanales held his H&K on him while Schwarz applied a pressure bandage over the wound. After tying it in place, he took a set of plastic riot restraints from his side pocket. "Hands behind your back, pal."

The gunman looked up at the muzzle in his face and meekly complied. "Are you going to take me to a hospital?" he asked as Schwarz slipped the restraints over his wrists and snugged them down tight.

"Us? No." He shook his head. "The ATF and the FBI will be by here in a little bit to talk to you. What they decide to do to you is up to them."

"You guys aren't cops?"

Schwarz grinned broadly. "You haven't heard me reading you your rights, have you?"

Suddenly it sank in. Not only had they not read him his rights, they had opened fire without waiting to be shot at first. "Who are you guys?"

"Believe me, you don't want to know."

AFTER CHECKING THE REST of the bodies, the warriors heard a chopper approaching in the distance. Now that Able Team had taken care of the illegal gun factory, the Feds were on the way to clean up the mess and take the credit.

"That sounds like our swan song," Schwarz said, looking to the west.

"It sounds like we'd better get moving if we don't want to have to hang around here for the next two days answering questions," Blancanales agreed.

Looking at the hill he had to climb to get back to where they had parked their Blazer, Schwarz sighed. "The next time we do one of these things, let's do it in town so we can call a cab when it's over."

Blancanales grinned. "Maybe we can just rent a limo. You know how hard it can be to catch a cab in these small towns."

"Good point. I'll mention it to the Bear next time I talk to him."

"Can the chatter," Lyons growled. "We've got a long ways to go."

CHAPTER SIX

In the South Atlantic

Captain Jan Bergmann of the South African freighter the SS *Springbok* looked out over the choppy waters of the South Atlantic Ocean. The wind was freshening, but the weather-satellite reports didn't indicate that a storm was forming. Weather over the South Atlantic at that time of year was tricky, though, so he would keep a close eye on both the radar and the satellite reports. Even so, Bergmann knew that the *Springbok* had nothing to fear from anything less than a Force Eight gale.

The *Springbok* was the pride of the South African merchant fleet. Newly built, she combined speed with efficiency and all the wonders that modern maritime technology could provide. Not only was she equipped with the Global Positioning System, she had data links to both weather satellites and the home office in Durban.

A radar array on her masthead gave her a clear view of the seas around her by both day and night. Right now, the radar screen failed to show any shipping within the radar horizon, which was how the captain wanted it to stay until she reached her scheduled port in Brazil. Along with the consumer goods, agricultural products and raw industrial materials stowed in her holds, the *Springbok* carried another shipment worth more than both the vessel and the rest of her cargo combined.

In her video-monitored and computer-controlled secure hold, the ship carried almost a quarter ton of South African diamonds. Most of them were industrial-grade stones, but there were several thousand carats worth of first-class gemstones in the shipment as well. Now that the economic sanctions against his country were lessening, the demand for South African stones was on the rise again and the mines were back in full production.

Even with the secrecy that surrounded the diamond shipments, Bergmann still felt uncomfortable whenever his ship was carrying the precious stones. Not that he worried very much about piracy on the high seas; that was a little too much like James Bond for the practical-minded African. It was just the additional responsibility involved with the shipments that concerned him. Until the diamonds were picked up by their buyers in São Paulo, it was his duty to see that they remained safe.

The only good thing about these trips was that the *Springbok* would stay in port for almost a week while the return cargo was loaded. Bergmann had come to appreciate the slower pace of life in Latin America and was looking forward to shore leave. He was thinking seriously of settling in Brazil when he had to leave SA, and his bonuses from the diamond runs would make that possible.

"I'll be in my cabin if you need me," he told the helmsman.

"Aye, sir."

With one last look at the weather scope, Bergmann left the bridge.

FIVE MILES NORTH of the *Springbok*, the *Petlyura* slipped through the cold waters of the South Atlantic like a steel shark. The stealth sub had been running at her full speed, fifty-two knots, ever since entering the Atlantic outside of Gibraltar. If the timetable Oleg Yatkin had been given was correct, his target should be right in front of him. It was time to find out if the intelligence was correct.

"Sonar," he commanded, "go active."

"Sonar active, aye."

"Put it on the loudspeaker."

Suddenly the throb of a ship's propellers sounded in the control room. "Twin screws making twenty-two knots," the sonar man announced. "It could be her."

"Bring us up to periscope depth," Yatkin ordered.

"Aye, Captain," the helmsman answered.

The deck under Yatkin's feet tilted for a few moments before leveling out.

"Periscope depth, Captain."

"Up scope."

Moving over to the periscope control housing, Yatkin extended the mast until the optics head just cleared the wave tops. This far from the *Springbok,* there was little chance of anyone on her bridge seeing the small wake trailing behind the periscope head, but old habits died hard.

The South African ship was ahead of them and to the right, steaming away from them at an angle. At eight-power magnification on the optics, he was able to read the cutout steel letters welded to the ship's stern.

"That's her," he announced, "the *Springbok.*"

Major Omar Rashid was almost salivating. "How much are the diamonds worth?"

"Several million American dollars, I'm told," Yatkin answered curtly.

The Ukrainian didn't like the Libyan's talk about the value of the cargo. Regardless of what he was about to do, he didn't consider himself to be a pirate. He was a Ukrainian nationalist who had been forced to make an unholy alliance with the Libyans out of political necessity. The diamonds would be sold to provide foreign currency so his nation could purchase much-needed Western technology. In his mind, the end certainly justified the means and removed the stigma from what he was about to do.

"Prepare your men for boarding," Yatkin ordered.

"They are ready," Rashid replied. "They have been ready for hours now."

"Remember," Yatkin said, "we only have an hour and fifteen minutes before the satellite comes overhead again."

"It will not take us nearly that long," the Libyan officer promised. "We will be back in half the time. My men are well trained."

Yatkin didn't answer. He was getting a little tired of hearing how dedicated the Libyans were. "Close in on her at flank speed," he told the helmsman.

"Close at flank speed, aye."

Fifteen minutes later, the *Petlyura* was alongside and slightly ahead of the much slower-moving *Springbok*. Yatkin cut his speed to keep pace with the freighter.

"Rashid," he called out over the intercom to the Libyan officer waiting in the forward escape chamber. "We're in position."

"Maintain your speed until we're clear," Rashid replied over the intercom.

"I remember the plan of attack," Yatkin snapped.

"Good."

A muted clang told Yatkin that the outer door to the escape hatch had opened and the Libyan scuba divers were on their way to the South African ship. As soon as the allotted time had passed, Yatkin turned the sub away and went dead in the water to wait out the assault.

A tense forty-five minutes later, the radioman turned to Yatkin and reported, "That's the signal, Captain."

"Bring us up to the surface," Yatkin ordered, "and stand by to launch the recovery boats."

"Surfacing, aye."

This was the only part of the operation that concerned Yatkin. Even though he knew that the American recon satellites were behind the horizon, any time a submarine was on the surface, she was vulnerable. A few minutes later, the boatswain on deck reported that the boats were on their way back.

"It is done, Captain," Rashid said when he reported to the control room. "The diamonds are aboard and you can submerge now."

"Where are the *Springbok*'s officers?" Yatkin asked when he saw the Libyan officer was by himself. "I need to talk to them."

Rashid's eyes glittered for a moment. "They chose to resist."

Yatkin was stunned. He had specifically told Rashid that he was to take the ship's captain and crew hostage and return them to Split. "What did you do to them?"

"I told you." Rashid shrugged. "They resisted us so we killed them."

Yatkin felt a sick, sinking sensation in his stomach. Attacking a merchant vessel on the high seas was piracy enough. Killing the crew would see him and his own crew hanged if they were ever apprehended by international authorities.

His hand shot out, grabbed the Libyan's battledress jacket and pulled the smaller man closer to him.

Rashid stared the Ukrainian straight in the eye before glancing down at the hand clenched in his uniform. Chilled by the Libyan's gaze, Yatkin released his grip.

"Did you think that you and your men could save your country without shedding blood, Captain?" The major's voice was low, but his disdain was clear. "This is a war we are fighting, a war of survival. You have now become a blooded warrior in this fight. Just thank God that it was not you who was on that ship."

"You bastard" was all Yatkin could think to say.

Rashid was silent for a moment. "I will talk to you about this later," he said, his voice cold and his eyes colder. "But now we must finish off the *Springbok* and set course for our rendezvous. The mother ship is waiting for our cargo."

Yatkin had recovered enough of his composure to realize that the Libyan was right. He had to get the diamonds to the mother ship so they could be forwarded to the nationalists back in the Ukraine. Without them, this whole venture would go for naught. Turning away without a word, he ordered the helmsman to take her down to periscope depth.

As soon as they were safely under the surface again, he went to the attack board to work up a firing solution. With the *Springbok* dead in the water as she was, there was no need to work up a complicated firing solution to sink her. All he needed to do was back off and shoot.

Yatkin maneuvered the sub in a circle until he was two thousand meters away, bow on to the side of the freighter. "Open outer doors on tubes one and two," he ordered.

"Opening doors," the weapons officer replied. "Tubes flooded."

"Set running depth at three meters."

"Three meters, aye," the weapons officer answered.

"Fire tube one!" Yatkin commanded. "Fire tube two!"

"One away. Two away." The weapons officer paused for a moment. "Both torpedoes running true."

Through the plates of the hull, while he counted down the seconds to impact, Yatkin could hear the whining of the torpedoes' turbines as they streaked toward the *Springbok*.

Even though she was two kilometers away, the *Petlyura* was rocked by the detonation of the first torpedo warhead. Through the periscope, Yatkin saw the flame-shot geyser of water leap into the sir. A second explosion right under the bridge followed a few seconds later.

Yatkin watched as the *Springbok* quickly settled in the water. The two 533 mm, shaped-charge warheads had torn the ship's bottom completely out. As it slipped below the wave tops, the stricken ship was racked by secondary explosions when the cold water reaching the hot boilers caused them to explode.

The sonar man shuddered when he heard the shrieking sounds of the ship's hull collapsing as it headed for the dark bottom of the ocean thousands of meters below.

Yatkin released the periscope controls. "Down scope."

As the periscope slid back down into its housing, he turned to the small chart table. A few minutes later, he had plotted a course to the northern shipping lanes. "Helm," he commanded, "come to course three-one-eight, depth two hundred meters. Make revolutions for forty-five knots."

"Course three-one-eight, depth two hundred meters, aye," the helmsman answered. "Increasing revolutions."

"First Officer, you have the conn. I'll be in my cabin."

As he brushed past the Libyan, Yatkin felt the man's cold eyes on him. When he got back in touch with his superiors, he was going to request that Rashid and all his men be replaced by Ukrainians he could trust to obey his orders.

MAJOR OMAR RASHID watched Yatkin disappear down the narrow passageway toward the bow of the sub. As he had suspected, the Ukrainian was a good sub commander. But he was new to the realities of political struggle and he was too soft for the job at hand. It was a Western cliché that you couldn't cook eggs without breaking them first, and Yatkin had just broken his first egg.

It didn't seem, however, that he had the guts to finish cooking it.

There was a Libyan submarine officer standing by in case Yatkin had to be eliminated, but Rashid preferred not to have to do that just yet. The Ukrainian had been trained in the Soviet nuke boats, whereas his own countryman had only served in the obsolete diesel craft of the Libyan navy. Putting an untrained captain in charge of the stealth sub could seriously jeopardize the first part of the mission. Until the Libyan crewmen had more experience with the nuclear-powered stealth submarine, Yatkin would have to remain in command.

But it wouldn't be for much longer anyway. As soon as the Ukrainians had pirated enough ships to ensure the silence of their government, Captain Yatkin and his men would have an unfortunate accident. The *Petlyura* and her nuclear weaponry would be taken into the Libyan navy, and the world would see the real value of a stealth submarine. The four targets for the SS-N-19 missiles had already been selected. Cairo, Tel Aviv, Damascus and Baghdad would go up in mushroom clouds.

This second half of the mission could be accomplished under the command of someone other than Yatkin. All the replacement captain would be required to do was to get the sub in close to the Israeli coastline. If necessary, he could do that much himself.

The plan was to launch the missiles from the Israeli shoreline, then escape into the Mediterranean. The Americans and Russians would be able to determine the true location of the launch, but it wouldn't really matter. To many it would look as if the Jewish madmen had finally hit their Arab enemies and been hit back in return.

In the turmoil that would result, Libya would emerge as the banner carrier for the Arabic Islamic states. Under her leadership, they could finally be combined into one great nation, as they had been back in the days of the great caliphs. When that dream was a reality, the West would cease to be the power in the world. Once more the green banners of Islam would wave in triumph.

CHAPTER SEVEN

Stony Man Farm

Commander Ivan Zelev of the Russian navy stepped out of the civilian-marked helicopter at the Stony Man chopper pad and removed his blindfold himself. "Thanks for the ride," he said in almost accent-free English over the noise of the still-spinning rotors.

Jack Grimaldi, Stony Man's resident pilot and aviation expert, raised one gloved hand in acknowledgment as the blacksuit who'd accompanied the Russian on the flight handed the man his kit bag. Waiting until his passengers had cleared the rotor's arc, Grimaldi pulled pitch, lifted off and turned the nose of the chopper back toward Washington, D.C.

Zelev stood as the civilian Jeep carrying what looked to be farm workers drove up to him. When the vehicle got closer, however, he saw that the men looked a little too alert and too hard core to be laborers. A life lived in the former Soviet Union had taught him what security people looked like, and these men had the unmistakable look.

No one patted him down for hardware—that had been done before he'd boarded the helicopter. But except for the driver, no one took his eyes off Zelev on the short drive to the three-story farmhouse in the center of the compound.

Three more hard-eyed men in blue coveralls met the Russian when he stepped out of the Jeep in front of the house. One took his bag while another patted him down for weapons. The third stood well back to have a good field of fire.

Zelev didn't make a fuss when the stony-faced security man relieved him of his wallet, key ring, passport, cigarette case and even his pocket change and handkerchief. Under the circumstances, he would have done the same. He expected that his belongings would be returned to him after they had been examined. At least in the United States, he wouldn't have to worry about anything being pilfered. There was nothing he owned that any American would want.

When he was completely clean, two of the guards escorted him through the door to an entry hall inside. A big burly man in a wheelchair and a stunning blonde were waiting to greet him. The woman stepped forward, her hand extended. "I'm Barbara Price and this is Aaron Kurtzman. Welcome to Stony Man Farm."

"Commander Ivan Zelev," he said, bowing low over Barbara's hand. "At your service."

Releasing her hand, he stepped up to Kurtzman's chair. "I'm pleased to meet you, sir," he said and extended his hand low enough for the Bear to reach.

Kurtzman took Zelev's hand. "Welcome aboard."

"If there is someplace where I may clean up a little?" the Russian said. "I am prepared to brief you and begin assisting your efforts in any way that I can."

"We have a room ready for you," Price replied. "I'll show you to it."

"Thank you very much."

WHEN ZELEV WAS ESCORTED into the briefing room a few minutes later, he found his kit bag and personal effects waiting for him. He filled his pockets again before opening the bag and taking out a locked briefcase.

"Here's what we are looking for," the Russian said, handing over a photo of a submarine tied up to a shipyard slip. "This was taken right before work was halted on her. In the Russian navy, she was simply called Hull Number 3865—no name had been assigned to her yet. We don't know what the Ukrainians are calling her now."

"What's this about it being a stealth sub that can't be detected?" Kurtzman asked.

"See the faceted shape of the conning tower and the fins at the stern?" Zelev said. "That was done to deflect sonar pulses the same way as your stealth fighter deflects radar. Also, it doesn't show in this photo, but the shape of the hull itself has been changed to do the same thing."

He pulled out a three-view drawing of the sub to show the flattened profile.

"These shape changes, however, are only one aspect of its stealth capabilities. The second and probably most important thing is that this sub is very quiet."

The Russian paused and looked embarrassed. "A couple of your countrymen passed information about your very quiet Seawolf submarines to us and we incorporated the improved machinery in our design."

"You will give us their names, of course," Price said.

"Of course."

"Thirdly," the Russian continued, "the ship's screw was redesigned so that it does not cavitate at high speeds and leave a bubble trail that sonar can detect."

"So you're saying that this thing really is undetectable," Kurtzman said.

"Not totally," Zelev replied. "But it is difficult to detect her unless you know exactly what you are looking for."

"And what is that?"

The Russian went into his briefcase again and pulled out what looked like graphs of some kind of sound wave. "Since the sub was never completed, we don't know exactly how she will actually look to sonar. But—" he passed over the graphs "—these were worked up on a scale model of the hull and sail design and show how she should look."

"Can I give these to our Naval Intelligence," Price asked, "so they can disseminate this information to our fleet?"

"Certainly," Zelev replied. "The sooner we find this ship, the better off all of us are going to be."

"What about the missiles and nuclear torpedoes?" Kurtzman asked. "How did they get away with them?"

This was the question Zelev had been dreading because it made his navy look more than incompetent, it made them look criminally negligent.

"We, too, have traitors in our country," he admitted. "It seems that the officer in charge of security for the nuclear weapons storage facility was too fond of the good life. For a few thousand of your dollars, he allowed Ukrainian nationalists access to the weapons."

"I'd like to get my hands on that bastard," Kurtzman growled.

"You're a bit late," Zelev said grimly. "Unless you have a free pass to Hades. He was tried and executed the day I left Moscow."

Two HOURS LATER, Aaron Kurtzman frowned as he read through the South African maritime report that his new computer program had highlighted for him. When the search started for the missing Russian stealth sub, he had created a new program to read through naval and merchant marine reports from around the world. He hadn't known what he was looking for when he wrote the program, but he did now.

"Where's Zelev?" he asked when Barbara Price walked into the Computer Room.

"Still sleeping off the jet lag. Why?"

"I think I've found where his missing sub was."

"Was?"

"The South Africans just lost a freighter carrying a load of industrial diamonds."

"What do you mean 'lost'?"

"It disappeared in the South Atlantic yesterday."

"How does a ship disappear nowadays?" she asked frowning. "Was there a storm?"

"No storm, and there weren't any radio messages of mechanical problems, either. It just simply disappeared."

"And you think the sub sank it?"

"Either that or a sea monster got it, and I stopped believing in fairy tales a long time ago."

"Have you run it through the recon tapes yet?"

One source of vital information that came into Stony Man Farm every few hours were copies of the tapes from the Keyhole series recon satellites that endlessly circled the Earth every day. Whatever happened around the world, if it happened when one of the satellites was overhead, the happening would be caught on the tapes.

"Not yet, but I know what they're going to show."

"What's that?"

"They're going to show the SS *Springbok* steaming along on one pass and then the next time the satellite comes over, there'll be nothing down there but water."

"How do you know?"

"Call it a hunch. Plus, I've always had a weakness for pirates. And what better use of a stealth sub than high-seas piracy."

"I don't think that Hal's going to buy a hunch like that, even coming from you."

"You tell me where the *Springbok* went then. She was a new ship and the pride of the South African fleet. She didn't just disappear."

"Run the tapes, Aaron," Price repeated. "Get the proof, and then I'll call it in to Hal."

Kurtzman's fingers flew over his keyboard. "I'm on it."

When the recon tapes were played back, they showed exactly what Kurtzman had predicted they would. On the first pass, a ship was plainly visible in the upper-left-hand quadrant of the satellite's lens, where the *Springbok* should have been at that time.

Computer enhancement clearly identified the ship as being the South African vessel.

The next time the satellite passed over the South Atlantic, roughly an hour and a half later, the ocean was empty except for a tramp steamer heading in the other direction and a large oil tanker steaming due north. The *Springbok* had disappeared without leaving a trace.

He made hard copies of the satellite tapes so Price could fax them to Hal. Slipping the photos into an envelope, he wheeled his chair out of the room in search of the mission controller.

MACK BOLAN STILL WORE his blacksuit and combat cosmetics when he walked into the Israeli war room at the command post a few klicks back from the security zone bordering Lebanon. His weapons and assault harness, however, had been left with the no-nonsense security detachment outside the bomb-proof door.

Their armed escort took them to a briefing room where a tall Israeli officer waited. Katzenelenbogen stepped forward to make the introductions. "I would like you to meet Colonel Dov Stielmann of the Mossad. He's the man who made our mission possible by getting the target information for us."

Bolan extended his hand. "I would like to thank you for that, Colonel."

"No," Stielmann said in faintly accented English, "it is I who should thank you and your men." He nodded to the others, who had followed Bolan into the room. "You have done us all a great favor and we are in your debt."

Stielmann had an idea who Bolan and his men were, though not by name specifically. These commandos were legends in the inner circles of the Israeli Defense and Intelligence establishments. Nonetheless, this was the first time he had met them in person, so Katzenelenbogen made the introductions using their current cover names.

Stielmann fully appreciated the need for that. Two of Abu Askari's most recent victims had been American and Russian nationals. With Bolan's team posing as international mercenaries hired by the families involved, the Israeli government's hands were officially clean and the payback raid wouldn't disturb the shaky peace negotiations with the Palestinians. Like Katz, he had had enough of war and was willing to give peace a chance.

"Before we start the debriefing," Stielmann said as soon as the introductions were over, "I have a message for you from someone called The Bear. You're to contact him as soon as you can."

"May I use your secure communications?" Bolan asked. "I should make that call now."

"Certainly," the Israeli replied, pointing to a bank of electronic consoles behind a glass partition at the end of the briefing room. "Tell the men inside to leave you alone while you make your call."

As soon as the Israeli radiomen cleared out, Bolan changed the radio frequency to one of the Farm's general-use channels. Aaron Kurtzman came on the line almost immediately. "Is this a secure line?" he asked.

"It's an Israeli facility," Bolan replied. He didn't have to explain that his hosts were recording everything he said and would unscramble it later. Allies or not, that was standard Israeli practice.

"Understood," Kurtzman answered. "Barbara needs you to get to a secure line as soon as possible. You'll be staying in Europe for a little longer than we had planned, and Ironman's people will be joining you shortly."

"What's the mission?"

"We'll talk about it later. How much longer do you think it will be before you're wrapped up where you are?"

Bolan glanced at his watch. "I can be at the embassy in Tel Aviv in about two hours."

"That's plenty of time," Kurtzman answered. "I'll have your air transport on hand by then."

"Where are we going?"

"You're joining the Navy for a while."

Bolan frowned. Naval operations could mean anything.

"You'll be going to the USS *Kitty Hawk*," Kurtzman continued, "where you'll join up with a Russian liaison officer. Your mission packs will be waiting there for you, and he'll have all the extra details you'll need."

"I'll call you from the embassy as soon as I can."

"Do that. The Man is anxious about this one."

CHAPTER EIGHT

In the Atlantic

The Libyan-flagged supertanker was keeping only enough speed to maintain steering as it turned into the wind. The mid-Atlantic sea was choppy, but the big ship cut through the waves as if it were sailing in a bathtub.

Through the *Petlyura*'s periscope, Captain Oleg Yatkin watched the big ship complete her maneuver and awaited the signal to surface and pilot his sub inside the tanker. He had seen this very same operation in one of those Western movies about the secret agent James Bond. In the movie, though, the ship had been capturing submarines rather than serving as a mother ship for one.

He had to admit that it was a clever idea. Hidden inside the ship's converted oil tank hold, the *Petlyura* could transfer her hijacked cargo and be replenished without ever having to risk being caught in port by one of the American or Russian recon satellites. Now that he was commanding a pirate ship, his only

chance of remaining alive was not to be seen by anyone.

As the Libyan tanker pumped the water out of her
false bottom, she rose in the water until the top of the
doors in her bow were above the surface of the
waves. Hydraulic rams forced the massive doors
open against the water pressure until the entire bow
of the ship was gaping open like a huge maw waiting
to suck the submarine inside and swallow it whole.
Yatkin thought that it rather looked like the Bible
story about Jonah and the Whale that his mother
had read to him when he was a child.

When the signal finally came, he ordered the sub
to the surface. As soon as the top of the sail broke
through the water, Yatkin transferred the conn to the
small control room in the top of the sail. From there,
he would pilot the *Petlyura* into the mother ship
himself.

With the sub's screw barely turning, Yatkin deli-
cately steered the sub through the choppy seas. Unlike the tanker, the sub wasn't large enough to shake
off the waves. Though the opening in the mother
ship's bow had looked huge from a distance, when
he got closer he saw that it was going to be a tight
squeeze. Nonetheless, he managed to thread the
needle without scraping the hull.

Once inside, Yatkin blinked, trying to adjust to the
dim light of the cavernous hold of the ship. Now he
really felt like Jonah inside the whale. As soon as the

bow doors closed behind the boat, lights came on, illuminating steel walkways on both sides of the interior.

When men with lines jumped onto the sub's hull to tie her off to the bollards welded to the walkway, Yatkin ordered the reactor shut down. As soon as it was secure, he told his first officer to take over and headed for the conning tower hatch leading outside.

Omar Rashid smiled to himself when he saw where Yatkin was headed. The Ukrainian was due for a rude shock when he got in contact with his superiors. Several aspects of the alliance between Libya and the Ukrainian Republic had been kept secret from the young sub captain. Certain facts of life were too hard for someone so young and politically inexperienced. But the Libyan mentally shrugged. He would have to learn fast or he would die.

When Yatkin stormed into the mother ship's radio room, he found half a dozen men at the consoles. "Out of here!" he growled. "All of you!"

The Libyan radiomen looked to their officer who shrugged and headed for the door. As soon as he had the room to himself, Yatkin switched the radio over to the frequency that was being monitored back in the Ukraine. As soon as his call was answered, he demanded to be patched through to the chairman of the Nationalists' secret council.

WHEN YATKIN WALKED OUT of the radio room, he looked pale. He had known that he would command a pirate ship for his homeland, but he hadn't expected that he would have to become a murderer for his beloved Ukraine as well. He was ready to die for his country, but to kill innocent merchant seamen for her was something else entirely. This wasn't what he had worked so hard to do.

It hadn't been easy to turn Hull Number 3865 into a fully operating submarine. The team of engineers and shipyard workers who had been smuggled on board the abandoned ship had worked long hours under the constant threat of discovery and imprisonment to make it happen.

As the sub's captain, he had been there almost every minute of that time as well. When not supervising the work, he had kept watch, signaling for silence every time someone approached close enough to hear the sound of the machinery at work. Then had come the loading of the weapons.

That had been even more dangerous, as it had had to be done in broad daylight. To accomplish that, they had first brought dummy ordnance into the sub over a period of several nights. The next day, they had loaded the ordnance barge with the real weapons and brought it alongside the sub. They had rigged the torpedo crane and brought out all the dummy weapons one at a time.

The thing was, for each dummy weapon the crane took out, it left a real weapon in its place. From a distance, it was hard to tell if the crane was taking them out, or putting them into the hatches. After a nerve-racking three hours, the ordnance barge was towed back to its berth and the sub was armed.

It had been both dangerous and thrilling work that he had thought was being done for the good of his homeland. Now, though, he wasn't so sure, but he was committed. Even if he told his superiors that he wanted out, in the eyes of the world, he would still be held responsible for the first sinking. His only option was to stay with the sub and see this through to the bitter end. He just hoped that it would all be worth it.

BACK IN THE *Petlyura*, Yatkin found that the Libyans had already taken the diamonds away for safekeeping. He was beginning to have doubts about what would be done with them, but he was helpless to do anything about it. His orders were specific on that point. He was to turn over all of his pirated cargoes to the Libyans for disposal.

Inside the sub's control room, he found Rashid waiting for him. "You have the information about the next target?" the Libyan asked.

Yatkin nodded. "A Japanese freighter carrying electronic equipment."

"Advanced electronic equipment," Rashid corrected him. "Both our nations desperately need high-speed computers if we are ever going to be able to develop our own high-technology industries to compete with the West."

"How many crewmen will be on that ship?"

The Libyan smiled thinly. "Not as many as were on the *Springbok*. The Japanese have automated their ships as well as their factories, so you won't have as many deaths on your conscience this time."

Yatkin turned away without speaking.

WHEN MACK BOLAN and Phoenix Force walked into the American embassy in Tel Aviv, they were wearing casual clothing. Showing up in public in their combat dress would have attracted unwanted attention, and that was the last thing they needed right now.

News of their hit on Abu Askari and his Soldiers of God had been leaked to the press, to show the Palestinian radicals that they couldn't get away with disturbing the peace process. As had been planned, mercenaries had been credited with the hit to keep the Israelis off the hook.

After Bolan presented his Mike Belasko passport to the Marine sergeant on the security desk in the lobby, the team was immediately escorted to the secure briefing room down the hall. The CIA station chief for Tel Aviv had been alerted and was waiting impatiently for them. He knew when an operation was going down, and he didn't like to be kept in the dark about it—particularly when it was going down in his territory. The call he had received from Langley had told him only to cooperate completely with these people.

He would do as he had been told, of course, but not without getting answers to his questions. Not even the desk jockeys back at Langley could fault him for wanting to know what was happening on his watch. He was a field man, the station chief, and couldn't do his job if he didn't know what in the hell was going on.

"Which one of you guys is Mike Belasko?"

"I am," Bolan stated, stepping forward.

The CIA chief studied the man in front of him and the five hard cases standing beside him. They looked like refugees from a chain gang, not anyone connected with any part of the United States government he was familiar with.

"I'm Jim Pritcher, station chief," he finally said.

Bolan quickly ran through the cover names for the Phoenix Force warriors.

"I don't know who in the hell you people think you are," Pritcher snapped after the introductions had been made, "but the next time you are operating in Israel, you might want to coordinate with me before—"

"It's not who we think we are that counts." Bolan stepped up to the CIA man. His eyes shifted to take him in from head to toe. "Nor do I think that it's really any of your business who we are. My understanding is that you've been asked to assist us."

The CIA chief looked away for a moment. He wasn't used to being challenged in his own station, but his orders had been specific. Anything these guys wanted, they got. No questions asked, or even allowed. Orders or not, though, he was going to use his own judgment on this one.

"I have been ordered to assist you," he grudgingly admitted, "and your men. So, what can I do for you?"

"I need to use your secure communications, and we all could use a cup of coffee and a sandwich."

Pritcher stiffened. Who in the hell did this guy think he was, a lunch counter waitress? "I'll have the kitchen send something up."

"Thank you," Bolan said. "Now, if I can use your comm room."

"Follow me."

Pritcher led Bolan down the hall to a room secured with an electronically locked metal door. Slipping his magnetically keyed card through the lock, he opened the door and led the Executioner inside. "Here," he said. "Help yourself."

"I need all the recording devices turned off."

The CIA chief smiled. "I'm sorry, but it's station SOP that we record all communications so that—"

"If you have a problem with my request," Bolan said, "I suggest that you contact Langley immediately and reference Hal Brognola."

Bolan allowed the trace of a smile to cross his lips. "Then you can pack your personal effects and say goodbye to the staff, because you'll be on the next plane back to the States and civilian life. This request is not negotiable."

For a split second Pritcher considered telling this Mike Belasko guy to stuff his request and get the hell out of the embassy. Something in the big man's eyes, however, told him that it would be a mistake to press the issue. He would, however, get in contact with Langley as soon as they cleared out and file a complaint about the incident.

Without saying a word, Pritcher reached down to the master control board and turned off the recording devices. "There."

"Thank you," Bolan said dismissively.

As soon as he was alone, he switched frequency on the radio and got through to Kurtzman.

WHEN BOLAN RETURNED to the briefing room, he saw that Pritcher had posted a young Marine sergeant to watch over Phoenix Force.

McCarter looked up in disgust when Bolan walked in. "The chaps in the kitchen here could sure use a few lessons in exactly what constitutes a proper sandwich," he growled. "The plastic cheese is definitely not on. Neither is the tuna-fish mash. Whatever happened to roast beef and horseradish?"

Bolan walked over to the table and poured himself a cup of coffee. After running an eye across the sandwich tray, he decided to take McCarter's advice and pass on the embassy cuisine.

"As soon as you're finished with lunch here, we've got a plane to catch," he told the men. With the guard in the room, no one asked him where they were going.

He turned to the Marine. "Tell your boss that we will need transportation to the Israeli IDF airfield in ten minutes."

"Yes, sir." The Marine turned to go.

"And tell him that we need an unmarked vehicle with Israeli plates."

"What's the drill?" Katzenelenbogen asked when the door closed behind the Marine.

"We're transferring our operations to the *Kitty Hawk*. The Russians have lost a submarine and Hal wants us to find it for them."

"What's on this missing sub that we have to find?"

"Aaron's not sure yet, but it might be carrying nuclear missiles."

"Bloody hell!" McCarter exploded. "Why can't the Russkies keep better track of their hardware?"

"It was the Ukrainians this time," Bolan told him. "And I'm sure Aaron asked them the same question. As well, the missiles are on board a sub that can't be detected."

"Say again?" James queried.

"Aaron says that it's some kind of stealth sub that's invisible to sonar."

"So how are we supposed to find it?" Katzenelenbogen asked. "Use magnets?"

"Actually," James broke in, "that's not a bad idea. Did Aaron say anything about finding it with Magnetic Anomaly Detection?"

Bolan shook his head. "No, he didn't, but that will be my first question to the Russian submarine specialist we'll be working with."

CHAPTER NINE

Southern Oregon

Able Team didn't stop in for a couple of well-earned cool ones at the Stewed Owl on their way back through Benton. By now, the locals were sure to know that several of their drinking buddies were dead, and that the Feds had another one of them in custody because of them. News traveled fast in a small town. If they didn't want to have to stack up more bodies, it was best that they just keep on driving.

As soon as the Blazer reached the north-south I-5 freeway at Ashland, Carl Lyons turned off at the service station and truck stop right by the on ramp. While the pump jockey filled the Blazer's tanks, Rosario Blancanales went to the men's room and Hermann Schwarz headed into a convenience store for a soft drink and something to eat.

As soon as Blancanales returned to keep an eye on the contents of their vehicle, Lyons headed for the pay phones in the corner of the lot. Using one of

Schwarz's portable scramblers, he put in a call to Barbara Price back at Stony Man.

The mission controller came on the phone immediately and took his report on the Benton mission. Then, she had new instructions. "Aaron says that you guys might as well drive on back to Portland. With the local flight schedules the way they are, you'll get there just as quickly as if you try to catch a flight at Medford or Eugene to PDX. He says that if you hump it, you should be able to catch the red-eye to Washington National. Grimaldi will be there to pick you up."

"What then?"

"He'll also have a change of clothes for you guys and tickets for a nonstop to Rome."

Lyons groaned to himself. That meant close to sixteen hours in a plane. "I hope these are first-class tickets this time. I'm a little tired of traveling back in baggage class."

"It's first class out of PDX and then an Air Force C-141 to Rome."

"Aw shit."

"Can't be helped," Price stated. She knew that flying an Air Force C-141 Starlifter wasn't anyone's idea of a comfortable ride. On top of that, the flight attendants usually had to shave every morning. But they were faster than anything going across the Atlantic except the Concorde. "Striker needs you guys in Rome ASAP."

"When do we get the mission packs?"

"Grimaldi will have them for you."

"What do you want us to do with the hard-ware?" The back of the Blazer was full of weapons and ammunition, so it couldn't just be abandoned.

"I'll have someone meet you in Portland and take the rig off your hands."

"Tell him to meet me outside on the departure deck."

"Good luck."

Back at the Blazer, Schwarz was just finishing up a ham-and-cheese sandwich served in a bubble pack with two limp slices of pickle.

"Not bad," he said as he crumpled up the plastic wrapper. "Last week was a good week for the sand-wich concession here. The mayo wasn't too rancid and the ham was a delightful shade of iridescent green. Maybe I should do another one."

Lyons shuddered. As far as he was concerned, convenience-store sandwiches could only be consid-ered food if you were starving to death.

"If you guys are done, we have a long drive ahead of us and then an even longer flight."

"Where are we going?" Schwarz asked.

"Rome."

"Georgia or Italy?"

"They don't have fried chicken and sweet-potato pie where we're going."

That perked up both Schwarz's and Blancanales's ears. Neither one had been in Europe for some time now. "Why are we being honored with a vacation?" Schwarz asked.

"I don't know yet," Lyons said. "Grimaldi will have our mission packs when we hit D.C."

"Why is it that I don't think we're going to get much time to enjoy the sights in the Eternal City?" Schwarz asked, sighing. "You know, the 'Three Coins in the Fountain' bit—sipping espresso, poisoning the pigeons in the square, diving for loose change and all that. I've always wanted to see Rome."

"Because it's our turn in the barrel again, that's why."

"It's always our turn in the barrel."

"You can always phone in a complaint if you don't like it. Just dial 1-800-who-gives-a-shit."

"I read somewhere that a leader is always supposed to keep his men's welfare in mind at all times."

"You've been reading the wrong book," Lyons said.

"Damn, I knew something wasn't right."

"WHY IS IT ALWAYS raining when we fly into this place?" Schwarz asked no one in particular as Able Team deplaned at Washington, D.C.'s National Airport in the middle of the night.

"Aaron ordered it especially for you, Gadgets," a familiar voice said from the bottom of the boarding ramp.

"Jack Grimaldi!" Schwarz feigned surprise. "How nice to see you. How long has it been?"

"Can the crap," Lyons growled, "and let's get out of this rain."

Even though their seats on the flight from Portland had been in the first-class cabin, the ex-L.A. cop was in no mood for chitchat. Between Blancanales trying to get a phone number from a beautiful young flight attendant and Schwarz living the high life on the "company" credit card, he hadn't gotten a hell of a lot of sleep. And he didn't expect to get much on the next leg of the flight either.

"Come on over to the car." Grimaldi glanced at his watch. "I've got your stuff in the back, and I'll brief you on the way to Andrews. Our C-141 is waiting."

The car turned out to be an unmarked four-door sedan parked in the security zone next to the terminal building. The driver was in civilian clothes, but the short haircut and black low quarter shoes gave him away as being some kind of Fed, probably one of Brognola's Justice Department agents.

As soon as the car pulled out into traffic, Grimaldi turned on the dome light and handed out the mission packets. "Like Barbara told you, Hal's sending us to Italy."

"We?" Lyons questioned.

"Yeah." The pilot grinned. "He wants me to tag along on your vacation to keep you out of trouble."

"What are we going to do on our vacation," Schwarz asked, "lie on the beaches or visit the wine factory and the pasta groves?"

"We're going to find a stealth submarine."

"Just what in the hell is a stealth sub?" Lyons frowned.

"It's a sub that you can't find with sonar," the pilot answered simply. "The Russians were working on it in their big Ukrainian shipyard, and now it's missing."

"Who made off with it?" Schwarz asked.

"The Russians think the Ukrainian nationalists were responsible for the snatch, but Aaron is holding out for Libyan involvement."

"What is it with those people?" Blancanales said. "Every time you turn around, they have their hands in crap like this."

Schwarz shrugged. "I guess some people are just no damned good."

"What are we going to be able to do about finding a sub?" Lyons asked. "If you'll remember, that's not exactly our area of expertise."

"The sub's turned pirate ship," Grimaldi stated, "and it's attacking freighters on the high seas. Aaron thinks that you three guys might be able to work on the traditional Mediterranean smuggling connections and pick up a tip from the fences.''

Lyons looked at the pilot like he had three heads. "He wants us to bump heads with the Italian Mafia on their own home turf? What's he been smoking? If he hasn't been watching CNN lately, those guys are having a full-scale shooting war with the government right now. You know, car bombs, political assassinations, that kind of thing.''

"He's got papers for us and a cover story.''

"All that means is that if we go in as hoods, the Italian police will be on our asses instead of the Mafia.''

"Into each life, a little rain must fall," Grimaldi replied, smiling.

"Well, it's going to be raining on you, too, if you go with us, old buddy.''

Grimaldi grinned. "As McCarter would say, I'll just be sure to wear my rubbers.''

"You'd better make sure that they're made of Kevlar.''

WHILE GRIMALDI and Able Team were winging across the Atlantic in the Air Force C-141, Bolan and the Phoenix Force commandos were touching down on the flight deck of the USS *Kitty Hawk*. The nuclear-powered aircraft carrier was the most powerful ship in the Mediterranean and the flagship of the U.S. 6th Fleet. When there was trouble in the Middle East or Europe, the Navy jets of the *Kitty Hawk* were the hard-hitting, mailed fist of American diplomacy.

This time, though, the *Kitty Hawk* had a new role. For the first time in her history, the carrier was serving as the home base for a clandestine attack force searching for a stealth sub.

The twin turboprop, C-2 Carry On Delivery—COD—carrying the Stony Man team hooked the first landing wire with her tail hook and slammed down onto the *Kitty Hawk*'s deck. As soon as the tractor had pulled the plane to her tie-down spot on the deck, Bolan and Phoenix Force picked up their flight bags and deplaned.

Waiting to meet them was a Navy officer in fresh khakis, the twin silver bars of a lieutenant pinned on his collar. "Mike Belasko?" he asked, scanning the men in front of him.

"I'm Belasko," Bolan said, stepping forward and extending his hand.

The lieutenant shook his hand. "I'm Jim Billings, sir," he said. "Welcome to the *Kitty Hawk*."

"Glad to be aboard."

"If you gentlemen will come this way, the captain is waiting for you in his cabin."

The lieutenant showed Bolan to the captain's door and knocked. When a voice inside told him to enter, he opened the door and waved the warrior through.

"I'm Ron Wilford," the captain said, extending his hand, "and this is Commander Jack Dibbles, my Intelligence officer."

Bolan quickly introduced the rest of the team, and the captain offered them seats around the small conference table in the side room. "To what do I owe the pleasure of your visit, Mr. Belasko?" he asked.

The encrypted, classified message he had received from COMLANT, which stood for the admiral commanding the Atlantic fleet, had merely told him to extend every courtesy to his mysterious visitors without telling him who they were. It had also ordered him to take part in an operation they would brief him on once they arrived.

Bolan quickly outlined the information he had about the missing Russian submarine and its deadly cargo.

"A stealth sub." The captain frowned. "I'm not sure that I understand what you're talking about."

"It's a submarine that's undetectable to sonar."

Suddenly the light went on. "You mean that it could get past the destroyer screen undetected?"

"That's what I've been told."

"Holy Jesus, Mary and Joseph," the Intelligence officer said softly. "That makes us sitting ducks."

"That's about it," Bolan agreed.

"Where was this sub last reported?" Captain Wilford growled.

"She hasn't been spotted since she left the shipyard in the Ukraine," the Executioner replied. "But now that we're aboard, if I can use your communications room, I'll be able to get more information for you and an update."

"By all means," the captain said. "Commander Dibbles will take you there right now."

He looked at the other men sitting around the table. "And, I will have your men billeted with my Marine contingent."

"If it's possible," Bolan said, "I would like them to be quartered separately and isolated. We like to work that way, and we need to keep this as classified as possible."

"I don't see a problem," Wilford replied. "Is there anything else you need?"

"A secure briefing room and quarters for another officer who will be joining us shortly, a Russian."

That raised more than one eyebrow.

"We're expecting a Russian naval officer," Bolan explained. "A submarine expert who's going to help us track this thing down."

''How is he coming aboard?''

''My understanding is that he will be flying in from Russia tomorrow morning. I'll get a confirmation as soon as I can get to a fax machine.''

''A Russian landing on my carrier.'' The captain shook his head. ''And I thought that this was going to be some kind of a political junket.''

''I wish it was.''

CHAPTER TEN

In the Mediterranean

The dark gray, two-seat Sukhoi Su-27N Flanker jet fighter with the white-outlined red star insignia looked more than a little out of place as it made a low pass over the nuclear carrier USS *Kitty Hawk*. The Russian fighter's weapons pylons were empty, and her gear and flaps were down to slow her speed as she made the flyby. Keeping pace off both her wings were two F-14D Tomcats from the *Kitty Hawk*. Their job was to guide the Russian pilot into the landing slot.

"You're not looking too happy this morning, CAG," Captain Wilford commented when he stepped out onto the observation platform overlooking the flight deck.

Lieutenant Commander Greg Connors was the Commander of the *Kitty Hawk*'s Air Group and was usually addressed as "CAG," the acronym for the initials of his title.

"Sorry, sir," Connors replied, shaking his head slowly. "It's just that I never thought I'd see a Russian Flanker landing on our decks. If he screws up the touchdown, we're going to be in a world of hurt."

"According to the message I received," the captain replied, "this guy's supposed to be fully carrier-landing qualified, as well as one of their hotshot pilots."

"Hotshot pilot or not, I don't like it. He might be qualified to land on the *Varyag,* but he's sure as hell not carrier qualified in my Air Group."

"CINCLANT says that we've got to take him on board."

"'Ours not to reason why. His but to do or die.'" The aviation officer purposefully misquoted Tennyson.

"That's more or less exactly what CINCLANT said. And what is said at the operational headquarters of the Atlantic fleet is what goes."

When the Flanker was in the slot for landing, the two Tomcats peeled off and left the Russian pilot to the chancy business of landing on a carrier deck. The huge angled deck of the supercarrier was more than twice the size of a WWII flattop, but jet aircraft landed at high speeds and carrier landings were still controlled crashes.

The firefighting and recovery crews in their fireproof suits were standing by in case the pilot blew it and turned his Flanker into a ball of flame in the middle of the flight deck. A rescue chopper with divers on board was also hovering next to the ship in case the Russians wound up in the sea. Everyone else had been cleared off the deck. There would be no gawkers for this landing.

Following the colored lights on the Frensel lens equipment of the landing signal officer, the Russian pilot made a textbook approach. Nose high, he came in over the fantail, engaged his tail hook on the first arresting wire and chopped his engines. The massive Sukhoi fighter was jerked to an abrupt halt and settled down onto the deck.

Connors let out the breath he had been holding and turned to the captain. "I'll see to getting them squared away."

"Invite them to join our other guests at my table for lunch."

"Aye, sir."

"And I want you there, as well, CAG."

The aviator smiled. "I wouldn't miss it for the world."

On the flight deck, the Flanker's twin canopy opened and the rear seat passenger climbed out first. The Russian officer was dressed in a black coverall uniform with the shoulder boards of a lieutenant commander and the insignia of a submariner on his chest. Stepping away from the fighter, he waited for the American officer who was approaching him.

"Commander Greg Connors," the sailor stated, stepping up to him and extending his hand. "I'm commander of the Air Group. Welcome aboard the *Kitty Hawk*."

The Russian stiffened to attention as he took Connors's hand. "Lieutenant Commander Viktor Solikov, Russian navy," he said in almost accentless English. "I'm glad to be here, sir."

He turned to the pilot, who had silently joined him. "This is Senior Lieutenant Dmitri Gorbunov, my pilot for this journey."

The pilot saluted before taking Connors's extended hand.

"His English isn't that good," Solikov said with a smile, "so I'll translate for him. He says that he enjoyed his landing very much and would like to do it again."

Connors laughed. "If you gentlemen will follow me, I'll see you to your quarters."

"A latrine would be nice, too," Solikov stated. "It has been a long flight."

Connors laughed. "There's one right inside the passageway. I'll lead you to it."

"THIS GLASNOST STUFF is going to kill me yet, sir," Connors said when he reported to Captain Wilford later. "Our Russian guests are reluctantly drinking coffee because we don't serve vodka in the wardroom. I've already turned down a request to take the pilot up in the back seat of a Tomcat and had to explain that we don't have any Playboy movies."

"Just wait until you meet our other guests," the captain said. "They'll make your Russians seem almost normal."

"Who are they?"

"Their leader says they're civilian, but I think they really work for the Company. Whoever they are, though, the admiral says that I'm to do anything he asks short of letting him conn the ship."

"I hate these spook operations," Connors said. "I thought the cold war games were supposed to be over."

"Apparently not," Wilford stated, shaking his head. He wished that he could take Connors into his confidence and explain the stealth sub problem, but Belasko's instructions were specific on that point. Only those with a "need to know" would be told about it, and he reserved the right to decide who those people would be.

A BRIEFING ROOM HAD BEEN made available for Bolan and his team deep within the bowels of the ship. Two Marine guards were on duty outside the door to make sure that only those who were on the access list even came into the passageway outside the room.

After seeing that his pilot was settled down with the Air Group, Solikov was escorted to the briefing room. Bolan turned when the door opened and the Russian walked in. "Here you are, sir," the Marine sergeant told the Russian.

"Thank you, Sergeant."

The Russian stiffened to a position of attention and introduced himself. "Lieutenant Commander Viktor Solikov, Russian navy."

"Mike Belasko."

Bolan quickly made the introductions for the rest of the team, using their current cover names. Solikov shook each man's hand in turn.

"Can I get you a cup of coffee before we get started?" Bolan asked.

"Thanks," Solikov said, moving toward the table with the coffee cups and hot drink canisters. "I can help myself, thank you."

"What can you tell us about this missing submarine of yours?" Bolan asked as soon as the Russian took a chair at the table.

Solikov opened his briefcase and pulled out a stack of documents marked with bold red stripes and words in Russian that had to translate as "top secret." Pulling out glossy photographs, he passed them around and then proceeded to give the men at the table a five-minute briefing on the submarine and its unique capabilities.

"So there's no way of tracking or locating this thing when it's submerged?" David McCarter asked as soon as the Russian was finished.

Solikov shrugged. "That's about it."

"Bloody hell!"

"How long can it stay at sea?" Rafael Encizo asked.

"That depends on how much expendable supplies it has stocked inside. But, like any nuclear-powered submarine, it can stay submerged for several months at a time."

"How did you people 'lose' this thing anyway?" Calvin James asked.

"As you are well aware," Solikov replied, "things are difficult in Russia right now. Particularly with regards to the pullout of our military forces from the so-called break-away republics, like the Ukraine. In most of these areas, the political situation is delicate to say the least. To a great degree, we have to rely on the cooperation of the nationalist forces involved. In this case, they pulled an end run, I think you call it, on us."

It was an end run all right, Bolan thought. But usually the quarterback wasn't carrying nuclear weapons. "What's your command doing to try to locate this sub?" he asked.

"We have all our recon satellites searching, and our naval forces are ordered to be on the lookout for it."

"How about Russian Military Intelligence?" McCarter spoke up. "Has its spy network been able to come up with any leads?"

"No. The problem there is that we have had to cut back on our foreign operations to the point that we have very few operatives outside our own territories now."

"Even in the Ukraine?"

"There most of all. The political animosity makes it particularly dangerous for our agents to operate in that nation."

McCarter grinned. "It's a bitch losing an empire, isn't it?"

"Yes, it is." Solikov smiled thinly before adding, "As you British should know."

"Okay," Bolan interjected before the conversation got out of hand. "Let's get back to the stealth sub."

After giving the Stony Man warriors more technical information about the sub, the Russian sat back in his chair. "That is about all I can tell you, gentlemen. Do you have any questions?"

"Where does this leave us, Mike?" Katzenelenbogen asked Bolan. "What are our options?"

"It leaves us waiting for whoever has that sub to make a mistake we can exploit, or until someone can get a lead we can follow up. Until that happens, we're just going to have to sit tight."

Bolan allowed a smile to cross his face. "The good news is that Lyons, Schwarz and Blancanales are arriving in Italy to work the smuggler connection for us."

"Who thought up that one?"

"Aaron. He thinks that since the sub has turned pirate, the Italian-Libyan connection is the most likely way for them to dispose of their looted cargo."

McCarter looked puzzled. "You mean to tell me that Gadgets, Pol and the Ironman are going undercover with the Italian Mafia?"

"And Grimaldi," Bolan added. "He went with them."

"God help us all."

Rome, Italy

HERMANN SCHWARZ PRESSED his face to the window as the C-141 Starlifter made its landing approach over the Italian countryside. "I think I'm going to like this place," he said. "It's nice and flat."

Lyons grinned. Italy boasted some of the most rugged mountains in Europe outside Switzerland. But, since airports were usually built on flat land, Gadgets had a surprise coming to him. Hopefully, though, they wouldn't have to get up in the Italian Alps. The smugglers they were targeted against worked the ports and coastlines.

After landing at the American Air Force base, the C-141 taxied into an empty hangar where the four Stony Man warriors were met by an escort. Their escort took them into a briefing room in the hangar occupied by three men.

The one who stepped forward with his hand out had to be an American. The white shoes and used-car-salesman look, however, meant that he was a political appointee instead of a foreign service professional.

"I'm Bob Brown, U.S. chargé d'affaires," the man said. "Glad to meet you boys. Anything the embassy can do for you while you're in Italy, all you have to do is call me. Ask for Bob."

Lyons shook his hand and introduced the rest of the team. Brown then introduced the other two men in civilian clothes as Dan Whelan, the head of the local DEA office, and Major Juliano Andrani, an Italian police officer. Then the embassy man looked slightly puzzled and turned to the DEA agent who nodded toward the door. Brown quickly made his exit.

"Sorry about that," Whelan said. "But Bob was cruising the classified-message log again and learned that you were coming in. He likes to think he's actually in charge of what goes on around here and insisted on meeting you."

"Can he be trusted to keep his mouth shut?"

"Actually he can. Which is more than I can say about almost anyone else you'll meet here, either U.S. or Italian.

"Because of that," Whelan went on, "Major Andrani here will be the only Italian official who will know who you really are. He and he alone can be trusted.''

"I knew things were bad here," Lyons said, "but I didn't know they were that bad."

"We might be overreacting," the DEA agent admitted, "but in your case, it's better to err on the side of caution. If word got out that you four people were here, you wouldn't make it off the air base."

The Italian officer nodded his confirmation. "The Mafia is very concerned about U.S. efforts to shut down their new heroin network. If they learn that you are connected with the U.S. Justice Department, they will not give you time to explain that you are not working on that particular problem."

"Thanks for the warning."

"My pleasure."

CHAPTER ELEVEN

When the embassy man ambled out of the briefing room the DEA agent handed four thick packets to the Stony Man warriors. "Here's the passports and documents we prepared for you," he said. "Along with credit cards in the same names and a few thousand dollars walking-around money. Mr. Grimaldi, your packet also has a current pilot's license in your passport name and logbook with an Italian endorsement. You'll be able to fly anything here except commercial aircraft."

He pointed to a stack of upscale, but obviously used suitcases resting on the table over against the wall. "If you'll repack your clothes into this luggage, we'll keep your other bags for you until you return. Four DEA agents matching your physical descriptions and booked on your passport names flew into Leonardo da Vinci International Airport an hour ago, and they were carrying this luggage."

"You guys are very thorough here." Blancanales nodded his approval.

"Unless you guys want to get killed, we have to be. Any Mafia contact you make here will check you out from top to bottom before telling you anything."

"What's the story on our hardware?" Lyons brushed the edge of his coat aside to show the Colt Python resting in his shoulder holster. With the Ironman it was always first things first.

"Your weapons?" He shrugged. "They're illegal in Italy. If you're caught with them, you'll be in deep shit until I can bail you out. And Italian jails aren't fun places."

He held up his hand. "However, this isn't like England. Everyone here is armed, particularly the people you'll be dealing with."

"We keep them then," Lyons said flatly.

"That's fine with me. You might need them before this is over."

Lastly Whelan handed over another thick packet. "You're going to want to go over this material carefully before you get started. It's the latest Intelligence printout on known Mafia players, hangouts and what they specialize in. If it's in that packet, you can pretty much count on it being accurate. The only surprises you'll have to worry about are the things that aren't in the report.

"Unfortunately though, that covers a lot of ground. Even though we have quite a few informers in the Families now, it's not like it is in the States. Back home, we know everything we need to know to put the Mafia out of business for good anytime the courts will let us. Here, it's only been the past few years that the Italians have been able to make any inroads against them at all. No offense, but I don't see how the hell Justice thinks you guys are going to be able to just fly in here and make a contact.''

''I know what you're saying,'' Lyons said. ''But we're not here to try to put the Mafia out of business. We're here to look for a stolen submarine.''

''A submarine?'' The look on the agent's face was comical. ''You're kidding, right?''

Schwarz grinned. ''And you thought we were here on a Justice Department junket.''

The man raised his hands. ''Don't tell me any more about it. I won't be able to resist telling my bar buddies.''

''You'd better keep this one to yourself,'' Lyons advised. ''It goes a lot higher than Justice.''

''I can believe that.''

LEAVING THE NATO AIR BASE without being seen was a snap. As soon as the men of Able Team were ready, they simply walked back out into the hangar bay, climbed into the back of a closed van and were driven away.

The ride south into the hills overlooking Naples took two hours. After threading its way through the narrow streets, the van stopped in an alley and the four men stepped out with their luggage. The hotel around the corner was a tourist trap, but four American hoods visiting Italy would hardly stay anywhere else.

After checking in, the four went down to the desk and rented a car to start the infiltration process. Though they were tired from the long flight, it was only early afternoon and it was never too soon to start scouting out the local situation.

As the team's wheelman as well as pilot, Grimaldi picked the car and chose a midsized Alfa-Romeo sedan. "We may need the speed," he explained, "and it never hurts to travel in style."

"You're getting a red one, I hope," Schwarz said. "Italian cars look good in red."

"We're in Italy," the pilot replied with a grin, "and it's red."

The port of Naples was a maze of narrow streets lying below the hills. Once at dockside, it looked like any modern port on the Mediterranean. In a word, it was crowded, dirty and ugly. Any charm it might once have had was gone in the name of concrete and modernization. Grimaldi pulled their rental up to the curb in what had to be the worst part of town.

Stepping out of the car, the team looked around for a minute or two before Lyons decided to try the place right in front of them.

"George's?" Schwarz said to himself as he read the painted sign on the wall. "What kind of Italian name is George?"

A sailors' bar in Naples should have been about the same as a sailors' bar anywhere in the world, but this place was in a class of its own. It looked tough in the extreme.

"You sure we want to have a drink here?" Schwarz asked when his eyes adjusted to the dim light. "We didn't get our shots updated before we left."

"We've been in worse places before," Blancanales observed.

"I know." Schwarz sounded weary. "But I've been trying to quit. The last time I was in a place like this, some asshole didn't like my boots and I had to counsel him about cultural diversity."

They chose a table away from the other solitary drinkers and ordered beer when the bartender came over. Right after he returned with their drinks, a tired, middle-aged prostitute walked up to their table and in broken English offered her professional services.

"Sorry, sweetheart," Lyons said, smiling as he shook his head.

She leaned over and, placing a hand on his shoulder, tried to bite his ear.

"Dammit!" he growled, jerking his head to the side. "I said I'm not interested."

Schwarz and Blancanales both stifled their laughs. That was what he got for coming into a dive like this.

The prostitute didn't even blink an eye when Lyons told her to leave. It had been a long time since she had been able to successfully work the tourist trade. But then, very few tourists ever made it to her part of town anyway, particularly American tourists. It was too bad about these guys though. The big blonde had been around the mountain a few times, but he looked like he still had a lot of juice in him. Being from northern Italy, she had always liked blondes.

She made her way back to her station at the end of the bar, whistling an old folk song from her hometown: "Tutti Mi Chiamano Bionda"—They all call me blond.

"What's the story with those guys?" the barkeep asked as she sat on her stool.

"Them," she replied, tossing her head. "They're just Americans who don't know how to treat a lady."

The barkeep sneered. "I can't see any ladies in here."

She ignored his gibe. In her work, she had long ago learned to ignore men who didn't appreciate that she provided a necessary social service. "Also, I think they are connected. When I tried to get friendly with the big blonde, I felt a shoulder holster and a big pistol."

The barkeep frowned. He didn't like to have armed men in his establishment unless he knew who they were. Tourists didn't carry guns, they didn't look like cops and they sure as hell weren't from the

Camorra, the local version of the Mafia. They could be from one of the American Families, however. Rome's anti-Mafia crackdown was making the American cousins nervous, and they were keeping a close eye on their business interests.

He leaned against the back bar, slowly polishing the fingerprints off of a dirty glass, and tried to remember if any of the local capos were holding a meeting that might include Americans, but he couldn't think of any. There were forty-two Camorra clans in Naples, and it was difficult to keep track of all of them.

As soon as these guys finished their drinks and left, though, he would call his district leader and report them. That would take care of his all-important obligation that allowed him to stay in business. In Naples, a man prospered or not depending on how much attention he paid to his obligations, and every man had at least one.

''Buttercup,'' he said to the hooker who was back into her Chianti, ''wiggle your behind outside and get the plate number for the car your blonde is driving.''

The woman pushed herself away from the bar, grabbed her purse and walked past the tables to the door. She had her obligations, too, and one of hers was to do the dirty work for the pig who ran the bar. The other was to sleep with him whenever his fat wife was mad at him.

"If I heard right," Grimaldi said softly, "the barkeep just told Sweet Thing there to go outside and take down our plate number."

"You sure?" Lyons asked.

"They speak a dialect here I'm not familiar with, but that's what it sounded like to me."

"Great," Schwarz said. "We just got our first entry in the opposition's data bank."

"We can always take the car back and rent another one."

"No," Lyons stated. "We came here to get noticed."

WHEN IVAN ZELEV was fully recovered from his jet lag he joined Aaron Kurtzman and Barbara Price in the War Room. Yet despite all the information that was coming in, they were making zero progress. But this was no surprise to any of them. How were they going to find a single submarine when so much of the planet's surface was covered with deep water? If the sub didn't want to be found, there was little they could do about it.

That single fact was the reason that the American ballistic missile submarine force had been such a potent nuclear deterrent during the long years of the cold war. Modern antisubmarine warfare was the art of trying to decide what target a submarine would hit and then trying to guard that target from attack.

In this instance, however, they had no way of knowing what the next target was going to be. The pirate sub could be anywhere in the world's oceans. Somehow, though, Zelev told them, he felt certain that it would turn up again in the same area. The Ukrainians were a provincial people with no interest in the vastness of the Pacific or anything else too far from their homeland.

So they would have to keep monitoring all incoming data, and hope that some indicators would provide a clue.

"WE JUST GOT ANOTHER LEAD on our pirate sub," Aaron Kurtzman told Barbara Price over the intercom. "A Japanese freighter carrying electronic gear went missing in the South Atlantic this morning."

"The same circumstances as the first one?"

"I've already run the tapes and it's the same story. She was steaming along in an empty ocean on one pass, and on the next there's no trace of her."

"I'm coming up."

Price quickly joined Kurtzman and Zelev in the Computer Room. "Do we have a manifest for the Japanese cargo?" she asked.

"Not yet, but it's reported to be high-speed industrial computers, state-of-the-art stuff headed for a car factory in Germany."

"Have you reported this to Striker and Hal yet?"

"No, I was waiting for the manifest."

"Get it to them now."

"Will do."

The nice thing about having Striker and the team on board the *Kitty Hawk* was that the carrier had secure communications gear able to accept even the most top-secret transmissions including encrypted faxes. It made keeping him informed easy for a change.

After Kurtzman updated Bolan and Brognola, he settled down to the matter at hand.

Now that there was a second missing ship that could only be explained by an attack of the pirate submarine, he had the beginnings of a pattern to work with. It was a scanty pattern to be sure, but it might be enough to give to the computers to see what they could find. First, though, he wanted to war-game it and see what he, Price and the Russian could come up with.

"Okay," Price said, "we've had two incidents now, and it's time that we tried to figure out what these guys are doing. The stolen diamonds are easy. They can be sold for hard cash almost anywhere in the world, no questions asked. The computers are a different matter. They are serial numbered, which makes them difficult to fence."

"And, they have limited application," Kurtzman pointed out. "These are the kind that are only used in industrial applications. Or in scientific research.

Therefore, they are more than likely to be used by whoever took them instead of being sold.''

"Which means a developing nation trying to hide some kind of research and that usually means forbidden weapons, nukes or chemical.''

"That's a safe assumption.''

"There is one other thing about the computers," the Russian spoke up. "They are bulky and there isn't that much storage room on board a submarine. The diamonds are easy, they're small and can be put into small packages and stored anywhere. But the computers are shipped in big packing crates, and they will have to be transferred soon if the sub is to continue being a pirate ship. One more hijacking like that, and they won't be able to crew the boat because the boxes will be in the way.''

That was the missing piece of the puzzle they had been needing. Now that they had it, maybe they could figure the rest of it out.

"Okay, what do you think they're going to do with them?'' Price asked. "What's the best way to trans-ship something like that?''

The Russian shrugged. "Since they can't risk making port, any port, in a stolen submarine, my guess is that they will try to transfer the cargo to another ship at sea. Something like what I think your Navy calls a submarine tender. We call them mother ships.''

Kurtzman and Price locked eyes. A mother ship, it was perfect. But just exactly what did the mother ship for a stealth submarine look like?

"What kind of ship do you think they'd use for that?" Kurtzman's fingers flew over his keyboard, bringing up a list of merchant ships.

"Actually almost any ship would do that has enough room to store the cargo."

"Great. Now I have to try to keep track of every tramp steamer in the Atlantic."

"Just be glad that the sub's not operating in the Pacific," Price pointed out.

"Bite your tongue."

A few keystrokes brought up on the monitor a list of ships plying the Atlantic. "Okay," Kurtzman told the Russian. "Help me find this mother ship of yours."

"Not mine, theirs."

WHILE THE TEAM at Stony Man was searching for Zelev's postulated submarine mother ship, Able Team was still trying to make headway in Italy. They found, though, that no one wanted to talk about anything other than such generalities as the weather.

But, while they had made no contact, their arrival in Naples hadn't gone unnoticed. As he was paid to do, the bartender at George's had reported their presence in town. So had the barkeeps at the next two clubs they'd visited. That evening, the waiter at their table in the hotel's restaurant reported their conversations as he had been instructed to do.

The next day, the four drove out to the civilian airport at the edge of the city. There, they rented an Augusta Bell helicopter and took a long flight up and down the coastline. Several times, they set the chopper on the beach and got out to walk around. Their object in the flight wasn't as much to scout anything out as it was to be noticed, and they were.

That evening, they dined again in the hotel's restaurant. Again, their waiter passed on their conversations. By the next morning anyone who was anyone knew that there were four new American players in town. Being Italians, though, those who knew of their presence preferred to speculate on what the strangers wanted rather than ask them, and Able Team still couldn't get a lead.

IT TOOK AWHILE for Kurtzman to get all the recon tapes he needed to make the search for the mother ship. Once they were on hand, though, it took very little time for the computers to run through them and find a vessel that fit Zelev's idea of what a mother ship should be and where it would have been during the two hijacking incidents.

"But that's a supertanker, a crude oil tanker," Kurtzman protested when the Russian pointed to an image of the ship on the screen. "It can't service a submarine."

"It was originally built as a supertanker," Zelev corrected him. "It could be anything right now."

He studied the big ship's specifications and dimensions in a Jane's reference book. Its power plant, tonnage, length, width and keel depth were given in both imperial and metric measurements.

"This ship," he said slowly, as if still thinking while he spoke, "is big enough that it could hide the submarine inside of it." He flashed a grin. "You know, like the ship in that movie about your superspy James Bond."

"You're not serious," Kurtzman said.

The Russian shrugged. "Why not? They have to have a place to off-load the stolen cargo and can't risk going into a port. You have to remember that a submarine remains safe only as long as it is hidden under water. On the surface, it's the same as any other ship, a target.

"This ship, though," he went on, "can go into any port it likes and no one will notice. Tankers are in ports all the time. They can even rig the hoses to it and pretend that they are pumping oil."

"He might have something, Aaron," Price said. "We've gone up against stranger things than this before."

"But that ship's full of internal oil tanks. There's no way to fit that sub inside of it as well."

"If the tanks have been taken out," Zelev pointed out, "there is more than enough room inside."

Kurtzman's fingers worked his keyboard. "Let's see if that ship has been in port lately."

It took no time at all to learn that the supertanker had recently been in port for a refitting. Even more interesting, the refitting had been done in a Libyan port rather than at a more efficient European facility. But if the Russian was right, doing the conversion work in Europe would have given the game away. Someone would have been bound to ask why a supertanker was having her oil tanks taken out.

"I think I'd better put in a call to Hal," Price said.

"Better yet," Kurtzman suggested, "why don't you ask him to fly down here for a briefing. We're going to have to convince him that we're right, and we have the best chance of doing that if he's sitting in front of us."

"Good point. I'll do that."

"A MOTHER SHIP that a submarine can hide inside?" Hal Brognola shook his head. He was in no mood for flights of fancy today, not even from Aaron Kurtzman. "Didn't I see something like that in one of those James Bond movies?"

"Almost," Kurtzman replied. "Except that in the movie, the ship was capturing submarines. This time, it's carrying one around inside."

"Do you have any hard evidence I can take to the Man?"

"Not exactly."

"So what does that mean? Either you have proof or you don't."

"I don't have a picture of the sub inside the ship I can show you, no," Kurtzman admitted. "But I do have the recon tapes of the mother ship hovering in the vicinity every time one of those freighters has disappeared.

"And," he added, "the Russian you sent down here agrees with us. In fact, he's the one who came up with the idea in the first place."

"Just because he's a Russian submariner, it doesn't mean that he knows what in the hell he's doing."

"The second-best piece of evidence we have," Price interjected, "is that this ship just came out of a long overhaul in a Libyan port. Because the work took place in Libya, we don't know exactly what was done. It very well could have been gutted and refitted to hold our sub."

"And you want me to take this off-the-wall, circumstantial evidence to the President and try to get an okay for a military strike against a foreign ship, is that it?"

Kurtzman grinned. ''Once again you've proven that you've got what it takes to be a crackerjack operations officer, Hal. That's exactly what we want you to do. And the sooner we take it out, the better.''

Brognola grunted. ''I'll give it a shot.''

CHAPTER TWELVE

In the Mediterranean

Presidential permission for the strike against the Libyan mother ship was quickly sent to the Stony Man team at its *Kitty Hawk* command post. The news jerked everyone out of their lethargy as they rushed to put an assault plan together. The first thing Mack Bolan did was to have Barbara Price put in a call to Grimaldi in Italy. On a mission as dangerous as this one, he wanted someone he trusted implicitly to fly for them and he didn't know a better aviator.

As soon as the preliminary plans and coordinations were made, a Sikorsky Sea Stallion helicopter transferred Bolan and Phoenix Force to the USS *Lewis B. Puller,* an assault transport carrying a Marine landing force battalion and an attached SEAL team. For this mission, it was the SEAL team that Bolan wanted to talk to.

Storming a ship as large as the supertanker would require more men than just the six Stony Man warriors. Along with the tanker's crew, there would be the sub's service and support staff, as well as her crew. To deal with that kind of numbers, they would need specialized help and that help was at hand in the 6th Fleet. Of all the nation's Special Forces units, the Navy's SEALs were the best suited for this mission, and Bolan was confident that he would have no trouble getting them to volunteer.

To keep Viktor Solikov's part in this venture as unobtrusive as they could, the Russian submariner went undercover. Before he left the *Kitty Hawk*, he had been given a Navy flight suit with American rank insignia to wear instead of his black Russian uniform.

The eight SEALs waiting in the *Puller*'s briefing room looked like finalists in an Iron Man competition. They were fit, alert and confident as only highly trained young warriors could be. They didn't know why this mysterious man and his team wanted to talk to them, but anything that broke the monotony of duty afloat was welcome. Particularly if it gave them a chance to bust some caps.

After introducing himself, Bolan quickly read the SEALs into the situation by giving them the background of the stealth sub, how it had come up missing and what it had been doing since then. Then he told them what they were going to do to stop it—fly out to the mother ship, rappel onto her decks, fight their way into the hold if necessary and place demolition charges on the sub inside.

"But," he concluded, "I only want to disable that sub without sinking the mother ship. The Russians still want to get it back when this is over."

"Then why aren't the Russians doing this, Mr. Belasko, instead of us?" one of the SEALs asked.

"That's a fair question," Bolan admitted. Were he in that SEAL's position, he too would want to know why he was laying his life on the line for someone else's ship.

"The answer is simply that we can get to the mother ship right now and the Russians can't. We need to take out that sub immediately so it can't slip away from us again and sink more ships and kill more people. After we've done that, we'll let the Russians get it back themselves."

He looked over the SEAL team. "Are there any more questions?"

There was none. They were all professional fighting men and the mission Bolan had outlined was the kind of thing the SEALs did best—fly in, complete their task and fly out. The fact that there might be people shooting at them while they did their thing wasn't of great concern. They had been shot at before.

"Now my demo expert will tell you about the special explosive charges and where you'll need to place them on the sub's hull."

"I know that all of you have had demo training," Manning said. "But since this isn't going to be your usual 'bash it and smash it' job, here's how we're going to handle it.

"Helping me with this lecture is Commander Viktor Solikov. Disregard the flyboy uniform he's wearing. He's actually a Russian submariner and knows how best to put this thing out of action."

Having a Russian in on the job got the SEALs' attention real quick. Even though it had been several years since the "evil empire" had fallen, a Russian military officer was still a novelty.

As soon as the briefing was over, Solikov took Bolan aside. "Where do I draw my weapons and equipment?"

"You don't." Bolan's voice was flat. "You're not going with us."

The Russian took a deep breath. "That submarine is of vital interest to my country. That's why I'm here. Not only was it stolen from us and we want it back, the missiles it carries could start a war and we would be blamed for it."

"I understand your concerns," Bolan said. "But the last time we took a Russian officer on a mission with us, he ended up dead."

"I'll take the risk."

"That's not the problem," the Executioner explained. "The problem is that my government doesn't want to have to explain the death of another Russian national."

"I will get the permission for you myself." Solikov's jaw was tight.

"No. I'm the mission commander, and I say who goes and who stays back. I know how you feel, but you're staying behind this time."

Knowing better than to push it any further, the Russian capitulated. "Okay. But at least let me stay in radio communication with you. That way, in case there is a problem with the demolition procedure I'll be able to advise the demo squad."

"That's fair enough," Bolan agreed. "I'll get you into the radio room."

Manning and the SEAL team's demo man spent the rest of the afternoon making up the special charges they needed to punch through the sub's pressure hull. The titanium hull would shrug off a normal explosive device, so they would need a special kind of shaped charge known as a cutting charge.

The rest of the strike force checked their weapons, ammunition and equipment one last time. With the exception of Katzenelenbogen, all the raiders would be armed with Heckler & Koch MP-5 subguns. Katz always carried his silenced Uzi no matter what. Pistols, fighting knives, grenades—both fragmentation and concussion—and a double basic load of ammunition made up the balance of their loads.

JACK GRIMALDI touched down while the SEALs were running through their mission prep. Bolan met him on the helipad and took him directly into the pilot ready room. "Get changed into a flight suit," he instructed. "You and David need to make a familiarization flight in one of the Ospreys."

"Outstanding. That's a hot bird."

As soon as Grimaldi was suited up, McCarter led him out onto the helipad. The Briton would fly as the copilot and weapons officer for the mission. Though a skilled pilot himself, he didn't mind riding the right-hand seat for a top-notch flyer like Jack.

A V-22 tilt rotor Osprey assault transport was waiting for them on the helipad with its turbines spooled up and its rotors turning. This particular machine had had all of its national markings painted out, even the serial number, to create plausible deniability for the mission.

It was a ploy the Stony Man teams had used many times in the past, and it hadn't failed them yet.

Accompanying them on the test flight was a Marine Osprey pilot who was more than a little apprehensive about turning one of the sophisticated aircraft over to these two unknown civilians.

"Don't worry," Grimaldi said with a grin when he saw the Marine grimace at his less than smooth transition from vertical to level flight. "If I crash it, I'll make sure that they don't take it out of your paycheck."

"Are you going to bleed for me, too, if you crash it?" the Marine aviator snapped back.

Once they were miles away from the ship, McCarter activated the weapons' sight and pulled the firing controls into position in front of him. "Give me a rundown on these," he said to the Marine.

"Are you familiar with the weapons systems on current chopper gunships?" the man asked.

McCarter nodded. "I'm checked out in the D-model Apaches."

"Good. This is the same look-and-shoot system the Apache uses. The turret is slaved to the helmet sight, and the pylon mount weapons will fire either from that or from the HUD display."

"Cool, as you Yanks would say." McCarter grinned as his right hand reached out to switch the weapons systems off safe. "Let's give it a try."

A ripping sound filled the cockpit as the 20 mm chain gun sounded off and a storm of high-explosive shells lashed the wave tops a thousand meters in front of them.

"Yup," McCarter said. "Just like the Apache."

"Who the hell are you people?"

"You don't want to know."

"I'M GETTING real time images piped directly in here now," Kurtzman told Bolan. "And the tanker is still continuing on her projected course. If you take off at 2200 hours, you should be able to intercept her by

0130. The thing is, she's sailing into a small storm. Is that going to be a problem?''

"No, we'll go anyway. The storm will probably help us by covering our approach."

"I'll tell Hal that you're a 'go.'"

"Take care, Striker," Price broke in.

"Always."

"And get that sub."

"We're going to."

THE LONE V-22 OSPREY flew low and fast over the storm-tossed South Atlantic. The tips of her propeller-rotors were only yards above the sea spray, and the mottled matte gray camouflage paint made her almost invisible against the crashing wave tops. Since Kurtzman couldn't tell them if the tanker was fitted with air-warning radar, it was the only way they could ensure that they weren't detected on the way in.

In the cockpit, Grimaldi sweated bullets as he concentrated on flying the aircraft. A sudden gust of wind or a downdraft would slam the Osprey into the cold, dark sea below, and no one would get out of the crash alive. Even if someone did, there was no one on hand to effect a rescue. In order not to spook the Libyans, the nearest U.S. ship was more than 150 miles away.

Bolan sat on the fold-out jump seat behind the pilot and watched the nav screen and the radar. Using the storm as cover for the attack had its drawbacks as well as its advantages. For one thing, the clouds were keeping the satellite cameras overhead from tracking the tanker. Therefore they were flying an interception course based on the ship's heading of a few hours earlier. If she had changed course, it might be difficult to find her.

Bolan looked up from the radar. "It should be on the horizon right about now."

"I've got her," McCarter stated. "Dead ahead."

The Executioner looked through the rain-lashed canopy and saw the bright running lights of the supertanker directly in front of them. He unbuckled his shoulder harness. "I'm going back. Give me a count to the touchdown."

"You've got it," Grimaldi replied without taking his eyes off his flying for even an instant.

In the rear of the Osprey, most of the SEALs strapped into their seats along the sides of the cabin were catnapping. Like all veteran troops, they knew the value of sleeping whenever they could.

"Sir, what's our ETA?" the SEAL team leader asked before Bolan could speak.

"We've spotted the ship, so you'd better wake your people and get ready."

The team leader didn't have to say a word. The napping commandos instantly came awake. Their hands quickly made a well-practiced inventory of their weapons and gear. Storm or not, this was just one more air assault into a potential firefight, and they had been through this drill many times.

At the rear of the aircraft, Manning hit the controls for the ramp door, lowering it into the jump position. Now they could hear the howling of the storm over the whine of the turboprops. The SEALs and the men of Phoenix Force stood as one man and hooked their rappeling ropes to the three steel cables running along both sides of the aircraft and down the center. They would hit the ramp three abreast for the short rappel to the ship's deck.

With the wind coming from the northwest, Grimaldi swung wide away from the tanker before approaching it from the starboard side of the stern. There was a quarter-city-block-size platform on the fantail marked with the white H of a helicopter landing pad that was perfect for their purposes. Keeping the Osprey's nose pointed at the rear of the bridge superstructure, Grimaldi brought the aircraft to a hover a few yards above the deck.

"Go!" Manning called out to the men waiting on the edge of the ramp.

Bolan, Katz and the SEAL team leader were the first men on the ropes. Even with the weights on the ends of the rappeling ropes, they whipped in the wind until the men were most of the way down.

As soon as his rubber-soled boots touched the rain-slicked steel deck, the Executioner hit the release to disengage the rope from his harness. In the high wind, he grabbed the rope and steadied it until the second man started down. When he had unhooked, Bolan, Katz and the SEAL leader took up security positions facing the superstructure in front of them.

As Bolan had hoped, the howling of the wind had muffled the sound of the Osprey's rotors. The strike force was down on the deck without sounding an alarm. He didn't know what the bridge watch was doing, but they sure as hell weren't keeping an eye on the rear deck.

He just hoped that the rest of the tanker's crew was as slack. It would make their job much easier.

As soon as the last black-clad commando reached the end of his rappeling rope, Jack Grimaldi hit his throttle and the V-22's rotors clawed for altitude. Swinging away from the ship, the pilot went into a low orbit several hundred yards behind the stern. Not only was the Osprey the strike force's ride home, it was there to provide fire support if the warriors ran into anything they couldn't handle on their own. He needed to stay out of accurate small-arms-fire range, but still be close enough to deliver instant supporting fire from the 20 mm chain gun in the nose turret or the rocket pods under the wings.

In the copilot's seat, David McCarter already had his weapons sight down and locked, and his gloved hands almost caressed the firing controls. Considering how calm things had been lately, the Briton was almost hoping that something would go wrong so he would have someone to shoot at.

AS THE OSPREY VEERED OFF to take up its support position, Manning joined the SEALs. Following his hand signals, they silently headed belowdecks to hunt their target. Solikov had extensively gone over the blueprints of the stealth sub to show them exactly where to place their explosive charges to do the most good. Or the most bad, depending on which side of the equation you were on.

As soon as Manning and the SEALs were safely on their way into the bowels of the tanker, Bolan led his half of the strike force toward the bridge and the crew cabins in the superstructure on the main deck. Regardless of what Manning and the SEALs ran into inside the tanker, they had to secure the upper decks to keep the rest of the team from being trapped. Their first stop would be the ship's bridge to prevent the watch from sounding an alarm; the second would be the radio room.

Only two men stood watch on the bridge when Encizo slipped the dogs to the hatch and pushed the steel door open to let Katzenelenbogen rush in. One of the Libyans immediately put his hands up when he saw the silenced Uzi. But when the second one made a sudden move, Katz triggered a short burst. The trio of 9 mm slugs took the crewman high in the chest and spun him before he crumpled to the deck.

''Don't move,'' the Israeli warned the first man in Arabic, ''or you're dead.''

The Libyan looked down at his shipmate's blood seeping out onto the deck and froze. Encizo slipped a pair of plastic riot cuffs over his wrists and cinched them tight. Leading the crewman to the corner, he made him sit, then taped his mouth and ankles. Two down and God only knew how many left to go.

''The bridge is clear,'' he radioed Bolan.

''Leave it and start clearing the cabins.''

The ship was sailing on autopilot so, even without human hands on the wheel, she would keep her nose into the wind. Even if the huge ship drifted a little off course, it wouldn't really matter. She was big enough to ride out anything short of a Force Eight.

Securing the crew cabins went quickly, the unarmed sleepy men obviously not up for a fight. Even the Libyan captain wisely chose not to resist when he saw the muzzle of Katz's silenced Uzi in front of his face. He meekly allowed his hands to be secured behind his back and his mouth taped before he was marched off to join the rest of his captive crew in the galley.

Bolan's group was securing the last of the above-deck cabins when Manning reported in. ''This is the right ship,'' he said, ''but the docking bay's empty. The sub isn't here.''

''Get out of there as fast as you can.''

"That might be a bit difficult." Manning's voice was calm, but Bolan could hear the rattle of small-arms fire in the background. "There's a couple dozen Libyans down here who don't want us to leave."

"We're coming down."

"Come in from the bow end," the big Canadian radioed back. "If you come down from the stern the way we did, you'll get pinned down here, too."

"Which side of the hold are you on?"

"The port side."

"Just hang on," Bolan said, as he, Katz, James and Encizo headed out.

DEEP IN THE CAVERNOUS HOLD the men of SEAL team 16 were doing what they did best—fighting as a unit.

The Libyans didn't have the advantage of being team players, but they made up for it with sheer numbers. The strike force had expected to find, and to have to deal with, a large crew on board the converted Libyan tanker, but these men were anything but merchant sailors. From their distinctive camouflage uniforms and green berets, they were part of Colonel Khaddafi's handpicked Islamic shock troops, the so-called Green Warriors.

Nonetheless, they were still men, and men could die. They were even helping the SEALs kill them by making suicidal attacks across the open walkways into the Americans' blazing guns. But with their greater numbers, they could afford to lose men as long as it kept the commandos pinned down.

When Mack Bolan reached the landing at the top of the A Deck companionway leading down into the docking bay, he halted for a moment before opening the door. "Gary," he radioed, "we're at the top of the stairs and we're making our move now."

"Watch your left flank," the Canadian radioed back. "There's a mob of them on a walkway between you and where we're at."

"We'll clear them out," Bolan replied.

No sooner had he spoken than a squad of camouflage-fatigue-clad men carrying AKs burst around the corner of the passageway leading back to the stern. Not expecting to find anyone there, the Libyans were slow to bring their weapons into play.

They paid for that slight hesitation when Bolan, Katz, James and Encizo opened up on them at the same time. For a brief moment, the passageway rang with gunfire, the screams of dying men and the whine of bullets ricocheting off the steel bulkheads.

When the brief gunfight ended, the four men stepped over the corpses and continued on toward the docking bay.

SLOWLY THE LIBYANS were closing in on the outnumbered SEALs. When one of the Navy commandos took a hit in the head and went down, one of his teammates leaped to his rescue only to take a savage burst himself.

Seeing that both men were still alive, Manning snatched a grenade from his harness and pulled the pin. "Cover me!" he yelled as he tossed the bomb.

Under the cover of the explosion, he dashed forward, his MP-5 subgun blazing. Reaching down, he snatched one of the wounded men by the back of his assault harness and dragged him back under cover. He was a little slow getting back down himself and a savage blow to his leg sent him sprawling to the floor plates.

A SEAL grabbed him in turn and pulled him back. "You okay?"

"Yeah," Manning gasped in shock as he took physical inventory.

The bullet hole in his right thigh looked bad, but it wasn't spurting blood. His entire leg was numb, but he could move his foot, so it couldn't be that bad. He'd still be able to run if he ever got the chance. He fumbled at his assault harness for his field dressing. He wanted to get it tied over the wound before the shock wore off and the leg started to hurt.

He had just finished tying off the dressing and had retrieved his subgun when all hell broke loose on the other side of the hold. Bolan and his comrades in arms had arrived. Now that they didn't have to conserve their ammunition anymore, the SEALs unleashed a storm of fire as well.

Caught between the two groups, the Libyan assault faltered. Frantically firing in both directions, they broke and ran for the bow of the ship to get as far as they could from the black-clad raiders.

"We've got wounded over here, Striker," Manning radioed to his rescuers.

"I'm sending Calvin over to help," Bolan replied. "Get your wounded ready to pull out as soon as he shows up."

"We're ready now."

While Bolan, Katz and Encizo kept up a steady stream of fire, James dashed across the walkway to the SEALs' position. As soon as the medic gave them a high sign, Bolan radioed to Grimaldi. "I'm sending the wounded up," he said. "Meet them on the foredeck."

"I'll be there."

SINCE THERE WAS NO NEED to keep out of sight now, Grimaldi brought the Osprey down as close as he could to the bow of the ship with the nose pointing back toward the bridge and crew's quarters. Holding the aircraft motionless in the air took everything the pilot had. The tanker was large enough that the wind broke over the side in strong gusts, threatening to slam the Osprey onto the deck.

"We're coming out," James radioed to the pilot. "Get it down on the deck."

"On the way," Grimaldi sent back. Touching down on the deck made the Osprey even more vulnerable, but it couldn't be helped. Wounded men couldn't climb up the ropes.

When a figure appeared on the walkway in front of the bridge, McCarter didn't even take the time to see if the man was armed. The man was in the wrong place at the right time, and life was full of little uncertainties.

Centering the glowing diamond on his helmet visor display on the unfortunate, a twitch of his finger sent a burst of 20 mm rounds from the turret-mounted chain gun in his direction. The explosive bullets chewed the crewman to bits and slammed his pulped remains against the bulkhead behind him.

To discourage any further sight-seeing, the Briton sent another long burst across the bridge windows shattering the glass and blasting through the thin sheet metal of the wheelhouse.

Seconds later, the first of the wounded appeared on the main deck. Manning was being supported by two of the SEALs, one of whom was also wounded. James and two more SEALs followed, bearing the limp body of one of their comrades.

Switching control of the weapons over to Grimaldi, McCarter unbuckled his harness and rushed back to help the men into the cabin. The way Manning was cursing as he helped him into a seat told McCarter that the big Canadian wasn't hit badly. One of the SEALs, though, was seriously wounded.

"Get him buckled down," the copilot told his teammates. "It's going to be a rough ride out of here."

"I've got all the wounded on board, Striker," Grimaldi radioed to the rear guard. "You guys'd better get your asses outta there."

"We're on the way up," Bolan sent back.

When the wounded had been evacuated, the two remaining SEALs had linked up with Bolan, Katz and Encizo to fight as the rear guard. After slamming full magazines in place, the five started laying down a withering fire as they pulled back. When they reached the top of the stairs, they tossed grenades back down into the hold before racing for the main deck.

A minute later, five figures in night-black combat suits rushed out of the hatchway onto the main deck. The last man turned long enough to snatch a grenade from his harness, prime it and toss it back through the hatch before he turned and ran. In seconds, a gush of smoke and flame blew out.

Bolan and Encizo hung back long enough to let Katz and the two SEALs board the Osprey before leaping on themselves. "Pull pitch!" Bolan yelled over the radio as he jumped for the ramp door.

Grimaldi hit the Osprey's throttles and collective control at the same time. Turbines howling, the V-22 leaped from the deck, her prop rotors clawing for altitude. As with any rotary-wing aircraft, the Osprey couldn't accelerate as quickly as a fixed-wing plane. It would be several long seconds before it could attain enough speed and altitude to be difficult to track with assault rifles.

Alert to the danger, Bolan and Encizo quickly snapped the rappeling ropes to their assault harnesses and leaned out of the open ramp. Katz and one of the SEALs took up positions at the sides of the ramp to back them up.

No sooner were they in place than a midships hatch slammed open and Libyan commandos stormed onto the deck. Before they could bring their weapons to bear on the retreating Osprey, the four men were pouring fire into them.

Bodies tumbled to the deck in bloody ruin. But rather than running for cover, the Libyans returned fire. AK rounds smashed through the aircraft's thin aluminum skin and sang through the troop compartment. "Go! Go! Go!" Encizo yelled over the radio.

In the cockpit, Grimaldi studiously ignored his teammate's urging. Both of the Osprey's turboprops were wound up as high as they could go, and he was playing the rotor tilt control like a Stradivarius. Since the rotors provided both lift and forward thrust at low speeds, increasing either one too much would rob the other. And right now he needed both the speed and the altitude. It seemed to take forever for the Osprey to get clear of range, but it was only a few seconds before the Libyans stopped firing.

The four men on the ramp stepped back inside the plane's cabin and raised it back into flight position. The closing of the ramp hushed the roar of the wind, and they heard the moans of the wounded. As they walked forward to get to the radios in the cockpit, James and the SEALs' medic were already working on them.

"That was just a piece of bad luck, Striker," Katzenelenbogen said. "It happens every now and then."

Bolan nodded grimly. He knew full well that luck played a big part in combat. The roll of the dice occasionally went against you no matter what you did to prepare for it. It didn't make it any easier to take, though. Not when young men were bleeding because of it.

CHAPTER THIRTEEN

Over the South Atlantic

"How're you doing back there?" McCarter called out as the Osprey sped north for the rendezvous with the *Puller.* Grimaldi was flying much higher this time to ease the piloting chores and to get the highest speed he could out of the tilt rotor assault transport. Flying that high put him on any radar screen that was watching the area. But with the wounded in the back, speed was the critical element right now.

"I'm busy," Calvin James replied. "I'll talk about it later."

The Phoenix Force medic was kneeling beside the most seriously wounded SEAL, trying to stanch the flow of blood from the fist-sized hole above the man's left hipbone. One of his teammates held an IV bottle of blood expander while the SEAL medic bandaged a lesser wound to his lower leg. "He's going into arrest," James said curtly. "I can't save him."

"Come on, Parnell!" the SEAL holding the IV drip bag yelled. "Hold on, man! Hold on!"

The wounded man gave the death rattle, his leg spasmed and his jaw went slack. He was dead.

There was nothing else to be done, so James moved away from him and went to treat the next wounded SEAL. This man's skull had been creased by a round that hadn't penetrated the bone. A bandage had been tied over the wound to control the bleeding, but he was nauseous and was having difficulty seeing clearly. James shone a small flashlight in each of his eyes in turn and saw that one of his pupils wasn't constricting properly.

"You've got a slight concussion," he told the SEAL, "but it's not serious. Just lie back and take it easy until we get back to the ship."

The SEAL tried to sit up and James put his hand on his shoulder. "Lie back down. This is no time for macho SEAL shit."

"Parnell?"

"He didn't make it."

The last wounded SEAL had a slight shrapnel wound in the shoulder, probably from one of their own grenades. A hand grenade didn't have any friends and could bite the hand that threw it as easily as it could the man it was thrown at. The wound wasn't serious and required little more than a bandage to protect it.

Now that the last of the SEAL casualties had been seen to, James turned to Gary Manning. The big Canadian had taken an AK round through the meaty part of the outside of his right thigh. James took off the bloodied field dressing and cut the pant leg to examine the wound. There was a clear exit hole, and the wound wasn't spurting blood.

"You're not hurt," James told him as he tied a fresh field dressing over the wound. "A few stitches and a couple weeks off the leg and you'll be okay."

"This son of a bitch hurts," Manning said through clenched teeth.

"This'll help." James took out a morphine Syrette and injected the painkiller into Manning's good leg.

The wounded man's eyes glazed over as the powerful drug hit his brain. "It doesn't hurt anymore."

"It's not supposed to, bonehead. That's what this stuff's for."

"I can go along with that."

Now that the last of the wounded had been taken care of, James went forward to the cockpit, where Bolan was on the radio to the *Puller*.

"They're standing by," the Executioner said when he saw the medic. "And they're steaming toward us to cut the distance as much as they can."

"What's our ETA?"

"We'll be touching down in about forty minutes," Grimaldi answered.

"One of the SEALs died, but the rest of them will make it until then."

"How's Gary?" McCarter asked.

"He's okay, just a hole in the leg. Shot through and through as we say in medical lingo. A few stitches and two weeks off the leg and he'll be as good as new."

ALMOST THE INSTANT Grimaldi touched down on the helipad on the aft deck of the *Puller*, Navy medics were swarming over the Osprey to get to the wounded. Since the ship was a Fleet Marine assault transport, it had a sizable medical bay and a staff able to handle any kind of combat emergency.

Even though James had declared the one SEAL dead, the medics checked him one more time before zipping him into a black body bag. The wounded were rapidly loaded onto gurneys and taken down to the sick bay and the waiting surgeons.

"It wasn't your fault, sir," the SEAL team leader said to Bolan as he watched his wounded and dead teammates taken away. "It was a good mission, but it just went bad."

"It's not over yet, son," Bolan told the young Navy commando. "We'll get them for you."

"I know you will."

KURTZMAN'S JAW was clenched tight as Bolan made his report from the *Puller*'s secure communications set. Finding the supertanker's internal docking bay empty was a big blow to the operation. Even worse, though, was the news of Manning's wound. The risk

of casualties was part of every mission they under-
took, but it was always a shock when someone was
hit.

"At least we know where they've been hiding that
sub," Brognola said. The big Fed had been standing
by in the Stony Man War Room as the President's
representative in case anything came up during the
sensitive mission that required direct input from the
Man.

"I knew that before those guys got shot up,"
Kurtzman snapped in frustration, as he pounded his
fist on the desk top next to his keyboard.

"Gary will be okay," Price said. Though she tried
to sound soothing, concern showed in her voice. This
wasn't the first time that one of the Phoenix Force
commandos had shed blood in their clandestine war,
and it wouldn't be the last. But that didn't make it
any easier to take. Every wound they took, no matter how slight, was one wound too many.

"We're back to square one now," Brognola stated
as he closed his briefcase and snapped the locks shut.

"No, we're not," Kurtzman said slowly. "Not
quite. The mother ship ploy is out for them now. Our
guys and the Russians will be all over that Libyan
tanker, and they'll never be able to use it again."

He reached out to his keyboard and called up a
map of the Mediterranean on his big screen monitor. "And that means that they'll have to bring that

sub into a Libyan port to off-load the pirated cargo and resupply her next time."

He studied the map for a moment. "And, when they do, we'll be able to trap her in the Med."

"But it's a very big place," Zelev reminded him. Throughout the entire mission, the Russian had kept silent while the Stony Man warriors and the SEALs laid their lives on the line to recover his Navy's missing submarine. He felt there was little he could do to advise professionals of their caliber. Now that they were back in the planning stage, however, he could contribute again.

"There are dozens of ports and hundreds of coves where she can come up to sail depth to off-load her loot and take on supplies. Even with the best satellite pictures, a submarine's sail is hard to spot."

"That's true," Kurtzman acknowledged. "But with both our nation's satellites looking for her, there's not too many places she can hide."

"I wouldn't be so sure of that," the Russian said. "But that might not matter one way or the other. I don't think that her captain will risk sailing through the Strait of Gibraltar to get to Libya. Stealth sub or not, with your Navy's top-secret underwater detection system in operation now, I don't think he'll risk it."

"How do you know about that?" Brognola asked, frowning.

Zelev smiled. "It's getting harder and harder to keep secrets anymore, isn't it?"

MAJOR OMAR RASHID CURSED when he heard that commandos had attacked and damaged the *Petlyura*'s mother ship. Though the United States had made no announcement regarding the raid, according to the survivors, the commandos had flown to the tanker in one of the Americans' V-22 Osprey tilt rotor assault transports. This particular aircraft was new in service, and it was unlikely that the Americans had sold any of them to other nations. Yet the raid sounded more like an Israeli operation—quick in, quick out and leave nothing incriminating behind, not even bodies.

If, in fact, it was an Israeli operation, the Jews would pay dearly for the attack. As would the Americans for having aided them by supplying the V-22 Osprey. The fact that Rashid's Ukrainian allies would also pay the price was of no concern to him. Regardless of what the Ukrainian nationalists had been told, they were still infidels and they had no place in the new world the colonel would create for the glory of God.

When the *Petlyura* concluded her final mission, Islam would once more sweep its enemies before it like a storm. But, for that to happen, he had to complete the rest of the hijacking operations. While the submarine's primary mission was to launch the missiles that would bring the final jihad, the hijacking operations were every bit as important, if not more so. The international economic embargo against Libya had crippled the country's fledgling industries, particularly the weapons-making facilities that were so vital for her survival. Everything from the most basic machine tools to computers were prohibited goods under the embargo. Now that supplies from the old Soviet Union were no more, Libya was falling further and further behind the developed nations. Even Egypt's industries were more advanced now.

For Libya to exploit the chaos that would result from the nuclear strike, she had to be ready to provide the weapons to secure her new territories. With the mother ship disabled and unable to transfer the pirated cargo, the rest of the planned hijackings would be much more difficult to accomplish.

But Rashid wasn't about to abandon the operation. Too much time and energy had gone into its planning to give it up. Even more importantly, the cargo was vital for the colonel's long-range plans. He would simply switch over to using regular Libyan cargo ships to transport his loot and make the transfers on the surface.

It would take longer to do it that way, which meant an increased danger of exposure to the satellites. But, since he had the orbit schedules for both the American and Russian recon birds, it would still work even if they had to submerge briefly whenever a satellite came overhead.

Even more determined to carry out his mission, Rashid made for the control room to give Yatkin the coordinates for the next target. This time, the *Petlyura* was targeted against an American-flagged cargo ship. The SS *San Juan* was home-ported in Seattle, Washington, and had been built as an ore carrier before its conversion to a rare metals container ship. Her cargo of metallic cobalt was vital for one of the colonel's pet projects, so she was slated to die.

This time, though, the *San Juan* wasn't going to die without a fight.

EVEN WITH THE NEWS BLACKOUT about the piracies, word had gotten around the shipping community that merchant ships transporting high-tech cargoes were vanishing in the Atlantic Ocean. Captains of vessels carrying such cargoes grew concerned, including Captain Bud Marshall of the SS *San Juan*. Part of the cargo being loaded onto his vessel in Charleston was cobalt, a rare metal that had uses in certain nuclear and laser industrial applications. He wasn't carrying much of it this trip, only one container destined for a lab in France. But if the pirate was after high-tech materials, that one container of cobalt could be enough to make him a possible target.

Marshall wasn't the kind of man to stand by and wring his hands when his ship was threatened. He had done two tours in Vietnam with the Brown Water Navy and knew how to fight to protect what was his.

On the weekend before he was scheduled to leave port, Marshall had gone to a gun show in Charleston and purchased a crate of twenty brand-new Chinese-made SKS semiautomatic infantry rifles. He also bought five crates of Chinese 7.62 mm military ammunition for the rifles.

His primary reason for buying the SKSs instead of something more modern was simple—they were dirt cheap. By the crate, they had cost him only $69.95 apiece. Dollar for dollar they were the firearms buy of the century. Secondly, he had come across the SKS in Vietnam and knew that it was not only an effective weapon, but simple and easy to use. He would have no problem training his mixed crew how to use them.

As soon as the *San Juan* left port and was in international waters, Marshall called a crew meeting and explained the situation and what little he knew about it. "I really don't expect any trouble on this run, boys," he said, "but it never hurts to take precautions. If trouble comes, I want to be ready for it."

An hour later, Marshall and his first mate were on the ship's fantail showing the off-duty crewmen how to load and fire the Chinese infantry rifles. By their second day out of Charleston, every crewman on the vessel had cleaned and fired his SKS, loaded two hundred rounds of ammunition into the chest-pack magazine carrier that came with each rifle and was ready to defend the ship.

Most of the men didn't believe there was any danger from submarine pirates, but none of them was about to tell Captain Marshall that. He had a way of running his ship that didn't make that a wise move.

Plus, it was fun to shoot the guns.

CHAPTER FOURTEEN

In the Atlantic

By now, the approach run to a target ship was routine to the Ukrainian captain of the renegade submarine. Using the shipping route information forwarded from Rashid's Libyan agents in London, Yatkin simply placed his sub in the path of his intended victim and waited until the ship appeared on the horizon.

Once more, the approach went like clockwork. As soon as he was in position behind the *San Juan,* he came up to periscope depth to check out the ship before committing to the attack. Seeing nothing out of the ordinary, he surfaced to let off Rashid's assault teams, then submerged again to wait until the Libyan radioed that he was ready to transfer the hijacked cargo.

He no longer watched through his periscope, though, as the Libyans took over the target ship and did whatever they were going to do. It was bad enough to know what they were doing without having to watch it. He had already decided that as soon as he could make port, he was going to turn his back on the *Petlyura* and walk away from her and the Ukrainian nationalists.

He considered himself a Ukrainian patriot as his father and grandfather had been before him. He was ready to give his life so that the Ukrainian people could live. He wasn't ready, however, to give his soul.

WHEN RASHID ENTERED the control room, he had a man with him, a crewman from the *San Juan* by the looks of him. The captive was wounded in the left thigh, and his right arm hung limp at his side. A bruise on the side of his face looked like the outline of an AK butt plate.

"Are you the bastard in charge of this sardine can?" the American snarled when he was brought before Yatkin.

The Ukrainian didn't know what a sardine can was, but his limited knowledge of English allowed him to figure out the rest. "I am the captain, yes," he said in heavily accented English. "Who are you?"

"I'm Bud Marshall, master of the *San Juan*. Or at least I was before you bastards came aboard."

He leaned toward Yatkin, his eyes blazing. "They're going to hang you if they catch you. You know that, don't you? I had twenty-six men on board that ship—" he jerked his thumb at one of his camouflage-uniformed guards "—and these fucking raghead butchers murdered them all."

Rashid started forward at the American's use of a pejorative slur against his Islamic warriors, but Yatkin stepped in front of him.

"They were armed this time," the Libyan explained. "And my men took casualties before we could subdue them. It could not be avoided."

"You murdered them, you bastard," the American snarled. "Some of them surrendered and you shot them down in cold blood."

"Is that true?" Yatkin asked in Russian.

"What difference does it make?" The Libyan shrugged. "We have the cargo on board and that is what we came for. Do your job and send the ship to the bottom before the satellite comes over again."

Yatkin had always prided himself on doing good work whatever the job was. But having a wounded sailor dripping his lifeblood onto the deck plates of his control room was a harsh reality check about what he was doing now. Ships and cargo didn't bleed when they were pirated and, since he hadn't witnessed the slaughter of the crews, he had been able to put the reality of being a pirate captain in the back of his mind. Now, he had to act like a man.

"Take this man to the sick bay and see to his wounds," he ordered one of the Ukrainian crewmen.

"Aye, Captain."

"It is dangerous for that man to live," Rashid warned.

"That will be my responsibility," Yatkin said.

Rashid didn't answer, but spun and left the control room.

Bringing the *Petlyura* around in a wide circle, Yatkin placed the stealth sub in a ninety-degree firing position to deliver the *San Juan*'s coup de grace. By now, the torpedoing was also routine.

"Flood tubes one and two," he ordered.

"Tubes flooded, Captain."

Centering the cross hairs of his scope on the *San Juan*'s hull, he gave the fire command. "Fire one. Fire two."

"Firing torpedoes, aye."

A few seconds later the weapons officer announced that the torpedoes were running true. Shortly after that, both of the 533 mm torpedoes struck the freighter amidships. Their detonations broke her in two, and she slipped beneath the waves before Yatkin could even retract his periscope.

NOW THAT an American flagged vessel and her crew had fallen victim to the pirate sub, Hal Brognola was caught between a rock and a hard place. As with all Stony Man operations, it would have been best for all concerned if this mission could be kept completely under wraps, even after it had been successfully concluded. This time, however, the loss of the *San Juan* was about to become headline news.

It had been decades since the media had been an ally in America's fight against international terrorism. In the *San Juan* incident, as in almost every other terrorist attack, the best he could expect from a hostile press was that they would twist the tragedy into another demonstrated failure of American foreign policy. And that would only be if they couldn't find a high-profile scapegoat in the armed forces or the CIA or a defense contractor to pillory in endless sneering editorials and talk shows.

Normally he was able to keep the media totally unaware of SOG operations. That success was due, in large part, to the fact that Congress knew absolutely nothing about the Stony Man Farm operations center. If the United States could ever eliminate the need for a Congress, the nation's security would improve several hundred percent overnight. This time, though, it wasn't a Congressman who had leaked the story, so Brognola couldn't take comfort in placing the blame there.

The problem this time was that the bodies of two of the *San Juan*'s crew had been discovered floating in their life jackets in the North Atlantic. And both of the bodies bore bullet holes.

Had the bodies been recovered by the Navy, Brognola could have taken care of it, but that wasn't the case. They had been fished from the water by a South American freighter with a sharp-eyed lookout on the bridge. The bodies had been taken to the ship's next port of call, where they had been identified as American merchant seamen from the missing *San Juan.*

Even though it could compromise the mission, Brognola knew that he had to convince the President to release some kind of statement about the pirate sub. If he didn't, sooner or later, the President's press secretary would have to try to explain yet another government cover-up to a room full of reporters out for his blood. It was evens up, though, which would cause the most damage to the government and the SOG operation, in the long run.

In the short run, making the threat public might allow the Navy to take a greater role in protecting American shipping and maybe discover the sub's whereabouts at the same time. And having the Navy in a high-profile role might help mask Stony Man's involvement in the long run.

He would have to coordinate this closely with the Russians, however, and make sure that not a single word was leaked about the sub's nuclear weapons. The antinuclear fanatics in both the United States and Europe were already out in full force because of persistent rumors of the ex-Soviet weapons disappearing from Russian control and then reappearing on the world arms markets. They would go completely ballistic if they learned that feared doomsday weapons were actually in the hands of people whose opinions couldn't be swayed by sign-carrying demonstrators.

The protesters wouldn't blame the terrorists for putting the world in danger, though. They never did. Once more they would twist the facts and claim that the world was again threatened because of Western imperialism, racism, capitalistic profiteers, or other such left wing, liberal psychobabble. Like all liberal protesters, they would never blame a problem on the people who were actually causing it. That would be too simple and it wouldn't get them the coverage they craved on the six o'clock news.

Popping another antacid tablet, Brognola started drafting a carefully worded statement for the President to release. His information was that CNN would air the story at six, and he needed to have something ready to throw to the White House media wolves.

BY NOW, Ivan Zelev was fully integrated into the Stony Man Farm routine. He had even taken to drinking coffee in the morning like an American instead of tea. And, since he was drinking Kurtzman's special industrial-solvent-grade brew instead of real coffee, it showed the strength of his personal commitment to improving cooperation and trust between their two governments. The first time he had tried some, he had thought they were trying to poison him.

Now that the existence of the pirate stealth sub was public information, the Stony Man team was inundated with reports of its sighting. Most of them were hysterical rantings, more on the order of UFO sightings, but a few of the reports bore closer investigation and had to be checked out.

Even though the Russian hadn't had the opportunity to work with sophisticated state-of-the-art computer equipment like what Kurtzman had at his command, he knew his way around electronics. And, with the things he didn't know, he still knew enough about them to ask intelligent questions.

At the moment he, Kurtzman and Price were reviewing one more time the tapes of the SS *San Juan* on her last voyage. The furor over the murder of the ship's crew had the President demanding answers immediately, and it was their job to find them for him. The first question they had to answer was what was the renegade sub using for a mother ship now that the supertanker had been put out of action.

Zelev leaned forward at Kurtzman's side and studied the monitor. "Can you widen the view so we can see more of the surrounding area?"

"No problem."

A few keystrokes changed the picture on the big screen monitor. "That's a little more than two hundred miles from side to side now."

"Outstanding." The Russian studied the screen. While his English had been good when he arrived, he had picked up enough colloquial Americanisms to sound almost like a native. "Okay, can you go back to the last time we can see the freighter?"

The tape ran backward until the slow-moving shape of the freighter appeared in the center of the screen.

"Okay," the Russian said. "Hold it right there. Now can you mark the positions of those other ships?" He pointed to the images of three other ships that shared the screen with the *San Juan.*

Blinking red blocks appeared on the screen over the images of the ships.

"Good. Now store those positions and go forward to the next satellite pass."

This scene showed no trace of the *San Juan.* Two of the three other ships were still showing on the screen, and the Russian studied them for a long moment. "Can you superimpose the positions of the ships you marked on the last pass on this view?" he asked.

A few keystrokes brought the three red boxes back.

"There it is," Zelev said triumphantly, pointing to the small speck of a ship in the upper-left corner of the big screen. "That's their new mother ship."

Kurtzman shook his head. "That can't be it. It's just a small freighter, a tramp steamer."

"That's right. She's only a small freighter, but she shouldn't be there."

"How can you tell?" Price asked.

"How long is it between passes of the satellite that took these shots, an hour and a half?"

"An hour, twenty-six minutes," Kurtzman answered.

"Even at twelve knots, which is a slow cruising speed for a ship that size, she should have gone twenty miles between those two passes. But, as you can see, she's traveled less than a quarter of that distance. She went dead in the water for some reason before getting under way again."

"So you think that's the sub's new mother ship?"

"She could be, and I think it should be investigated."

Barbara Price thought for a moment. "You were dead right the first time, Ivan, so I'll go along with you on this one, too."

She turned to Kurtzman. "Better make copies of those tapes and mark that ship's locations. This is going to be an even harder sell than the last one. Hal's going to think that we've completely lost our minds."

CHAPTER FIFTEEN

In the South Atlantic

On the strength of Stony Man's analysis of the *San Juan* incident, the President authorized the Navy to stop the freighter Zelev had tagged, and search her hold for evidence of pirated cargo. He had even gotten an emergency meeting of the UN Security Council to put its stamp of approval on the mission. Since ships of three nations had been hit, for once the UN did what needed to be done.

When the word was flashed to the American destroyer USS *Hawkins* on patrol in the Atlantic that she was to pursue and stop the pirate sub's mother ship, cheers broke out all over the ship. The captain and crew of the *Hawkins* knew about the disappearance of the SS *San Juan* and the renegade sub that was believed to be responsible for the loss of the ship and her crew. They wanted payback. Pirating American merchant shipping on the high seas was not to be tolerated. They were ready to strike back, and it was looking like they were going to get the chance.

Six hours of steaming at flank speed had brought the *Hawkins* into position behind the merchant ship as it turned east to go into the Strait of Gibraltar.

"Look at her making smoke," the destroyer's XO said, peering through his powerful field glasses. "She's spotted us, and she's trying to run."

"She isn't going anywhere," growled Commander Bull Zimmer, the *Hawkins*'s captain, around the butt of the cigar clenched between his teeth.

The *Hawkins* was at General Quarters for the pursuit of what had been identified as the pirate sub's mother ship. The Lloyd's registry identified the vessel as the merchant ship *Sorya*, a South Korean-built, Libyan-owned, Serbian-flagged cargo ship. Considering her listed power plant, her top speed would only be some eighteen knots. The *Hawkins* could do thirty-five knots without straining her turbines.

Tipping back the steel pot he wore, the captain put his own field glasses up to his eyes and studied his prey. There was no sign of gun mounts on her decks, but that was no guarantee that she was unarmed. In the days of very effective antiship missiles, she could have a hideaway launcher tracking them at this very moment, waiting to pop up and fire a missile.

"CIC, bridge," Zimmer said over his throat mike.

"CIC, aye," came the voice of the combat information center's officer in charge.

"Status on the target."

"She's making seventeen and a half knots and still no sign of targeting radar, sir."

"I'm going to hail her now," the captain said. "If she cranks up any kind of targeting radar, sink her. Don't give her a chance to get off a shot at us."

"Aye, Captain."

"We're in range, sir," the XO stated.

"Gunnery," the captain said.

"Guns, aye."

"Put one across her bow a hundred yards out."

"One on the way."

The five-inch radar-directed gun in the single turret forward barked once. A geyser of water appeared a short distance in front of the fleeing freighter, but there was no sign of her reducing revolutions.

"Put another one fifty yards out."

"On the way."

This five-inch round landed close enough that water sprayed onto the forward deck of the freighter.

"She's slowing," the XO observed.

Captain Zimmer turned to the lieutenant standing by in a steel helmet and flak vest. "Prepare for boarding, Mr. Hernandez."

Hernandez grinned and picked up his M-16. "We're on it, Captain."

"Good luck, keep your head down and don't let them get the jump on you."

"They won't, sir. Count on it."

"I have their captain on the horn, sir," the radio rating announced.

"Put it on the speakerphone and record it."

"Aye, sir."

"This is Captain Berton Zimmer of the USS *Hawkins,* who am I speaking to? Over."

"This is Captain Mohammed Rasuli of the Serbian merchant ship *Sorya.* Why have you stopped me?"

"I am under orders to halt you and search your holds for evidence of piracy. Stand by to receive a boarding party."

"I refuse to be boarded," Rasuli transmitted. "Keep off or I will not be held accountable for what happens."

"I have a UN sanction," Zimmer sent back. "We will board and conduct our inspection. If you resist, I have authority to do whatever is necessary to carry out the UN directive."

When the *Sorya*'s master didn't reply, Captain Zimmer put down the microphone and took up his field glasses again.

"That doesn't sound to me like he has a Serbian name," the XO said. "Or a Serbian accent, either. That guy sounds like he's an Arab."

"I don't care if he's a Martian," Zimmer growled. "I'm going to search that ship from top to bottom. And if he's working with that pirate sub, I'm towing his ass back to the States."

The *Hawkins*'s auto-loading five-inch gun turret was swung over to the side and trained on the *Sorya*. The 20 mm Phalanx system was put on directed-fire mode and aimed at the bridge of the ship as well. Every man who could be spared from his post had been armed and was standing along the starboard deck of the destroyer. One false move, and Zimmer intended to sink the ship on the spot.

Zimmer had also posted two men with video cameras to record whatever happened. If things went bad and he had to fire, he didn't want to go through the same drill the captain of the *Vincennes* had gone through when his cruiser had shot down that airliner in the Persian Gulf.

"Away boarders, Mr. Hernandez," he radioed to the waiting boarding party.

"Boarders away, sir."

When the boats were only halfway to the *Sorya,* an explosion rocked the freighter and a gaping hole appeared in her plates at her waterline.

"What's going on?" Zimmer dropped his cigar.

"We didn't do it, sir," the XO confirmed. "None of our weapons have fired."

The captain lunged for the radio, but before he could key the mike, more explosions racked the ship. This time, smoke and flame appeared as the hatches blew open.

"She's sinking!"

Zimmer looked and saw that the *Sorya* was settling in the water. "Mr. Hernandez," he radioed to the boarding party officer, "search for survivors."

"Aye, sir."

The *Sorya* slipped beneath the waves in less than five minutes, leaving only small bits of floating debris to show that she had ever passed that way. In minutes, the OIC of the boarding party reported that there were no survivors.

Zimmer retrieved his cigar from the deck, stuck it back in his mouth and relit it. "God!" he said. "Those poor bastards didn't have a chance."

"Why'd they do it, sir?" the helmsman ventured to ask. This was the first time he had watched a ship die, and it made him want to seriously rethink his chosen profession.

Even though he had been in the Navy for several years himself, the captain had also never seen a ship sink before, and knew how the helmsman felt. "I don't know, son," he answered. "I really don't know."

"Let's hope to hell that those video cameras were working," the XO said, breaking the silence. "This will go before a board of inquiry or I don't know the Navy."

The captain took off his steel helmet, closed his eyes and rubbed the back of his neck. "I really didn't need this. I was having a nice career and I was kind of looking forward to getting my fourth stripe before I hung it up and retired to the chicken farm.''

"It wasn't anything we did, sir," the XO said. "Her captain sank her himself."

"I just hope the board sees it that way."

"They will, sir."

"WE'VE REALLY GOT a mess on our hands now," Hal Brognola announced. In the aftermath of the sinking of the *Sorya,* the big Fed had flown to the Farm from Washington for a special conference with Price, Kurtzman and their Russian liaison officer.

"The entire Libyan navy has put to sea," he said. "Their mission is to 'protect peaceful merchant shipping from American aggression,' as the colonel has put it. He has invited other Third World nations to join with him in this crusade against American imperialism on the high seas."

He shook his head. "The worst part of it is that even after making the Navy's videos public, there is a great hue and cry on the floor of the UN blaming us for an 'unprovoked attack' against an innocent merchant ship."

"Are you surprised?" Price asked.

Brognola shook his head. "Then, we've also had strong protests from the government of the Serbian Republic. They're claiming that most of the crew of the *Sorya* were Serbian nationals, and they're demanding reparations for their deaths."

"I really didn't need to know that," Kurtzman said. "If the Serbs are involved, that means that I've got yet another coastline to keep an eye on as well as Libya."

"But we have the NATO naval blockade to do that for us, don't we?" Brognola asked.

"Don't forget," Kurtzman said, "that the stealth sub can't be picked up on sonar. For all we know, she's been in and out of what are now Serbian ports a half a dozen times already and no one noticed it."

Kurtzman wheeled his chair around to face Zelev. "If you were the sub's skipper, where would you be docking in Serbia?"

"Split," the Russian answered without hesitation. "It's an old Soviet naval base and one of the few places where our subs used to make port. It still has all the facilities to service and resupply a sub, even a nuclear boat."

"Isn't that rather a strange mix?" Brognola asked. "Ukrainian nationalists, Serbians and the Libyans."

"Not really when you think about it," Price answered. "The Ukrainian nationalists are making sure that they'll still have nuclear weapons to threaten Russia with when the government gives the rest of them back. Then, the Serbian leaders have already gone public saying that if the West intervenes in Bosnia that they will retaliate with nuclear weapons, and apparently this is where they think they will get them. And Libya? They've been involved with this kind of thing for decades. They're a perfect partner for a nation that needs to learn the ropes about the terrorist business."

"It's gotten entirely too complicated when the Islamic fundamentalists start allying themselves with the emerging Europeans."

"I've got another piece of news for you to chew on while you fly back, Hal," Kurtzman added. "According to the Mossad, several members of Kessler's nuclear weapons team have been spotted in Tripoli."

"The Red Baron and his Flying Circus. That's just what I needed. How the hell did that bastard ever survive the fall of the wall? I thought the West Germans had him on their pickup list?"

Wilhelm Kessler was an East German Communist nuclear physicist and weapons designer. His nickname came from the fact that he was the heir to one of Germany's old baronial families, but still a dedicated Communist. When European communism failed, Kessler gathered a team of out-of-work chemical- and nuclear-weapons technicians from several ex-Communist nations and disappeared. When he surfaced again, he was offering his team and his services for hire to the highest bidder. Reports had placed him in Iraq right before Desert Storm, in North Korea and in Iran.

"The KGB pulled him out right before things went tits up."

"And now he's in Libya?"

"He hasn't been spotted there himself, but a couple of his team have. The Israelis recognized them from their work at the Osirak nuclear reactor in Iraq back in the early eighties."

"It's too bad that air strike didn't take them out as well as the reactor."

"The IDF had to be real careful not to hit the labs where the foreign scientists were living. They knew they were going to get a lot of grief from the bleeding-heart liberals anyway and didn't want to get the Communist nations down on their heads as well. You'll remember that there was still a Soviet Union as well as an East Germany at the time."

"What do you think it means?"

"I think that the good colonel has gotten his hands on at least one of those nukes from the sub and is up to no good. Again."

Brognola didn't say a word, but reached into the inside pocket of his suit jacket and pulled out a half-used roll of antacid tablets. He peeled off two, popped them in his mouth and swallowed them dry.

"Thank you for sharing that with me," he said. "I didn't need to sleep for the next week anyway."

He pushed his chair back and stood. "Get a report together about Kessler and fax it to my office. I'll take it over to the Man as soon as I get back."

Barbara Price added one more thing for him to think about. "Remember to tell him that the Egyptians and the Israelis both have offered their services if we want to go after Kessler and his boys."

"What about the peace treaty?"

"The Libyans haven't signed on to it anyway, so there'll be nothing lost if we have to go up against them again. It's been a long time since the colonel had his beauty sleep interrupted with the F-111s. Maybe he needs another wake-up call."

"Damn! I thought we were looking for a missing sub, not trying to start a war with Libya."

"The way this thing is shaping up," Kurtzman said, "I'd say that we're in for a twofer this time."

"Twofer?"

"Yeah," Kurtzman said with a grin. "Two high-risk confrontations for the price of one. And since they're both in the same theater of operations, it'll cut down on the battlefield logistics involved."

"Humor doesn't become you, Aaron."

He shrugged. "A man's got to have a hobby."

CHAPTER SIXTEEN

Naples, Italy

Hermann Schwarz had brought along a portable scrambler and a fax machine, and every evening, he checked in with Barbara Price at Stony Man Farm. He didn't have much to report, so far, but he was hoping that Kurtzman would have developed something they could follow up on.

The only thing from the news about the sinking of the *Sorya* that affected their part of the operation was the fact that the Serbians were apparently involved. That was welcome information, but it only complicated the picture.

"If the Serbians as well as the Libyans are in on this gig," Blancanales said, "we're working the wrong Italian port city to be keeping an eye on either one of them. Serbia is on the other side of the boot and Libya is directly across the pond from Sicily, not the mainland. Any Italian traffic with the colonel will be going through the island before it comes here."

Lyons thought for a moment. "Maybe that's where we should go. We aren't coming up with diddly around here, so we might as well try something else."

"Is our cover good enough for Sicily?" Schwarz asked. "The Cosa Nostra Families there are in close contact with their cousins in the States, and they're bad news."

"Let's give it a try and find out," Lyons stated.

"Just like that?" Schwarz said. "Don't you want to run it by our DEA contact first?"

"I'm not so sure that he knows any more than we do."

"If you get me killed, man, I'm going to come looking for you."

"If you get killed in Sicily," Lyons pointed out, "you won't have far to look because we'll all buy it together."

"This is certainly not what I had in mind when you talked about coming to Europe."

THE PORT OF PALERMO looked like a nastier version of the port of Naples. It was more run-down, sun-baked and dusty. It was easy to believe that it was the second-largest smuggling port for the Mafia. The Mafia had its origins centuries ago in Sicily. It had been born of bandit families that had resisted the various nations that had occupied and tried, and mostly failed, to rule the island. In fact, La Cosa Nostra meant "our thing" in Italian.

Modern Sicily was still very much in the hands of the traditional bandit clans. Nothing of any importance happened that escaped their notice. Even with all the tourists who visited, the arrival of three Americans was reported. But then, a contact in Naples had passed the word that these particular three Americans bore keeping an eye on.

The morning was spent walking around the dock area and talking to every sailor and dockworker they could find who spoke English, and learning nothing. To take a break, Lyons drove up into the hills to a small village for lunch.

"This is more like it," Schwarz said as he set down his wineglass. "A table under a tree in a quaint village square. Fresh bread and a lovely salad with our pasta. And," he added, refilling his glass, "this wine is a real find. I'm beginning to like this place."

"Don't get too comfortable," Lyons warned. "We've still got work to do after lunch."

"Considering the luck we've had so far, maybe we should just stay here and enjoy the view. I'm sure their dinner menu is just as good as their lunch."

A well-dressed young man walked up to their table. "My grandfather wants to talk to you three," he said in accentless English.

"Who's your grandfather?" Lyons asked, easing his jacket aside so he could get at his Colt if it came to that.

The young man saw the move, but didn't react. "I will let him tell you that himself."

"And what if we don't want to meet him?"

The man nodded toward someone standing by a car on the other side of the street. Three more men piled out of the back and threw their coats back to reveal 9 mm Beretta submachine guns hanging on slings at their sides. The plaza instantly cleared.

"You will meet him one way or the other."

Schwarz kept his hands in plain sight as he slowly pushed his chair back from the wooden table. "Can I bring my bread with me? It's really good."

"By all means, and the wine. It's a long drive."

FROM THE MOMENT that they walked into the old stone villa on the barren hilltop, Schwarz decided that he didn't like this situation. He didn't like the looks of the high walls surrounding the courtyard with only one way out, and he sure as hell didn't like the hardmen with the Beretta subguns. Most of all, though, he didn't like not being able to understand what these guys were saying.

The young man who had approached their table had made the introductions, but then had left the room, leaving them with four bodyguards and the old man, the capo of the Family.

The man in the red velvet chair behind the massive oak desk looked like an Italian version of Anthony Quinn. He had the craggy face, barrel chest and booming voice of an older Zorba. He had introduced himself as Emilio Zappa, as if the name should have meant something to them. Schwarz tried to remember the Intelligence summary the DEA man had provided them, but came up with a blank.

Without Grimaldi to translate for them, Lyons was letting Blancanales do most of the talking. Even though the old man's English was halting, the Politician could usually charm the birds from the trees, but this guy wasn't buying it at all.

"He thinks we're DEA agents," Blancanales explained. "He says that his people checked us out in the States and came up with us working for the Feds."

"Great," Lyons said.

"I guess we're going to have to 'fess up," Schwarz stated. "Tell him everything and hope for the best."

"That might be a good idea," the capo said in much better English than he had used before. "Otherwise—" he shrugged and held out his hands in an expansively Italian gesture "—I might have to kill you. Nothing personal, you understand, it's just business."

"We work for the American government," Lyons admitted, "but we're not with the DEA. We work against terrorists."

"But I have nothing to do with terrorists," Zappa said. "So I don't understand why you were looking into my business."

"We were talking to your people hoping to see if they knew anything about a submarine that was stolen from the Russians in the Black Sea."

"Someone stole a Russian submarine?" The look on the capo's face was one of total astonishment. "I have never heard of such a thing."

"None of us had, either, before this happened," Lyons replied.

"Who has taken this submarine?"

"That's what we don't know. But we need to find it as soon as we can. It's important."

"From the tone of your voice, I think that whoever has stolen this submarine of yours has been doing bad things with it."

Lyons knew that the only way they were going to get out of this place alive was to convince this guy that he had nothing to fear from them. And that meant that he had to tell him about the hijackings. But he wasn't going to mention the missiles. If the Mafia got their hands on them, the world wouldn't be worth living in.

Lyons quickly ran down the list of hijacked ships, making sure to point out the crew loss as well as the ships and cargo. "This is why we were poking around the docks," he concluded. "We were hoping to get a line on whoever was fencing the hijacked cargo. If we could do that, we would snatch him and learn more about the sub's operations."

The capo studied him for a long moment. "There is something else." He leaned forward. "You have not told me the whole story. There is more to this than missing ships, sailors and cargo. Were that all there is to it, I would have read of this submarine in the newspapers, and you would not be here poking your fingers into my enterprises. I would like to know the rest of this strange story."

Lyons had no choice now but to tell him the rest of it. "The people who stole the submarine also stole four Russian nuclear missiles with it. These are only sea-launched tactical missiles, but they are big enough to wipe out a—"

"Basta!" Zappa lunged to his feet. "Enough! I have heard enough."

He started to pace the floor. "I have always hated the missiles," he said. "From the day I first heard about them. War is horrible enough without such things.

"I know," he stated, thumping his chest, "because I myself fought against the British in North Africa and they captured me at El Alamein. That is where I learned to speak English, in their prisoner of war camp. When Mussolini was killed, they released me and I vowed never to fight in a war again."

He halted in front of Lyons. "Do you swear that this submarine has those missiles on it?"

"Yes," Lyons said solemnly. "It has four Russian sea-to-ground nuclear missiles with a range of some six hundred miles."

"And you say that you don't know who is operating this submarine now?"

"Our best information is that Ukrainians and Libyans are in it together and maybe the Serbians, as well."

"That is a strange combination, I admit. But the world is not what it once was."

"You can say that again."

"Maybe I will help you find this submarine. But if I do, you will have to do something for me in return. Business is business."

"You name it," Lyons replied, "and we'll do it."

"Do not be in such a hurry, my young American friend. Wait until you hear what I want first."

The capo looked out his window to the barren hills surrounding his ancient stone fortress. The pile of rocks had been in his family for centuries and he wanted to hand it, and the business it controlled, over to his grandson intact when the time came. "There is a man on this island that I would see dead," he said.

"Wait a minute," Lyons growled. "We can't commit a crime in a foreign nation."

"You said that your job is to fight against terrorists."

"Right."

"This man is a terrorist and he has no honor. He makes war against women and children with bombs instead of dealing with me like a man does. He wants to take over my family's enterprises, but he isn't strong enough to do it in a face-to-face battle. He has started bombing the shops and boats of my people to test me. If you will kill this man for me, I will help you."

"Why can't you kill him yourself?"

"I can, but it is best that I do not. With the new push from Rome to wipe us out, my hands must be completely clean. That is why I sent my grandson out of the room. Not even he is to know of this."

The Able Team warriors looked at one another for a long moment. Basically they had two choices. They could agree to take out this other Mafia lord and, by doing so, get the lead on the submarine they needed. Or they could die. It wasn't really a choice.

"I'll take care of your problem for you," Lyons finally said, "in exchange for your help in finding that sub."

The capo reached for the decanter of brandy on his desk and quickly poured four glasses. Walking around the end of the desk, he handed each of the men a glass.

"To our friendship."

"To friendship," Able Team echoed.

"YOU AREN'T REALLY thinking of going through with this hit, are you?" Schwarz asked.

The capo had offered them the hospitality of his villa, and they had been in no position to refuse. His hospitality, however, had turned out to be a cell-like room in the basement where they were to wait until the hit could be made. It was a large room with all the comforts of home, but a cell regardless.

Lyons nodded tightly. "Yes, I am. I told him that I would, and they take a man at his word around here."

"Hal's going to have a fit. He sent us over here to track down criminals, not to commit crimes ourselves."

Lyons shrugged. "I'll be hitting a Mafia chieftain, so what will he care? If you'll remember, that's what we do for a living."

"But we do it in the line of duty, and with the sanction of our government," Schwarz protested. "And in case you haven't noticed, we're not quite in the United States anymore. From what that DEA man said, I don't think we're going to like an Italian jail if this goes wrong."

"The target's a Mafia boss and he's going to end up dead sooner or later anyway, so I might as well do it now. I don't think the Italians will mind having another one of these guys off their active list."

He looked around the stone walls of their room. "Plus, if you haven't noticed our accommodations, look around this place. I don't think we're going to be breaking out of here with anything less than high explosives.''

"There's another angle to this as well," Blancanales spoke up. "After we do this job, our host thinks that you won't be able to finger him without putting the finger on ourselves at the same time.''

"There is that," Lyons admitted. "But that's where we'll have the last laugh on that old boy. I don't think he knows what we really do for the Feds.''

"Are you going to burn him when it's over?'' Schwarz asked.

"That depends on what he comes up with. If he helps locate that sub, we'll have him in our pocket the way he thinks he is going to have us.''

"How do you mean?''

"Think about it. We'll have him on record as having helped the United States government and I'm not sure that he'll want that bit of information nosed around. It might be bad for the line of business he's in, you know?''

"Not bad, Ironman, not bad.''

"I have my days.''

CHAPTER SEVENTEEN

Sophia, Sicily

Lyons rested the forearm of the Russian SVD sniper rifle on the sunbaked rock and wiped the sweat from his eyes before taking the weapon up again. The sun was high in the sky, and the rifle was almost too hot to touch.

He hadn't been too surprised when Zappa had produced the specialized Russian weapon for him to use. Since the fall of the Soviet Union, their military hardware was for sale all over the world. The SVD wasn't quite the precision tool as was the .50-caliber Model 82 Barrett he had used in Oregon. But it was still one of the world's best rifle-caliber sniper pieces. The range to the target area was only a little more than three hundred yards, and he should have no trouble making the shot at that close a range.

Schwarz lay next to Lyons with his high-power binoculars focused on the mountain road below them. Blancanales was a hundred yards away, in a security position higher up in the rocks, guarding their escape route. If something went wrong and he wasn't able to make the kill, they would have to ex-filtrate over the top of the open, barren hill where a car and driver waited to take them back to Zappa's castle.

Sicily might have been a garden island back in Roman times, but it was a rocky, barren, sunbaked, almost desert landscape now and offered little cover and concealment for a sniper. The hilly outcropping he had picked was the only place that gave him the exact position he needed to make the shot. In snip-ing, as in the stock market, position was everything.

But while he had the position, he had little con-cealment if the target started firing back. And he had absolutely no concealment from the sun. Fortu-nately, however, if Emilio Zappa's information was correct, he wouldn't have long to wait. According to the capo, the target went to visit his young mistress every Wednesday afternoon arriving at exactly two o'clock. He would spend an hour and a half dally-ing with her, then depart.

Hitting him at the woman's villa would have re-quired a major operation, as it was well guarded. But the man made himself vulnerable by driving to the estate instead of flying his helicopter. He drove to his assignations with two of his bodyguards and a driver in an armor-plated Mercedes four-door sedan, but that shouldn't present a problem.

The 7.62 mm Russian ammunition Zappa had provided for the SVD was designated heavy ball rounds in Russian parlance. In the West, however, it would have been called armor-piercing ammunition. Under the copper jacket of the bullets was a hardened steel core capable of piercing light car armor and bulletproof glass. The plan he had come up with after reconning the site, however, didn't require him to shoot his way through the armor.

Lyons's position gave him a clear view of the coastal road as it rounded the crest of an outcrop that overlooked the sea below. The road had been cut into the face of the cliff and hugged it for two hundred yards before reaching a flat below and turning inland away from the sea. That two-hundred-yard stretch of road was his killing zone.

"Here he comes," Schwarz warned. "And he's coming on fast."

The big ex-cop looked up over the scope and saw that the Mercedes was doing at least sixty to sixty-five miles per hour as it approached the outcrop.

"That guy's in a real hurry to see his honey," Schwarz commented. "He must not have learned that anticipation is half of the pleasure."

Anticipation wasn't half the pleasure for Lyons. He had only a few seconds to make his two shots before the car passed the critical strip of land where the road had no shoulder on the seaward side and no guardrail to keep an out-of-control car from going over the edge. And, of those two shots, the first was the most critical. There would be only an instant when the car would be face on to him and he would have a clear shot at the right front wheel.

Taking up the slack on the trigger, he focused the scope low on the far side of the road and waited for the front of the Mercedes to fill his sight. Suddenly the car was in the cross hairs and he squeezed the trigger. The butt of the heavy rifle slammed into his shoulder as it ejected the empty brass and chambered a new round. It felt good, though; the Russians knew how to make a first-class shooter's piece.

His aim was true, and the car's right front tire blew out under the bullet's impact. As the heavy vehicle pulled to the right with the deflating tire, the rear end swung out slightly to the left crossing the unmarked center line of the road.

While it was still sliding sideways, Lyons refocused and put two rounds into the left rear tire before the driver could try to recover from the skid.

With the right-front and the left-rear tires gone flat, the Mercedes continued its skid to the left. On level ground, the driver still would have been able to recover from the slide and drive out of the killing zone on the flats.

The problem was that there was no place for the car to go on that particular stretch of the highway. The road was too narrow, and the car's forward momentum was taking it toward the unprotected shoulder on the water's side.

Lyons saw the brakelights flash as the driver tried to stop, but the Mercedes was still traveling too fast and went over the edge of the road. The heavy vehicle seemed to hang in the air for an instant as if it were attempting to defy gravity. The driver's door opened, suggesting the driver was going to jump, but it was too late.

The nose dropped and the Mercedes plunged into the rocks below. There was no explosion and no fire when the two-and-a-half-ton car hit the rocks.

Instead, the car seemed to flatten itself out, as if it had been stepped on by a giant, invisible foot. The wreckage rebounded into the air, losing a wheel and the hood in the process, and rolled over onto its side before it came down again. The vehicle then rolled over and over until it went off the rocks and into the pounding surf. It immediately sank out of sight beneath the waves.

"You want to go down and check it out?" Schwarz asked.

Lyons shook his head. "No one got out of that."

EMILIO ZAPPA POURED four glasses of brandy and passed them around to the men of Able Team. "You were as good as your word," he said, "so I will be as good as mine. It is a pleasure to meet men who know about obligations of honor."

The capo raised his glass. "To honor."

"Honor," the trio toasted.

"I have two pieces of information for you," the Mafia chieftain said when the glasses were empty. "The first is that a submarine was seen in Split harbor a few weeks ago. One of my blockade runners was delivering cargo there and saw it when it came in. He said that the Serbs built a shack over the conning tower, I think it is called, so it could not be seen. He also said that it was under heavy guard and the men working on it would not talk about what they were doing."

"That confirms the Serbian connection to the sub," Lyons said.

"It seems to," Zappa agreed. "The second piece of information is that a Libyan businessman is offering industrial-grade diamonds for sale or trade for certain items of electronic equipment. Since you said that diamonds were among the shipments that were hijacked, I thought you would like to know."

"Where can I find this Libyan?"

"That you cannot do." Zappa shook his head slowly. "This man has been useful to me in the past."

"But he is also tied to those missiles you said you hated."

"That is my concern and I will deal with it myself."

Zappa rang a small silver bell and two men entered the room. "My men will take you back to the village where you left your car. You will find that everything you left in it is still there. As long as you are on the island, you will be under my protection so you will be able to enjoy your stay without worrying about car thieves.''

Lyons knew that he could take Zappa at his word. As long as they stayed on Sicily, they would be under his protection, but they would be marked men as well. That meant that they wouldn't have to worry about talking to anyone about the Libyan businessman, because no one would talk to them. There would also be no way to confirm the rest of Zappa's information and no reason to look for more.

They were finished in Sicily, and Brognola and Price would have to come up with a new lead.

BACK IN THEIR HOTEL in Palermo, Lyons wasted no time in getting their hard-earned information back to Stony Man Farm. Kurtzman sounded grumpy when he came on the line, and Lyons realized that it was the middle of the night back in Virginia.

''I hope you have something useful for me,'' Kurtzman groused.

''I have confirmation that the sub was in Split,'' Lyons replied, ''and I have a line on some of the sub's hijacked cargo.''

''Give.''

As he went over the information, Lyons didn't bother telling Kurtzman how he had obtained it. The story of Emilio Zappa and the ''favor'' he had done in exchange for it would have to wait until he returned to Stony Man Farm.

"Better get it packed up, guys," Lyons said when he broke the radio link. "We're leaving tonight."

"Where're we going?" Schwarz asked.

"Back to the mainland. The Bear wants us to go to Brindisi to keep an eye on the Serbian connection."

"Damn, I was hoping to get more of that village bread."

"You're just going to have to fill up on pasta."

BOLAN FOUND Yakov Katzenelenbogen alone in the *Puller*'s officer's lounge. "What's up?" the Israeli asked when he saw the hard copy in Bolan's hand.

"The President got tired of waiting for someone to find that sub," he told him as he read the decoded fax he had just received from Stony Man Farm. "He's got another mission for us."

"What is it?" the Israeli asked.

"He wants us to hit a suspected weapons factory in the Libyan desert."

"A nuclear plant?"

"Apparently someone thinks so. And that someone is in the Mossad. Also, we have confirmation from the Ironman that the Libyans are trying to trade diamonds for electronics and that ties in with the other hijacked cargo. The President wants whatever's going on there shut down immediately."

"Doesn't he have enough problems with Libya right now?" Katz asked.

"Apparently not."

Everyone on board the *Puller*, including the Stony Man warriors, was well aware that after the sinking of the *Sorya*, the Libyan navy had sailed out into the Mediterranean in force and was harassing the American and NATO ships at every opportunity. They were playing "chicken" with their ships, training missile launchers and gun turrets on passing American vessels and generally raising the level of tension to a war pitch.

The crew of the *Puller* had been at General Quarters for some time now, and every weapon in the 6th Fleet was locked and loaded, ready to fire. For most of the officers and men, the question wasn't "if" a shooting war with Libya would break out, but when.

There was no doubt that the Libyans would come off second-best in any such encounter with the American Navy, just as their jet fighters had been defeated every time they had challenged the Tomcats of the fleet. Even in the Middle East, Libya's navy was a joke. But even if the 6th Fleet made a clean sweep of the Mediterranean, it wouldn't be without some cost in American lives. Trading young American casualties for Libyans even at a great ratio didn't seem to be a fair trade.

Even facing this threat, though, the President wanted to up the ante in this high-stakes game of brinkmanship with the colonel. If the past was any indication of how the Libyan leader would react, a strong response would send him scurrying for cover again. At least that was what the President's White House advisers were telling him would happen.

"When do we leave?" Katz asked.

"It will take us a day to get a task force together and steam to the launch point. We're scheduled for launch tomorrow night."

"Who are we taking with us?"

"No one," Bolan said. "This is to be a total Plausible Deniability scenario this time, no outsiders. Jack will fly us in one of the Ospreys, and there will be a Navy fighter cover for our exfiltration, but that's it. We're on our own when we reach the ground."

"What's the opposition?"

"Not much. There's a small security detachment and the foreign scientists. We're going after them."

When Katz raised one eyebrow in question, Bolan went on to explain. "The Mossad has reported that Wilhelm Kessler and his team are involved in this Libyan project."

"The Red Baron."

"Exactly."

As with the late Abu Askari, Wilhelm Kessler had a high rank on Phoenix Force's shoot-on-sight list. And with the death of the Palestinian terrorist, the former East German renegade scientist had moved up a notch on that list. Stamping his file Closed would make the world a much safer place for people to live.

"That's another bastard I won't mind having a hand in taking out."

"I rather thought you'd feel that way."

"I'll get the men going," Katz said. "When do you want to brief them?"

"Give me a couple of hours to go over this with the Navy first."

CHAPTER EIGHTEEN

Aboard the USS Lewis B. Puller

Planning the strike on the Libyan weapons-research facility went quickly. Kurtzman faxed spy satellite photos of the compound to the Stony Man team along with a plan of the site that had been put together by Israeli and Egyptian agents working undercover in Libya. After studying the material, Bolan and Katzenelenbogen decided to make a simple night air assault directly onto the grounds of the compound.

The plan lacked the stealth of a traditional ground infiltration, but made up for it with swiftness and the instant on-call firepower of the Osprey. Since the intelligence reports indicated that there was only a small guard force on duty, varying from eight to twelve men, the numbers were in their favor. Once the security force had been neutralized, they could take their time and make sure that they thoroughly destroyed the facility.

While Rafael Encizo and Calvin James went over the team's weapons and assembled the demolition charges, Jack Grimaldi and David McCarter helped the sailors prepare the Osprey for the long flight. The first thing they concentrated on was checking the aircraft's weapons systems and loading the ordnance. For this mission, Grimaldi chose Maverick tank-busting and ground-attack missiles for his underwing pylon loads. The nose turret-mounted 20 mm chain gun was loaded with a mix of HE and armor-piercing ammunition.

Since they would be operating at the extreme range of the tilt rotor assault transport, the two then helped the *Puller*'s airframe mechanics install an auxiliary one-hundred-gallon fuel tank in the rear of the Osprey's troop compartment. Grimaldi would use that fuel first, then jettison the empty tank before the final run into the target.

After Bolan finalized their assault plan, he went looking for the Russian.

"Have you seen Solikov?" he asked Katzenelenbogen.

"He's hanging around with the armorers, eyeballing the missiles and hardware. Why?"

"I need to talk to him about the mission."

"He usually doesn't like what you have to say about our missions."

"He'll like what I have to say this time."

"You taking him with us?"

Bolan nodded. "This raid isn't really connected with his country's missing submarine, but we need a demo man, and I don't want to use a SEAL this time. They've contributed enough."

"It's about time that he got his feet wet," the Israeli stated. "Nobody rides for free."

As Katz had said, Bolan found the Russian liaison officer watching the Navy aircraft armorers load 20 mm ammunition into the Osprey's ammo bays and fuze the missiles hanging from the pylons.

"How'd you like to go along with us this time?" he asked.

Solikov looked surprised. "Why the sudden change of heart about me risking my life?"

"With Manning laid up with that leg wound, I need a good demo man. The rest of us are going to have our hands full with the staff and the garrison. While we're doing that, someone has to get in there and destroy that facility."

"In that case," the Russian said, bowing slightly, "I'd be honored to accompany you."

"You'd better reserve that judgment until we're safely back here."

"Regardless, it is time that I did something more to help resolve this situation. After all, it is a submarine of my navy that we are chasing. And—" he shrugged "—the Libyans need to learn that they cannot get away with being involved in crimes against Mother Russia."

"You've done your part so far," Bolan reassured him. "You were just supposed to be our Russian submarine expert, not a Spetznaz commando."

Solikov grinned. "Did I ever tell you about the time I went through the naval commando school? I was the number-two man in my graduating class."

"That figures."

TO AID THE ASSAULT TEAM in reaching its target undetected, the *Puller* steamed to a position off the western coast of Egypt to launch the Osprey. By coming in on the wave tops from that direction and then skimming the desert the rest of the way in, the strike force should be able to make it to the target without alerting Libyan defenses.

As a further aid, the Navy was going to send up a large jet-fighter force to patrol the edge of Libyan airspace farther to the west, to draw the attention of their radar away from the low-flying Osprey. The Air Force was also contributing an airborne-warning-and-control-system aircraft—AWACS—to keep the aerial traffic organized, as well as to warn Grimaldi if the Libyans launched fighters against him.

"Are you ready?" Bolan asked Solikov when the strike force gathered on the flight deck of the *Puller* right after dusk. The Russian had been outfitted with an M-16 rifle, an assault harness and a rucksack borrowed from the SEALs. His face was streaked with night-black combat cosmetics, and his black Russian submariner's beret.

Solikov grinned. "I'm as ready as I can be. I have studied the blueprints thoroughly and it looks pretty straightforward. I shouldn't have any trouble blowing the place sky-high, as I think you say."

Bolan smiled. "That's the way we say it all right, and that's exactly what I need you to do."

"No problem." He patted the stock of his borrowed assault rifle. "We're ready."

A FEW MINUTES LATER, the V-22 Osprey lifted off from the aft deck of the *Puller* and banked away into the night sky for the two-hour flight to the weapons facility in the desert.

To pass the time, McCarter ran Solikov through the loading and firing procedures on the M-16 he had been issued. The Russian officer had been trained to use the Kalashnikov family of assault rifles, but the M-16 was different enough that it didn't fall to his hand naturally. Solikov's job was to set the charges to destroy the facility, and the assault rifle was only a backup for him. But if he needed it, he would have to know how to use it. In a firefight, a man either knew his weapons intimately, or he died.

"Feet dry," Grimaldi called out from the cockpit, using the Navy term for a strike force reaching land after an overwater flight.

"How's our cover?" Bolan asked when he went up to the cockpit.

"So far, so good. The Navy's air show is doing a good job of drawing their attention from us. There's no active radar anywhere near us."

"What's our ETA?"

"We should be on the ground in another eighty or ninety minutes at about 0130 hours local time."

Bolan turned to go back to the troop compartment. "Give me a fifteen-minute countdown."

"You got it."

WILHELM KESSLER WASN'T in a good mood when he walked out of his office at the secret Libyan research facility in the desert. Even though the sun had long gone down, the hot air was stifling as he made the short walk to his air-conditioned four-wheel-drive Toyota truck. The fact that he faced an hour-long, late-night drive through the desert to the villa where he was staying didn't help any.

He should have known better than to get involved with Colonel Khaddafi, but the pay was more than right and the target was even righter. The problem was that his schedule had been badly disrupted. The loss of the hijacked metallic cobalt on the *Sorya* would put his enhanced nuclear warhead program seriously behind schedule.

Fortunately, though, the scientist had a plan B to fall back on and would still be able to accomplish his mission. The one thing he had learned from working for volatile Arabs was that it was always necessary to have a plan in reserve.

His reserve plan in this case was the production of simple binary nerve gas artillery projectiles. He had the blueprints from such weapons he had developed in East Germany to use as prototypes, and the material he would need was readily at hand. Standard Russian artillery illumination projectiles and fuses could be easily reworked to disperse the nerve gas. The base chemicals were commonly used to make agricultural fertilizer and were easy to convert to something more deadly. All he needed to do was to finish setting up the machinery and start making them.

Even so, the conditions at the desert research facility weren't what he had asked for, and needed, if he was to produce the weapons he had contracted to make. Sophisticated weaponry couldn't be put together in a tent like black powder pipe bombs. There had been many minor holdups that were to be expected in starting an operation of this kind. The biggest problem, however, was that the air filtration system necessary to keep the desert grit out of the precision machinery didn't work as promised.

He had finally lost his temper, and the Libyan in charge of preparing the facilities had been very apologetic. He vowed to have a new filtration system on the morning supply convoy from Tripoli, but

Kessler doubted that he could come through with it on time. Everything else had been delivered late, so he expected nothing to change. He intended to report the incompetent to the colonel and demand that he be replaced. If he was going to do his work, he had to have the supplies he required and have them on time.

Kessler's Toyota was fifteen miles from the compound when he caught the shape of an aircraft passing in front of the moon, headed in the other direction. The only reason for a plane to be in the vicinity would be that it was going to land at the research facility. But as far as he knew, no one was scheduled to fly in tonight. More than likely, the visitor was another late-night emissary from the colonel with one of his last-minute demands or a request to fly to Tripoli to discuss another one of his mad schemes.

If that was what it was, though, it was too damned bad. The colonel's man would just have to wait until he returned in the morning.

Even if the colonel was paying him quite well for his services, the Libyan leader was going to have to learn that he was dealing with Wilhelm Kessler, not one of his cowering subordinates. He might be working for the colonel now, but he wouldn't be cowed by him or any other man.

FIVE MINUTES AWAY from the target, Bolan was back in the cockpit of the Osprey, watching their approach.

"You want me to take out that vehicle?" McCarter asked as he tracked the headlights moving across the desert floor below.

"No," Bolan replied, "let him go. I don't want to risk alerting the security force at the compound."

"That's too bad. I've got him locked in and I can take him out with three rounds. That won't even heat up the gun barrels."

"Save it for later. We might need those three rounds before this is all over."

"I've got a radar lock on," McCarter said suddenly, hitting the ECM module on the fire control panel. "It's an antiaircraft gun."

"Get us on the ground," Bolan said tersely.

Jack Grimaldi aimed the nose of the Osprey at the cleared area in front of the main building and rotated the turbine prop nacelles to let the plane land like a helicopter. If he came down fast enough, he might be able to dodge the fire.

While the pilot desperately tried to duck under the radar-directed gun before it could fire, McCarter was locating the threat with his infrared target seeker. The instant that his helmet visor pip blinked to indicate that he had a lock on, he squeezed the trigger.

The chain gun growled as a string of 20 mm tracers reached out from the Osprey's nose turret and connected with the ground. A twitch of the turret-control joystick walked the fire to the left and brought a bright secondary explosion that put the 23 mm out of action.

Turbines screaming on full-reverse pitch, Grimaldi dropped the rest of the way onto the sand. "Go! Go! Go!" he yelled, hitting the rear-ramp release.

James and Encizo were the first ones out of the open ramp, their subguns blazing. Katzenelenbogen, Bolan and Solikov were hot on their heels.

Even with the advance warning from the antiaircraft gun, the defenders were still running for their posts when the Stony Man force hit the sand. James and Encizo dropped their initial targets, then raced for the perimeter trenches, trying to get there before the Libyans. All the heavy firepower was in sandbagged positions along the trenches and, if they could take it out, they just might be able to stay alive.

CHAPTER NINETEEN

The Libyan Research Facility

As per Bolan's specific orders, Viktor Solikov ignored the firefight raging around him and raced for the main building, the rucksack full of demolition charges slamming against his back. When a camouflaged figure broke out of the shadows in front of him, he didn't even break his stride. He just stitched him with a quick burst of 5.56 mm rounds and kept on running.

When he reached the laboratory building, he flattened himself against the wall and tried the main door. When luck wasn't with him and he found the door locked, a quick burst from his M-16 blasted it open. He went in low and took cover behind a desk to check the place out. When a quick look around showed that the building was empty, he slung the rifle, dropped the ruck and went to work.

He set the first charge on a large tank of anhydrous ammonia by the far wall. What the explosives themselves didn't destroy in the lab, the corrosive chemical would. Switching the detonator to radio control, he activated the backup timer as well, setting it for two hours.

After checking to make sure that the timer was counting down, he looked around to see what he should blow up next. A large computerized turret lathe caught his eye, and he went for it. Precision tooling machines were hard to come by in Libya, and it would be difficult to replace.

As soon as Solikov ducked inside the main building, all hell broke loose in the compound. Racing through a hail of AK fire, Calvin James and Rafael Encizo reached the heavy weapons positions in the trenches before the Libyans. Settling down behind a 12.7 mm heavy machine gun, James opened up on the three Libyans running toward them, their AKs shooting flame.

The Libyans dived for cover, but it was too late. The inch-long slugs of the heavy machine gun caught two of them before they could reach safety and slammed them to the ground, bleeding and broken. The third hardman made himself small behind a light pole, his assault rifle lying forgotten beside him.

While James and Encizo kept the Libyans out of their own defensive positions, Bolan and Katzenelenbogen went into offensive mode. If the mission was to work, they had to completely eliminate the opposition before the Libyans realized how few attackers there were.

A Libyan stood by the open door of the guards' barracks shouting orders. From the Sam Browne belt he wore over his desert camouflage fatigues, he had to be the officer commanding the guard force. Bolan raised his subgun and triggered a 3-round burst.

The trio of slugs drilled through the officer's jacket right over his heart, and he crumpled in mid-shout.

Racing to the open door of the barracks, Katz tossed a grenade in through the opening and flattened himself against the outside wall as it detonated. The bomb was still singing through the air when he stuck the muzzle of his Uzi around the edge of the door and emptied a full magazine into the interior at waist height.

Even with their officer gone and their own machine guns turned against them, the remaining dozen or so defenders tried to rally. Bolan and Katz, however, didn't give them a chance to get their act together.

When Bolan saw them trying to work their way around to the main building, he radioed a warning to James and Encizo to keep them away from Solikov. With Bolan and Katz cutting them off on one side and James and Encizo coming in on the other, there was no place for the Libyans to go. Taking cover behind a stack of supplies, they tried to fight it out.

Now the Stony Man team had to take cover themselves, but their superior combat skills didn't make it even a contest. Every time one of the Libyans chanced a look, someone put a bullet in him. After losing more than half their number, the survivors emptied their magazines on full automatic, turned and ran.

Three of them made it into the sturdy concrete block building with air conditioners in the bottom of every window. Considering that the guards' barracks was a simple wood frame building, that had to be the quarters for the foreign weapons team.

"You want me to try to get them to come out of there?" Katz slapped a fresh magazine into the butt of his Uzi.

"Might as well give it a try," Bolan answered. "If they're alive when the relief force shows up, they can pass on a message."

"You inside the building," Katz called out in German. "If you surrender, you will not be harmed."

When there was no answer, he repeated the surrender demand in Arabic. A burst of 7.62 mm fire from an AK on full automatic was the only answer he got.

"Let's do it," Bolan said grimly.

"Wait!" Encizo pointed to a sandbagged bunker. "Let me see if that 23 mm over there is still working."

Settling into the gunner's seat, he tapped the foot pedal that controlled the twin-barreled weapon's traverse mechanism. Swinging the barrels around to bear on the building, he tripped the foot switch trigger. Only one barrel of the machine cannon was still working, but that one was enough.

The 23 mm HE rounds tore through the thin walls of the prefab building like a jackhammer. Glass and chunks of concrete blocks flew in all directions. After cycling through more than sixty rounds, the gun fell silent when its ammunition box ran dry. There was no return fire.

Bolan stopped to slam a fresh magazine into his H&K subgun. Transferring it to his other hand, he drew the 10 mm Desert Eagle from his holster and flicked the pistol off safe.

"Okay," he said. "Let's get in there and clear that place out."

There was little enough to clear up, however. The antiaircraft cannon shells had done more than simply tear gaping holes in the walls. Shrapnel from the exploding rounds and splinters of concrete had turned the room inside the building into a slaughterhouse.

WHILE THE STONY MAN force mopped up outside, Solikov was making good progress with his demolition project. More than half the explosive charges in his rucksack had been laid and the timers set. Rather than destroy things like the generator complex that could be easily replaced, he was concentrating on the specialized machinery. With the trade embargo still in place, it would be more difficult to smuggle the heavy machinery in. He had no doubts, however, that it all would be eventually replaced.

One of the evils of capitalism was that there were always men who were more than willing to make a dollar, franc or mark selling the tools of death to madmen. Unfortunately his own country was now full of such men. Russian-built weapons of all descriptions were reaching a wider market than they had ever done under the old Soviet regime.

The world would be a far safer place if weapons and, even more important, the tools used to make weapons and ammunition could be eliminated. But since that wasn't likely to happen in any future he could imagine, he went back to setting his last few demo charges. They would do a lot to make this particular part of the world safe for a few months at least.

LIBYAN ARMY Major Ali Jered jerked awake at the sounds of the explosions in the distance. Sound traveled far in the cool night air of the desert. The colonel had been right again. The Americans had come to raid the isolated weapons research laboratory.

Outside his tent, he heard the excited voices of his men and the sounds of the T-62 tank engines cranking up. As soon as the vehicles were started and the crews on board, they drove off at full speed toward the compound ten kilometers away, as they had been instructed.

God had told the colonel that the infidels had spies watching the research facility. Since he couldn't reinforce the security troops at the site itself without the spies learning of it, he decided to leave them as they were. But to make up for it, he had ordered Major Jered and his elite armored detachment into the desert within striking distance. They were to remain hidden in a deep wadi until they were needed to repulse the attack that was sure to come.

Not even stopping to lace up his combat boots, Major Jered grabbed his weapons and ran for his command vehicle. His driver had the door open and his foot holding the clutch pedal to the floor. The instant the major was in his seat, the driver dropped the clutch and they sped off.

Now that he was above the wadi's rim, the sounds of battle were louder. Jered could hear small-arms fire and the explosions of grenades. He was confident that the security force could hold on until he arrived. They, too, were handpicked troops and would die before running from Americans. And, while they were dying, his men were racing to avenge them.

"WE GOT COMPANY COMING, Mack!" David McCarter radioed Bolan from the cockpit of the Osprey. "There's an armor column coming in from the south."

Bolan no sooner looked out over the desert than a tank gun boomed in the distance. The round fell short of the Osprey, but the next one should have the range. "Get into the air!" he ordered Grimaldi.

The Stony Man pilot immediately pulled pitch, and the heavily armed tilt rotor clawed for altitude. A second tank shell exploded right where the machine had been sitting on the ground, sending red hot shrapnel singing through the air.

As soon as the Osprey lifted off, the raiders took cover behind the Libyans' perimeter defenses. James found an unloaded Libyan RPG-7 antitank launcher on the front berm of his trench and snatched it up. Taking an RPG rocket from the carrier in the bottom of the trench, he quickly loaded it into the front of the launcher. Grimaldi and McCarter should be able to handle their little problem. But if they couldn't, it didn't hurt to be prepared.

McCarter had a big grin on his face as Grimaldi quickly climbed to attack altitude. He was finally going to have a chance to work out with the Osprey's weapons systems, and he was ready for it. Flicking a switch on the fire control panel, he selected his underwing ordnance loads. This was where the laser-guided, armor-busting Maverick missiles the *Puller*'s Navy ordnancemen had loaded on his pylons were going to come in handy. As had been proved in the Gulf War, Mavericks were the world's premier tank-busting missile.

Flicking on his laser target illuminator, he slaved the Maverick's warhead guidance systems to the laser beam. Now when he illuminated a target with the laser, the number-one Maverick would lock onto it. Once locked on, the warhead's internal guidance systems could take over when the missile was fired. That way, McCarter didn't have to keep the laser designator on the target for its flight and Grimaldi could press the attack.

He lit up the lead tank with the laser, got an immediate lock on and fired. The missile dropped from the pylon and ignited a millisecond later, streaking for the Libyan T-62 tank below. At this short range, it seemed that it hit the target almost instantly.

The Maverick's shaped-charge warhead cut through the thick armor of the tank's turret as if it were so much cream cheese. The superheated plume of explosive gases melted the steel and added it to the destructive force. When it drilled through to the inside of the turret, the white-hot molten metal brought instant death to the tank crew. It also detonated the 155 mm rounds in the main gun's ready rack. The resulting explosion blew the turret completely off the tank and sent it tumbling through the air.

Before the turret came back to earth, McCarter had lit up the second tank and fired. This Maverick took out its target as well, impacting right in front of the driver's position. The T-62 didn't lose its turret this time, but all the hatches blew open as the stream of white-hot explosive gases blasted through the driver's body into the turret.

Grimaldi was banking around to line up on the third tank when a sudden stream of tracer fire from the 12.7 mm antiaircraft machine gun on the tank's turret flashed past the canopy a few yards in front of his face.

"Get that bastard!" Grimaldi yelled as he violently racked the Osprey up on one wing to escape the fire.

"I'm on him!" McCarter turned in his gunner's seat to look over his shoulder, and the Osprey's nose turret turned with him. Centering the diamond pip on the top of the tank's turret, he triggered the chain gun. The turreted 20 mm weapon growled like a tiger as it spit a mix of armor-piercing and HE rounds at the exposed antiaircraft machine gun and the Libyan gunner. All it took was a quick burst before the gun and the gunner were blown to mangled chunks.

Now that the 12.7 mm was silenced, Grimaldi swooped back down so McCarter could deliver another Maverick. With the laser designator on the target all the way, the missile flew fast and true. It impacted low on the turret and blew the hatches open again.

Now that all of the heavy armor was blazing on the desert floor, McCarter went after the APCs and the troops they carried.

The first one fell victim to the last Maverick on his underwing pylons. The missile unleashed its destructive force, and the APC disappeared in a ball of flame as its fuel tanks went off. A few flaming figures staggered away from the wreck, but quickly collapsed to the ground.

The three remaining personnel carriers were easily disposed of as well. Their light armor was no match for the 20 mm antipersonnel rounds. McCarter was careful to brush the chain gun's fiery touch across the antiaircraft machine guns mounted on the top of each track before getting serious about poking holes in it. A few 20 mm rounds later, they were each left as burning hulks in the sand.

The crew of the last APC bailed out before the Osprey could swing around, and took to their heels across the sand in the opposite direction. Seeing the Libyans escape, James slipped in behind the sandbagged 12.7 mm machine gun again and set the sights for the distant target.

"Let them go," Bolan said, placing a hand on his shoulder. "I want to finish this up and get out of here."

CHAPTER TWENTY

Eastern Libya

Major Ali Jered ran until he couldn't run anymore. His feet were raw inside his boots, and he wished that he had taken the time to lace them properly before leaving the wadi. The sawing sound of the chain gun still sounded in his ears. The desert behind him was lighted by the roaring fires from the burning carcasses of his armored detachment. The occasional explosion as a round of ammunition cooked off in the conflagration only added to the surrealistic glare.

The three T-62 tanks and the four APCs full of troops under his command had been destroyed by the mysterious aircraft that had swooped down on them from the black night sky. Except for a mere handful of men who had managed to get away on foot as he had, his entire detachment had been wiped out.

Dawn wasn't far off, and he realized that he had to make it back to the wadi before the sun rose too high in the sky. The supplies they had left back there would last him until someone flew out to see what had happened to him.

On second thought, however, maybe it would be better if he found a band of nomads and just stayed in the desert with them. Returning to Tripoli without being able to report a victory would be hazardous to his health.

DAWN WAS JUST BREAKING over the desert when Grimaldi lifted the Osprey off the ground and banked away toward the rising sun and the Egyptian border. The Libyans would be expecting them to try to escape to the south coast, since that was the shortest route out of their airspace. The Egyptian government, however, had agreed to allow the Osprey free passage over their country before they would turn north to make rendezvous with the *Puller.*

Behind them, columns of black smoke stained the still-dark sky over the destroyed weapons factory. Solikov had done a damned good job as the team's replacement demo man. Once more Colonel Khaddafi was going to have to build another secret weapons factory if he wanted to become a serious mass murderer. He was also going to have to find another group of foreign scientists who were willing to sell their talents to a man like him. Hopefully it wouldn't be so easy next time.

Thinner columns of oily smoke rose over the shattered hulks of the Libyan armored force. They had been too little, too late. And, as had been so graphically proved in the Gulf War, armor was no match for an attack aircraft armed with Mavericks. It still wasn't.

The message the Stony Man team was leaving in the desert behind them was plain—scientists who did that kind of work for paymasters like the colonel could expect to run the risk of being a target.

Even though the facility was out of action and the research team dead, Katzenelenbogen wasn't happy that Kessler hadn't been in the compound. "I wonder where he was?"

"Since it wasn't reported that he'd actually been seen here, maybe he had just hired out his team and wasn't leading them himself."

Katz shook his head. "We haven't heard the last of him, you know."

Bolan smiled grimly. "And he hasn't heard the last of us, either."

"That's something to look forward to."

"THE AWACS SAYS that we can expect company before too long," Jack Grimaldi announced a half hour into the flight back to the *Puller*. "They have three Libyan Fitters airborne on an interception course at Mach 1.2."

"Damn!" McCarter bent over his radar screen. "How close are we to the Egyptian border?"

"Not close enough. I'd better get us down on the deck so we can hide in the trees."

"What are you talking about? There aren't any bloody trees down there."

"I know."

The Libyan Su-22M-2 Fitter J wasn't a threat to be dismissed. The export version of the Russian swing-wing fighter was optimized for both air defense and ground attack missions and was a potent weapon in both roles. Back in 1981, a pair of Fitters had engaged a pair of Navy F-14 Tomcats over the Gulf of Sidra in one of Khaddafi's earlier saber-rattling exercises.

After waiting to be fired on first as the rules of engagement demanded, the Navy fliers then proceeded to mix it up with the Libyan Sukhois. In the world's first aerial combat between variable geometry fighters, the Fitters came out second best, with both of them going down to the Tomcat's air-to-air missiles.

This time, though, the score would turn out the other way. The Osprey was an impressive aircraft, but it was no match for a jet fighter.

TEN MILES inside Egypt's western border with Libya, a pair of MiG-21bis jet fighters patrolled a clear china blue sky at twenty thousand feet. In the lead fighter, Egyptian air force Senior Lieutenant Faud Kassem watched his British-installed airborne targeting radar screen light up with pips marking incoming traffic. Though his MiG was almost twenty years old, the Egyptian air force fighters had all been upgraded with the latest in Western-made fire control and targeting electronics.

The radar was showing four planes heading his way. The first was slow moving and should be the American Osprey they had been told to look out for. The other three were fast jets that read out on his IFF radar as Sukhoi Su-22s, the primary fighter of the Libyan air force.

"Here they come!" Kassem radioed to his wingman.

"Is the American going to make it?"

"I don't know, but it doesn't look like it. They're closing in on him too fast."

The flight leader instantly made his decision. "I'm going in to draw them off."

"The squadron commander told us he'd ground us if we cross the border."

"We'll survive," Kassem said, as he hit his afterburner. "I'm not going to let those Libyan pigs shoot those men down."

"Wait for me, Faud," the wingman radioed. "You need someone to watch your tail."

"You had better hurry then."

"I'M PICKING UP a pair of Egyptian fighters crossing the border." McCarter sounded jubilant. The Briton had his finger on the decoy-flare button, ready to start dropping flares as soon as he had a launch signal. Theoretically the decoy flares, which burned at more than two thousand degrees, would confuse a heat-seeking missile and draw the missiles away from the Osprey.

Since the flares were a passive defense measure, though, he didn't have much faith in them. McCarter believed in the old axiom that the best defense was a strong offense. But he didn't have a hell of a lot to go on the offensive with today, not against jet fighters. Firing assault rifles at them from the rear ramp wasn't going to cut it.

"They'd better put a rush on it," Grimaldi growled. "Those bastards are only a minute or two away from a launch."

Before he finished speaking, the lead Egyptian MiG triggered an American-supplied AIM-9L Sidewinder heat-seeking missile from extreme range. He didn't have a lock on and had no hope of downing one of the Libyan Sukhois, but he hadn't really intended to.

When the Libyan pilots detected his launch, they instantly threw their fighters into evasive maneuvers, giving the Osprey pilot a chance to put more distance between him and them.

After easily dodging the Sidewinder, the lead Sukhoi-22 bored in on the two Egyptian jets. At his command, the Egyptian wingman broke away, leaving the MiG leader to take on the Sukhoi himself. But the cocky flight leader had no doubts of the outcome. The heavy swing-wing Sukhoi fighters were no match for the Egyptian's lighter MiG-21s. The nimble 21 was well-known as being one of the world's best dogfighters, and Kassem knew how to put his mount through its paces.

A Mach 1 corkscrew maneuver kept the Su from locking on him before they passed each other at well over two thousand miles an hour. Immediately racking his MiG up into a split-S turn, the Egyptian ace reversed his course and came in behind his opponent.

The Sukhoi driver panicked and tried to bank away from the MiG, but to no avail. There was no way that he was going to shake the Egyptian off his tail. With the Su-22 hanging on the edge of a high-speed stall, Kassem easily turned inside of it and launched another Sidewinder from the Libyan's six o'clock position. This missile had lock on and flew straight up the Sukhoi's tail pipe at Mach 2.5.

The resulting fireball consumed the jet's aft fuselage and sent it heading for the ground.

"Splash one Libyan," McCarter gleefully announced.

"What's happening with the other two?" Grimaldi peered through the canopy, trying to spot them. Until all three Libyans were taken out, they weren't safe.

Even with the loss of one of their fighters, the Libyans still pressed the attack on the MiGs. Their orders were to destroy the raiders at all costs and that meant taking out the Egyptians first.

The lead Libyan launched one of the AA-2 Atoll heat-seeking missiles from his underwing pylons. Leaving a trail of dirty white smoke, it raced for Kassem's MiG at supersonic speed. The Egyptian heard the launch warning in his earphones and racked his fighter into a tight turn, aiming the nose of his jet directly at the sun.

One weakness of the Russian-designed Atoll missiles was that its heat-seeking warhead didn't have a discrimination circuit built into it. That meant that it would lock on to the hottest heat source in the area and follow it, even if that source was the sun. It was an old Israeli air force trick that wouldn't work against the newest American heat-seeking missiles, or even the newer Russian ones, but it was still effective against the AA-2.

After climbing for thirty seconds, the Egyptian pilot slammed his control stick hard over to the right and sucked it back into his belly. The MiG made a hammerhead turn to starboard and rolled over onto its back as it dived out of the line of fire with its hot tail pipe aimed away from the oncoming missile.

Locked onto the blazing desert sun, the Libyan Atoll missile streaked past him at over Mach 2, headed for the target it would never reach. Now, it was his turn.

The Libyan Sukhoi was still game and was maneuvering to a position on his tail again. After glancing over to see that his wingman was closing in on his prey, Kassem racked his MiG into a high G Immelmann turn. Panting hard to keep from blacking out from the punishing maneuver, he nosed over at the top of the turn and swooped back down on his target from behind.

With both of his Sidewinder missiles gone, it was time for the Egyptian to use the twin-barrel GSh-23L 23 mm revolver cannon mounted on the belly of his plane.

When the first burst was a bit high and wide, the Sukhoi went up on one wing and tried to turn into him. Had the Libyan been in another MiG-21, the maneuver might have worked. There was no way, though, that the heavy swing-wing fighter was going to be able to turn inside the nimble MiG-21.

Holding his MiG in a high-speed skid, Kassem triggered his belly cannons again. This time he saw the sparkle of 23 mm hits on the Sukhoi's outer wing panel. Turning even tighter, he walked the high-explosive cannon fire into the Libyan's fuselage center section.

One of the 23 mm rounds smashed into the Libyan's turbine rotors. The tempered steel blades snapped off, shredding the fuselage like a burst of shrapnel. Red-hot turbine blades sliced through the fuel tanks, venting the vaporized jet fuel to the slipstream. An instant later, the Sukhoi exploded in a ball of flame.

As Kassem banked away from the fireball in the sky, he saw that his wingman had also dispatched his opponent. It was time to go home. Spotting the American Osprey below him, he dropped his speed brakes and flew in behind it.

"PHOENIX ONE, this is Desert Eagle," came a British-accented voice over Grimaldi's earphones.

"Phoenix, go."

"This is Eagle. Your tail is clear. Welcome to Egypt. We will escort you to your destination. Over."

"This is Phoenix," McCarter answered. "Thanks ever so much, old boy. Phoenix out.

"Tell the boys in the back to relax," he told Grimaldi. "We're home free."

"Good men, those Egyptians," the pilot said with a smile. "I knew they would come in handy someday."

"It's rather nice to have them on our side for a change."

CHAPTER TWENTY-ONE

Stony Man Farm

As had been the case after President Ronald Reagan called Khaddafi's bluff back in 1981, the colonel's reaction to the destruction of his desert weapons facility was to cut and run. He recalled his navy to protect his territorial waters and was reported to have left his palace in Tripoli to take up residence in a nomad's tent in the desert again. Maybe this time he would figure out that the United States wasn't going to allow him to obtain weapons of mass destruction. More than likely, though, the lesson would have to be repeated in a couple more years. The colonel wasn't one to learn from his mistakes.

With the Libyan navy back where it belonged, the combined 6th Fleet and NATO ships were able to stand down from the war alert. This didn't mean, however, that everything was back to normal. There was still the pirate sub to be found and neutralized. The warships were quickly redeployed to keep a close watch on all the Libyan-flagged or Libyan-owned merchant vessels sailing the Atlantic and the Mediterranean. If the renegade sub planned on using any of them as a mother ship, it would be caught.

With the successful Libyan raid behind them now, the Stony Man staff went back to the primary problem, hunting for the elusive stealth sub. Although they had successfully cut off the pirate sub from two of her mother ships, they were no closer to knowing where she was or what her next move was going to be than they had been in the beginning. All they knew was that since the sinking of the *San Juan,* there had been no more unexplained shipping losses on the high seas.

The fact didn't make Aaron Kurtzman feel better, however. He liked to have his enemies out in the open. Or at least, he liked to have a clue as to what they were doing so he could find them and deal with them.

"What would you be doing right now if you were commanding that sub?" Kurtzman asked Ivan Zelev.

"I don't have any idea at all. I'm not a pirate and I don't think like one. When I was a pig boat officer, my job was to be ready to kill you Americans. Other than that, I had to keep from being killed. It was simple and straightforward, not at all complicated like this."

"I'm beginning to wonder if we should be concentrating on the missiles on the sub instead of the piracy," Price said.

"How's that?" Kurtzman asked.

"The piracy's small peanuts."

"Tell that to the crew of the *San Juan*."

"It's small peanuts compared to what that sub could do if it launched even one of those missiles."

"Okay," Kurtzman admitted, "you've got a point there. Let's war-game that aspect of it for a while and see what we have."

Fingers flying over his keyboard, he brought up the file showing the characteristics of the Russian designed SS-N-19 submarine-launched cruise missile. "Okay, those things can carry either a conventional warhead of a thousand kilograms of HE or a hundred-kilowatt nuke at a range of some six hundred miles."

"With that range," Kurtzman said as he called up a map of the Mediterranean and superimposed a red border six hundred miles wide around the entire coastline, "she can hit anything within the red zone."

More keystrokes enlarged the area the map covered to include the Atlantic coastline of Western Europe and the British Isles. The red zone grew to cover those coastal areas as well.

"There," he stated, turning to Price. "Is that enough target area to worry about? That's every major city of Europe and the Middle East, except for Berlin and Moscow.

"But," he added with a shrug, "if she sails into the Baltic, she can then hit Berlin and Moscow as well."

The extent of the red-marked area made the map of Europe and the Mediterranean look as if it had been slashed with a razor and left to bleed.

"Maybe we had better keep on the piracy angle," Price said. "There's no way we can ever cover all of that."

EVER SINCE THE SINKING of the *Sorya*, Oleg Yatkin had held his submarine off the northwest coast of Africa awaiting instructions from Libya about a new mother ship. There was no point in his hijacking any more ships if there was no way to transfer the cargo.

The inactivity didn't sit well with Major Omar Rashid. As far as he was concerned, every hour that the *Petlyura* sat idle was an hour wasted that could be better put to use bringing his leader's plans to fruition. A flurry of radio messages to his command in Tripoli had, however, gotten him a new target that he triumphantly took to Yatkin.

"This is the last one, though," Yatkin stated flatly. "After we take this cargo, I'm returning to Split until this mother ship situation can be settled. This boat is a lot of things, but it is not a cargo truck or a warehouse."

"After we get this cargo," the Libyan said, "I will call for further instructions about its disposal."

"I'M PICKING UP a second ship," the *Petlyura*'s sonar man announced as they closed in on their latest victim, a British merchant vessel with a cargo of machine tools, "and it sounds like a warship."

Yatkin took the headphones from the man and held them to his ears. There was a second ship up there and, from the sound of her heavier machinery and faster-turning screw, she was some kind of naval escort ship.

"Take us up to periscope depth," he ordered. "I need to take a look."

"Aye, Captain. Coming up to periscope depth."

Turning his cap around backward to clear the eyepieces, Yatkin guided the scope up from its housing, allowing the optical head only to break the surface of the water. If that was a warship, it would be on the lookout for submarine periscopes.

As soon as the optical head broke water, Yatkin had his eyes to the scope. What he saw ended any thoughts of even trying to capture the cargo ship.

A sleek, matte gray frigate flying a white British naval ensign from her fantail and a large white number 39 on her rakish bow was keeping pace with the freighter. Parked on the warship's fantail landing pad was a Westland Sea King antisubmarine helicopter with two sonar homing torpedoes hung under her belly. The heliport was large enough to hold two such choppers, which meant that the second one was probably in the air above him right now.

"Down scope," he ordered.

"There's a British antisubmarine frigate escorting your target," Yatkin told the Libyan. "I'm breaking off the attack."

"You can sink the frigate," Rashid replied. "Two torpedoes, and it will be finished."

"My country is not at war with the British," Yatkin said. "Attacking that ship would be an act of war, and I do not have orders to start a war. Plus, it had an antisubmarine-warfare helicopter parked on her fantail, and there might be a second helicopter over us right now."

"But, my colonel needs that cargo," Rashid insisted.

"Your colonel is just going to have to wait. I don't have orders to risk this vessel even for him."

"I'm getting pings, Captain," the sonar man broke in.

"From the escort?"

"No, sir. I think it's from an aircraft."

If the sonar man was right, that meant that the second helicopter that hadn't been on the frigate's flight deck was airborne and was towing her sonar array in the vicinity. And, since many of those choppers also carried MAD gear, he had to get out of the area as fast as he could.

"Break off immediately!" he ordered the helmsman. "Steer zero seven two and get us out of here at flank speed."

"Aye, Captain."

Yatkin turned to Rashid. "That does it. I'm taking this sub back to Split until this operation gets sorted out. Until your government and mine comes up with a workable plan, I am not going to risk this ship or my crew. This submarine is too valuable to risk for a few crates of machine tools."

Rashid didn't bother to mention that these were laser-guided remote-control machine tools used for machining radioactive materials. That was none of the Ukrainian's business.

"THERE ARE WARSHIPS patrolling the strait," the *Petlyura*'s sonar man reported as the sub approached Gibraltar and the entrance to the Mediterranean Sea. "They're destroyers or frigates from the sound of them."

This was what Yatkin had feared. Now that the world's navies had been alerted to the existence of a pirate submarine, they were actively patrolling the narrow path he had to take to get back to his home port.

"Rig for silent running," Yatkin ordered. "Passive sonar only."

Running the Strait of Gibraltar was always dangerous for a submerged submarine. At the bottom of the narrow channel between Europe and Africa, the currents ran from the Mediterranean into the Atlantic at several miles an hour. The surface currents, however, ran even more strongly in the opposite direction. Smaller surface ships steaming west had been known to almost stand still against the current around Gibraltar even though their engines were running at full revolutions.

The interface zone where the two currents of water met was the most turbulent spot in any of the world's oceans. And the deep channel they would have to navigate was very narrow. Usually submarines made the passage on the surface because it was safer—and a lot easier—than trying to run the deep channel.

On the way out of the Mediterranean, Yatkin hadn't been concerned about being discovered because no one had been looking for them. He had kept the *Petlyura* closer to the surface so she was sailing through the calmer water of the upper current. This time, however, he had no choice but to go deeper and try to stay in the current interface so its turbulence would further mask his passage from the surface ships searching for him.

"We're being pinged," the sonar man said.

Even with the sound-deadening material covering the hull, Yatkin could hear the muted metallic pinging of the active sonar pulses. "What's the range?"

"Four thousand meters and closing."

As the warship approached, the pings came faster and faster until they sounded like a heartbeat.

"He's just hunting," Yatkin said to calm himself as much as to reassure the bridge crew. "He doesn't have a fix on us yet."

"Should I go deeper, Captain?" the helmsman asked.

Yatkin glanced at the depth gauge, which registered fifty-three meters, then down to his chart of the strait. "No, hold where we are. We'll be entering the current interface any time now."

No sooner were the words out of his mouth than the sub shuddered as its pointed bow penetrated the turbulence of the interface zone. Overhead, the pounding of the warship's screws grew louder and louder.

"At twelve hundred meters," the sonar man sang out, "and closing fast."

Now the sub was being shaken like a rat in a terrier's jaws as the currents sawed at it. It was much worse than the shaking they had taken coming through the Dardanelles, but it was also their salvation.

"Ignore him," Yatkin said triumphantly. "We're completely safe now."

Yatkin's prediction came true. But the fading of the warship's screws didn't completely ease tensions in the sub. The hammering she was taking from the currents had the bridge watch nervously glancing up at the bulkheads to see if they were holding under the pressure. Fortunately, however, the passage went quickly. One minute they were being rattled and shaken and the next they were out the other side and all was quiet.

In the sudden silence, Yatkin could smell fear and fresh sweat over the normal submarine odors of stale cooking, unwashed men and the all pervading dampness. While the *Petlyura* was fully operational as far as her military duties went, not all of her water condensers were on line and there wasn't enough water for showers. Even with the CO_2 air scrubbers on full blast, the air was getting as rank as in the old diesel boats he had trained on as a cadet.

Nonetheless, it was a good smell now because it meant that they had run the gauntlet unscathed. "We're home free, boys," he said. "Secure from silent running."

"WHY THE HELL wasn't I given this report sooner?" Aaron Kurtzman fumed into the phone as he looked over the fax he had just received from Hal Brognola about a suspected sonar contact with the stealth sub in the Strait of Gibraltar. "This was recorded hours ago."

"It's a Naval Intelligence report," the big Fed answered from his Justice Department office in Washington. "They only sent it to me FYI as a courtesy."

"Damn those swabbies. When are they going to learn to do what they're instructed? We can't find that damned sub if the various Intelligence outfits don't make sure that I get whatever information turns up as soon as it comes in."

"It won't happen again."

"It shouldn't have happened this time."

After harassing Brognola for a few more minutes, Kurtzman hung up the phone. "I wish he'd get those damned people in line. It would make my work a hell of a lot easier."

"At least we know that the sub's back in the Mediterranean," Price said.

"Yes, but why?" Kurtzman asked. "It doesn't make much sense to me. The Med's not the best place in the world to try to make a living hijacking cargo ships. There's so much maritime traffic that it will be difficult for them to surface and raid a ship without being spotted."

"As I said earlier," Price pointed out, "I think we need to concentrate on those missiles she's carrying. There are quite a few places around the Med where a single nuclear missile could do a lot of good, or a lot of harm depending on which side of it you're on. Considering that the Libyans are involved again, I think we should notify the IDF that they might have a pirate sub carrying nuclear missiles headed their way.''

''The Israelis aren't the only ones who are threatened,'' Kurtzman said. ''We need to notify all of the southern NATO nations as well.''

''Plus, make sure that Lyons knows that the ball's in his court again. We're probably going to need access to the Serbian coastline before this thing's over.''

CHAPTER TWENTY-TWO

Brindisi, Italy

"This is more like what I had in mind when you said we were coming to Europe, Ironman." Schwarz grinned as he sipped a cappuccino and eyeballed a stunning blonde sitting at a nearby table. She was wearing sunglasses, a smile and a bikini that only a minimalist could have designed. "With a little bit of work, I think I could learn to like this place."

Carl Lyons and Rosario Blancanales ignored their partner's mindless banter. They were drinking double-strength instant coffee and studying the map of Brindisi's port and the surrounding area. Price's orders were for them to acquaint themselves with the port as soon as they could and start making contacts in case they needed to get a line on the situation in Split. She also wanted them to find a smuggler who would be willing to risk running the NATO blockade and keep his mouth shut at the same time.

Brindisi was a far cry from either Palermo or Naples. As befitted a major tourist port, it was a clean, modern town full of European vacationers on holiday and college students on break. Brightly painted cruise ships and ferries were tied up at the piers taking on cars and tourists headed for Greece and the Aegean islands.

Even though Brindisi was flooded with tourists, the port wasn't without its darker side. Smuggling was a major Italian passion and, even with the war in Yugoslavia, the Adriatic coast offered as many opportunities for a man in a small fast boat as did any other. Considering the situation with the new ethnic republics, maybe even more. There were arms and ammunition to be smuggled in, and refugees and drugs to be smuggled out. If Price ordered them to make a raid on Split, those same small fast boats could carry them as well for the right price.

"Okay," Lyons said as he drained the last of his coffee and folded the map, "let's head down to the docks and get to work."

Schwarz reluctantly got to his feet. "Can we come back here when we're done?" he asked plaintively. "I think I just got a date for tonight."

"You've got a date with sailors' bars and beer joints, you mean," Lyons said. "Barb wants us to get a handle on this situation as fast as we can."

"I hope we have better luck than we did in Naples or Sicily," Blancanales said. "We don't need any more Mafia chieftains on our case."

"Nor any more side trips to do someone else's dirty work," Schwarz added.

SINCE RUNNING the NATO gauntlet at Gibraltar, Major Rashid had had little to say to the *Petlyura*'s captain. Yatkin had halfway expected the Libyan to try to take over the boat or at least try to convince him to attack another ship. While he was glad not to have to argue with the Arab, he didn't trust the man's silence. Whatever Rashid was cooking up, he knew he wouldn't like it.

Being a firm believer in doing to others before they did unto him, Yatkin had made some plans of his own, and he had enlisted the assistance of his boatswain to help carry them out. Being more than two meters tall and weighing at least one hundred kilos, the boatswain was well suited for what Yatkin had in mind.

When Rashid left the control room to join his men in their afternoon prayer to Mecca, Yatkin nodded to his boatswain. In turn, the burly sailor nodded to two more of the Ukrainian crewmen who had been hanging around the control room for the past hour.

The three Ukrainians walked up behind the two Libyan crewmen still on duty on the bridge. The boatswain took care of his victim all by himself. One blow of his massive fist sent his Libyan sprawling to the deck plates, stunned. Before the other one could react, the two Ukrainian sailors jumped him as well. In seconds, both Libyans had strips of tape over their mouths to prevent them from shouting a warning, and short pieces of rope bound their hands behind their backs.

As soon as they were secured, the two struggling Libyans were marched down the passageway to the watertight door closing off the supply bay, which had been converted into a living area for the Arab commandos. When Yatkin jerked the hatch halfway open, the two Libyans were dumped through the opening and the door slammed shut behind them. The boatswain put his weight against the locking dog while Yatkin pulled a large padlock from his back pocket.

"I don't want any of them let out of there until we reach port," Yatkin said as he snapped the heavy lock shut and pocketed the key.

"Aye, Captain," the boatswain replied over the hammering of fists on the other side of the heavy steel door. "I'll tell the rest of the crew."

The big man smiled slowly. "I've had more than enough of those bastards myself. It'll be nice to have the stink of goat fat out of my face for a while."

Yatkin looked around to make sure that the other crewmen were out of earshot. "If I were you," he said softly, "I'd consider following me when I leave the boat at Split. As long as we're forced to work with the Libyans, we're going to go from bad to worse. If the Russians catch us, they're going to shoot us for stealing their boat. If the Europeans or

Americans catch up with us, we're going to hang for piracy."

"We're buggered either way we go then, Captain."

"Not if we get off the boat as soon as we can and try to make it back to the Ukraine."

He thought for a moment. "Or we could try to make it to Italy and pose as refugees from the fighting. All we would need is a small boat. Anything would do."

Having been a sailor all of his life, he was ready to cross the Atlantic in a teacup if he had to. He could sneak past the NATO blockade in his sleep.

"That might be difficult to find in Split, though. It's pretty heavily guarded."

"We made off with this one, Captain," the boatswain pointed out. "And it was well guarded, too."

Yatkin smiled. "We did, didn't we?"

"We sure as hell did, sir. And I think we can do it again. Next time, though, let's not stop and take on any fucking Arabs."

"You've got my word on that."

"What do you want me to tell the rest of the men?"

"Nothing until we make port. Then you can pass the word that we're abandoning the ship."

"Aye, Captain."

THE SUBMARINE'S NUCLEAR power plant was making only enough revolutions to maintain steerage when Yatkin passed the Greek island of Corfu and approached the blockade zone. Even with the sub's stealth characteristics, Yatkin had ordered silent running ever since rounding the heel of the Italian boot and entering the Adriatic Sea.

He was fully aware that running the NATO blockade off the Yugoslavian coastline wasn't going to be the same piece of cake that it had been on the way out of Split. Every navy in the world was now aware of the existence of his pirate stealth sub and would be actively hunting for it. Regardless, he also had more faith in his ship's ability to elude sonar than he had had before.

Even so, there was another danger now. Not only did he have to worry about sonar from the surface ships now, MAD-equipped aircraft could have also joined the search for the *Petlyura*. The submarine's designers had made her invisible to sonar, but there was nothing they could do to mask her magnetic field. Magnetic Anomaly Detection gear measured the background magnetic fields of the earth and recorded the changes in the fields that occurred when a large chunk of iron passed between the detector and the earth. And, for the purposes of MAD, a submarine rated as a large chunk of iron.

Before he started his run, he had to check to see if the skies overhead were clear of aircraft. The

Petlyura was fitted with a retractable radar array that could be sent up to the surface to check on aircraft while the sub remained safely submerged.

"Come up to radar depth," Yatkin ordered.

"Radar depth, aye, sir."

When the depth gauge showed fifty meters of water above the hull, the sub leveled out. "Release the radar array."

"Radar away."

A few minutes later, the radar screen came alive, showing the airspace over the sub. "I don't have any airborne radar returns, Captain," the radar man reported after several 360-degree sweeps. "The sky's clear above us."

"Retract the radar," Yatkin ordered, "and bring the reactor up to fifty percent power."

"Half power, aye."

Even with the advanced design screw that prevented high-speed cavitation, sonar returns from the churning water in the submarine's wake were still strong. The faster the screw turned, the stronger the return. The trick was to balance the advantage of using the *Petlyura*'s high speed to get through the blockade quickly against the increased risk of sonar detection.

He chose a conservative approach. "All ahead one-half," he ordered. "Make revolutions for thirty knots."

On fifty percent power from the reactor, the boat could make almost thirty knots, which was almost as fast as the fastest surface ships. Plus, the sub could accelerate faster than any pursuing destroyer if she was detected and had to make a run for it.

"Thirty knots, aye."

As the faint vibrations built up, he saw several of his crewmen cross themselves, and he felt a sudden urge to do the same. All of their lives were riding on his skills as a pig boat commander, and those skills would be tested as they had never been before on this run.

"Steer course zero-three-two," he ordered.

"Zero-three-two, aye," the helmsman answered.

Silent running meant turning the ventilator fans down and the control room soon took on the reek of a crowded jail cell. To make matters worse, a thick pall of strong cigarette smoke hazed the air. Yatkin had read somewhere that smoking had been prohibited on all American submarines, and he shook his head in wonder. Every submariner he had ever known, Russian or Ukrainian, had been a heavy smoker. The vice went with spending your life underwater, waiting for it to crush the life out of you. The Americans had to be men of iron to serve under the sea without smoking.

He could have done with a little less smoke right now, but he knew that the crew's stress level was high and he didn't want to add to it. And, if they were going to die, at least they all deserved a last smoke. Patting his pocket and finding it empty, he walked over to his boatswain's mate and bummed a cigarette himself.

"I'm getting approaching sonar, coming on fast," the sonar man announced. "She's six thousand meters out, and it looks like she's going to cross our bow."

"Reduce revolutions to ten percent." Slowing the sub would let the warship pass several hundred meters farther in front of them and reduce their risk of being detected.

"Reducing revolutions, aye."

The sounds of the ship's screws and the pinging sonar were fainter than they had been when they had made the run past Gibraltar, but they were still nerve-racking. The pounding of screws and the pinging of sonar were the sounds of death for a submarine.

With the *Petlyura*'s power plant making only ten percent, the NATO ship would pass well in front of them. Hopefully the stealth sub's sonar-deflecting design would work for them once again.

"He's going away." The sonar man's relief was evident.

"All ahead half."

The rest of the run was just as nerve-racking. Yatkin had had to slow the submarine two more times to allow a fast-moving warship to pass by them. Each time the pound of the ship's screws brought absolute silence to the control room. No one even wanted to breathe too loudly lest the sound attract unwelcome ears.

"We're through the blockade line, Captain," the sonar man announced finally.

"All ahead full," Yatkin ordered. "We're going in."

At the captain's words, a muted cheer broke out in the control room. He wasn't the only Ukrainian on board who was sick of being a pirate. Like their captain, even though the crewmen were staunch Ukrainian nationalists, most of them had a totally different idea of serving their country. And those ideas had nothing to do with sharing a submarine with murderous Libyan commandos.

The boatswain had said nothing to anyone about the captain's plan to leave the submarine as soon as it reached port, but locking the Libyans in their bay was a good indication that the situation on board the pirate ship had radically changed.

CHAPTER TWENTY-THREE

Split Harbor

When Oleg Yatkin entered Split harbor this time, he didn't bother to notify the Serbians so their hydrofoil patrol boats could come out and camouflage the *Petlyura*'s sail when she surfaced. He didn't care if the American spy satellites were overhead. Let them see where the pirate sub was. It simply didn't matter to him anymore. Regardless of what his superiors back in the Ukraine wanted, he was done with piracy and he was done with Libyan fanatics.

He realized that it meant he would also be done with submarines. Never again would he slip beneath the waves like a steel shark hunting for his prey, and he knew that he would truly miss the life of a submariner. But that was the price he would have to pay for having gotten involved in this mad scheme in the first place.

He also didn't care what Rashid would do with the sub once he and his men were safely away from her. That again was of no concern to him. More than likely, the *Petlyura* would get a new Libyan crew and continue her career as a pirate ship until she was finally discovered and sunk. He hoped, however, that no Ukrainians would be on board when she made her final plunge into the lightless depths. And he would do whatever he could to convince his men to leave with him.

He knew there was a good chance that the Ukrainian nationalist leaders would consider him a traitor for not giving in to Rashid, but again he didn't care. No good could possibly come from his country's unholy alliance with the Islamic fanatics. But he was out of that now as well. All he had to do was to get as far away from Serbia as he could, as fast as he could.

He also didn't care what happened to the four SS-N-19 nuclear missiles still loaded in the launchers in the forward hold. As far as he was concerned, they belonged to the Ukrainian nationalist movement. The movement's leaders in Kiev could do whatever they wanted to with the damned things. Even so, before he could leave the sub, there was one last thing that he had to do. Leaving the launch card behind might tempt Rashid to do something insane with the missiles, and he didn't want that on his conscience.

Reaching up to his neck, he pulled a small chain from under his shirt. On the end of the chain was a small plastic card with a magnetic code strip on the reverse side. For the nuclear missiles to be launched, the card had to be inserted into the fail-safe lock. No magnetic card, no launch—it was as simple as that. The missiles couldn't be fired without a total rework of the submarine's firing circuits.

Taking the card from the chain, he walked down to the small officers' galley next to his cabin and placed it in the microwave oven. Punching in five minutes on the timer, he hit the start button. In thirty seconds, the smell of hot plastic hit his nose. Peering through the glass window in the door, he saw that the launch card was being transformed into a bubbling ball of molten plastic.

Whatever else happened after he left the *Petlyura*, launching her missiles wouldn't be in the picture for quite a while. The launch circuits could be rewired to bypass the fail-safe card lock, but that would take the technicians several days to do. And, in that time, maybe the nationalists back home would come to their senses.

Satisfied that he had done everything he could do to keep the missiles out of Rashid's hands, at least for a few days, he turned around and headed for his small cabin to pack his personal belongings.

As SOON AS the *Petlyura* docked, Rashid knew without being told that Yatkin had returned the stealth sub to Split harbor. Since he commanded a pirate ship, it was the only safe haven available to him. And he was sure that the cowardly infidel was going to abandon the submarine as soon as he shut her reactor down. He also figured that most, if not all, of the other Ukrainians would go with him.

Even if they did, it would be only a minor inconvenience and only for a short while. Yatkin didn't know about Rashid's plan to replace him, and all of his countrymen, with Libyan submariners for the final mission. The sub would be his then, but first he had to get out of this compartment so he and his men could take over the ship.

From the minute Yatkin had locked them in their bay, his men had tried everything they could to break out, but had been unsuccessful. But he knew that God wouldn't let him fail and would give him a way out. All he had to do was wait, and he was a patient man.

THE UKRAINIAN CREWMAN who unlocked the hatch to the Libyans' sleeping bay thought he was doing the right thing. The captain had ordered the sub secured for dockside, and that meant opening all of the inside compartments to the fresh air. He hadn't wanted to bother the boatswain for the key to the lock, so he took the master key from its peg in the quartermaster's cubicle.

The first thing he saw when he unlocked the hatch dogs and opened the steel door was the muzzle of the Makarov pistol in Major Rashid's hand. The Libyan shot the crewman in the face and pushed the hatch the rest of the way open.

Seeing that the passageway was empty, Rashid signaled to the men behind him, calmly stepped over the body and started down the passageway toward the control room. God was with him today and would surely deliver the traitor Yatkin to him as well.

The Ukrainian crewmen busy securing the submarine's systems for their dockside stay thought nothing of seeing armed Libyans in the passageways. Even though the captain had locked them all in their bay for the trip back to Split, they still thought of them as their partners in piracy.

Rashid found his prey in the small captain's cabin with his back to the door stuffing his dirty clothing into a bag. Yatkin looked surprised when he turned around and saw the Libyan standing there with his men behind him. "The *Petlyura* is all yours now," he said.

"And so are you," Rashid grated.

"What do you mean?"

"I mean that you are to stand trial for treason against the Libyan state. The best you can hope for is a quick bullet in the brain."

When Yatkin's hand shot out for his small bag, Rashid instinctively fired three quick, unaimed shots at the Ukrainian's center body mass.

Yatkin looked surprised as he slowly slid to the floor, his back pressed against the bulkhead. The

9 mm rounds the Makarov pistol fired weren't powerful, but at point-blank range, it didn't really matter. All it meant was that he wouldn't die as quickly.

"The missiles," the Ukrainian gasped.

"What about them?" Rashid snapped.

"I destroyed the launch card." Yatkin's face had a faint smile as his last breath left him. He convulsed once, his feet kicked on the floor plates and he was dead.

"Get this infidel dog out of my sight," Rashid barked to the man standing closest to him.

"What do you want me to do with him, Major?"

"Throw him in the harbor with the other filth."

"Yes, sir."

The Libyan turned to his senior sergeant. "Secure this sub immediately."

"As you command, Major."

The man started to go, but paused. "What do you want me to do with the rest of the Ukrainians, sir?"

Rashid thought for a moment. Since the colonel was still playing at being allied with the Ukrainian nationalists, it might be best if they were kept alive for the moment. If they needed to be killed later, the Serbians could track them down easily enough.

"Let them gather their individual belongings," he said. "Then escort them to the end of the dock and turn them loose. If they try to come back, however, kill them. In fact, I don't want anyone on this dock without my permission until we leave. All the workmen are to be escorted when they come and go, and they will be guarded at all times.''

''It will be done.''

Brindisi, Italy

WHEN LYONS ANSWERED the knock on the door of their hotel room, he was surprised to see Emilio Zappa's grandson standing there. The young Mafia heir was alone and stood carefully with his hands open at his side.

''Greetings from my grandfather,'' he said. ''I have a message for you.''

''Come in.''

When the young man walked into the living room of their suite, he wasn't surprised to see Schwarz aiming a pistol at him. Under the circumstances, he would have done exactly the same thing. He stood calmly while Lyons patted him down and discovered that he was clean, as he had expected him to be. Zappa wouldn't have sent his grandson if he had thought he would be facing danger. And, if he was going to be among friends, he would have no need of a weapon.

''Have a seat,'' Lyons offered. ''Can I get you something to drink?''

''No, thank you,'' the young man said, taking a seat in the overstuffed chair by the window. ''I don't drink when I'm on family business.''

"So, what can we do for you?"

"Nothing," he answered. "This time, it's what I can do for you. I have news of the submarine you have been seeking. It sailed into Split harbor yesterday, and it is moored in plain sight at the old Russian submarine base. It is under heavy guard, though, by men believed to be Arabs. Maybe they are the Libyans you talked about."

Schwarz shook his head in disbelief. After all of the high-tech time and effort that had been put into this operation, to have an old-time Sicilian godfather be the one to deliver the goods was a fine irony. Maybe Hal should sign the Mafia chieftain on board as his new intelligence chief.

"Tell your grandfather that we thank him," Lyons said.

"He also wants me to tell you that if you want to go to Serbia, you should go down to the south dock and ask for a man named Mario. If you tell him that Emilio has a cousin in Rome who recommended him, he will help you."

"A cousin in Rome?"

"Mario will understand."

"How did Emilio know that we have been asking about a boat?"

The young man shrugged. "My grandfather has eyes here as well as in Sicily. In his business, he has to. And he says that you can trust Mario to keep his mouth shut and not to overcharge you."

"I appreciate that."

"If you have no other questions," the young man said, standing slowly, "I must be going."

Lyons walked him to the door. "Thank you again," he said. "This information will help eliminate a great danger for all of us."

"That's what my grandfather is counting on. I hope you do not fail him."

"We'll try not to."

The young man paused in the door. "I don't know if it means anything to you, but my grandfather has asked the priest in our village to pray to Saint Dismas for the success of your mission."

"Thank him for us," Lyons answered seriously. "We're going to need all the help we can get."

"Who's Saint Dismas?" Schwarz asked when the door closed behind Zappa's grandson.

"If I remember correctly," Blancanales replied, "I think he's the patron saint of thieves."

"That's rather appropriate."

"Isn't it."

MAJOR RASHID SEETHED with anger. The report from the Serbian electronics expert who was examining the *Petlyura*'s missile-firing circuits was anything but good news. The man said that it would be two or three days before he could bypass the fail-safe locks so the missiles could be launched without using the magnetic-coded launch key Yatkin had destroyed.

Even thinking about the Ukrainian officer made Rashid's teeth ache. The bastard had died much too easily.

Had it not been for Yatkin's treachery, the mission would be well on the way to its conclusion. Now it was seriously jeopardized by the submarine having to remain in port while the missile circuits were being reworked. The problem was that since Yatkin had brazenly sailed into Split harbor without taking protective measures, the Americans had to know where the submarine was. And since they did, there was hardly any point in trying to camouflage it now.

The Serbian military command had put the harbor defenses on full alert in case of an attack. Even so, if the Americans were willing to spill blood, they would be able to destroy the sub. His only chance of gaining enough time to finish the repairs was the threat of the nuclear missiles she carried.

As he knew only too well, with the missiles' firing circuits inoperative it was a hollow threat. But that was something his enemies had no way of knowing. And being the cowards that they were, they would hesitate before risking a nuclear confrontation over a few acts of high-seas piracy. Were they to get wind of the submarine's final mission, however, they might risk it.

The colonel's latest communication had brought him great honor—he had been named to the inner circle of the council of advisers. But with that great honor had also come an even greater responsibility. As soon as the missiles were operative again, he was to put to sea immediately with the skeleton crew of Libyans he had on hand. He was to break through the blockade and sail for a rendezvous in the Mediterranean.

Once the *Petlyura* was safe again in international waters, additional Libyan crewmen could join him for the final mission. The man who had been scheduled to take over command of the submarine had been struck down in Tripoli traffic and wouldn't be out of the hospital for several weeks. Another submarine officer was hurriedly being trained to take his place, but the man wouldn't be ready in time for the final operation. The honor would go to Rashid.

Even though all of the colonel's preparations weren't yet completed, Rashid had been commanded to fire the missiles and trust in God's mercy for the rest of it to happen as had been planned.

CHAPTER TWENTY-FOUR

Stony Man Farm

Lyons's report of the sub's sighting electrified the Stony Man staff. The decided lack of new information since the pirate had made her run through the Strait of Gibraltar had had everyone frustrated. When compared to the Atlantic, the Mediterranean was small, but there were still thousands of places to hide a submarine.

"We'll need to get a satellite confirmation on this before I send it to Hal," Kurtzman said as he started touching keys to bring up his menu of the U.S. spy satellites in space. "The problem is that it may take a couple of orbits before the Air Force can maneuver one of the K series into position to tape the area."

Zelev smiled. "We have a satellite we might be able to swing over to cover that area almost immediately. Let me get in touch with my people and arrange for that."

Kurtzman switched to calling up a list of the known Russian recon satellites and their orbital paths. "Which satellite would that be?"

Zelev laughed. "We call it Snow Rabbit Three. And I don't think that you have it on your list."

"Snow Rabbit Three? What kind of name is that for a spy satellite?"

"It's the name of something that can hide from its enemies without being seen," the Russian explained. "We knew that you were tracking our satellite launches, so we developed the Snow Rabbit program."

Kurtzman shook his head. "You're a wealth of startling information, Ivan. Just exactly what is this Snow Rabbit program of yours?"

"Do you remember a couple of years ago when we were having widely publicized problems with our satellite launchers blowing up in outer space? It got a lot of press here in the West and a lot of snickering in your defense industries."

"I vaguely remember," Kurtzman said, reaching for his keyboard to bring up the data.

"Anyway, each of those 'defective' rocket boosters actually released a satellite right before they were command detonated. The debris from the explosion masked the satellite's release and made it look like another piece of space junk to your radar."

"That was clever enough," Kurtzman said admiringly as he scrolled through a list of Soviet satellite launches.

Zelev bowed his head slightly and smiled. "We had our moments, too. Now, if you will let me get in touch with Moscow, I'll get those pictures for you."

WHEN HAL BROGNOLA arrived at Stony Man, he looked as if he had been ridden hard and put away wet as he hurried into the Stony Man War Room. The big Fed had been living on coffee and cold sandwiches for so long now that he had forgotten what a real sit-down meal tasted like. Or a long hot shower followed by a thick bathrobe, a cold drink and a warm bed.

"We have the confirmation," he announced abruptly. "The Russians faxed the photos, and the sub is in Split harbor. They aren't even trying to camouflage it, and it's tied up to a dock in plain sight."

"That's great," Kurtzman said with a smile. While he didn't look as worn-out as Brognola, he, too, had been putting in too many long, frustrating hours. With him though, since he always looked rumpled, it didn't show as much. "That makes it easy for an air strike. One two-thousand-pound smart bomb, and that boat is history."

"Air strikes are out," Brognola said grimly. "The Ukrainians have announced that they have signed a mutual defense pact with the Serbian Republic. Any attack by United States or NATO military forces on Serbian territory will be considered as an act of war against them. And since they still have the world's third-largest nuclear missile force, that's not a threat to be taken lightly."

"Will they do it?" Price asked.

Brognola shrugged. "Our intelligence analysis indicates that they have a couple of loose cannons in their military high command who would like to do nothing more than nuke somebody, anybody, just to prove that they can do it. Unfortunately the Russian analysis agrees with ours, so we just can't take the risk."

"How about using one of your subs to attack their sub?" Zelev offered.

"Same problem," the big Fed replied. "It will be considered a military attack against Serbia if it takes place in Serbian waters."

"Have the Ukrainians fessed up to having nukes on board that sub yet?" Kurtzman asked.

"We're still dancing around with them on that issue. They claim that the stealth sub was part of their half of the take when the old Soviet Black Sea Fleet was broken up. They say that it is armed, but they refuse to say if any of that armament is nuclear."

"They're lying, of course."

"There's little doubt about that," Brognola agreed. "The Russians have nothing to gain by lying to us about the missing missiles. But there's also no proof that they are still on that particular submarine."

"What about the Libyans? Could the missiles have been transferred to them?"

Brognola shook his head. "It's not thought so at this time, but we're keeping an eye on it. We have the Israelis and Egyptians working the Libyan end of it, and there has been no indication that they have the missiles." He paused. "Yet."

"They aren't that hard to hide, though."

"That's true, but the Israelis have promised to turn Libya into a real desert if Khaddafi gets any ideas about using them, and Egypt is siding with them on this one. In fact, the Egyptians have moved most of their armored forces to the Libyan border to show the colonel that they're dead serious this time."

"What does the President want us to do about that sub?" Price asked. "If it gets out to open sea again, we might never find it."

"The Man wants it taken out within the next forty-eight hours, or he's going to hit it with an air strike anyway and gamble on the Ukrainians not retaliating. He says we can't afford to take a risk with four nuclear missiles on board a pirate ship."

He looked at Price. "He wants to know if Striker and his people can take it out."

"They might not beat the odds on this one," she stated calmly.

"I know, Barb." Brognola spread his hands in a gesture of helplessness. "But I'm afraid I have to ask him. It's what the President wants."

"Before we talk to him," Kurtzman said, "let's war-game this thing and see if there's an easy way for them to get in for a change. Or at least one that has a good chance of success."

He put a map of the Split area on the big screen projector and studied the approaches to the harbor for a long moment. "How do they have the harbor defended?"

"According to the Russians, the Serbs have taken over the old Soviet navy harbor defenses, including the coastal missile batteries, the air defense weapons and some kind of command-detonated minefield system. They say they had a good system, and it's still intact."

"I wish they'd taken it all with them," Price said.

"So do we," Zelev broke in. "Believe me."

"How about a fast attack boat? The Italians have some that will hit better than sixty knots."

"No go." Brognola shook his head. "The Serbs took over the old Yugoslavian hydrofoil ferries and heavily armed them. They'll do almost eighty knots fully loaded."

"Can they paradrop someplace up the coast," Price suggested, "and make their approach overland? They could use the HALO glide chutes so the drop plane could stay out of radar range. Those chutes can glide sixty miles or so from the drop point."

"Split is completely under Serbian military control and it's crowded with hundreds of troops. There's checkpoints every half mile or so, and special passes are needed to get anywhere near the naval base."

"What you're talking about is an underwater approach, right?" Price said.

"That's what they came up with at Langley," Brognola admitted. "And the Joint Chiefs agreed."

"Which means that the vehicles are already on their way to the Mediterranean, doesn't it?"

Brognola nodded. "The minisubs left on a C-5A before I left Washington."

Price's eyes flashed. "I'm the mission controller, and I hate to send them out against such odds. Some day I hope that Mack tells those SOBs to take their suicide mission and stuff it. If he lives that long that is. Every time the politicians screw up it's always the same few men who put their lives on the line so we can all go to bed at night and not have to worry about waking up dead."

There was little Brognola could say in answer to that except that she was right on the money. But for now, he had to do his best to salvage what he could. He glanced at her with a rueful grin and shrugged. "I'll be staying here until the mission is concluded. The President wants me to be on hand in case the shit hits the fan."

"Why don't you take a shower and lie down for a couple hours?" Price suggested. "I'll send someone for you if anything comes up."

He rubbed his hand over his cheek stubble. "That might not be a bad idea."

"While you're doing that, I'll get in touch with Striker and give him his marching orders."

"They've already been faxed to him on the *Puller.*"

"Of course."

CHAPTER TWENTY-FIVE

On the USS Lewis B. Puller

"Probably the best thing about the Conger MS-3 minisub," said the Conger Underwater Enterprises representative as he enthusiastically tapped his pointer on the computer display screen showing his company's latest undersea product, "is that it is very fast. I understand that those Serbian hydrofoil patrol boats are fast, too. But you should be able to outmaneuver them if they get a sonar fix on you and escape."

CUE was more than delighted to have been contacted by the Navy to provide examples of their MS-3 minisub for a field test. Conger had been trying to get the Navy to commit to buying the machines for a couple of years now, but had run into the brick wall of the nineties defense cutbacks. If the subs performed well in this test, however, it might change some minds and release enough funds to keep the company in business.

"You should be able to get into the harbor," the rep continued confidently, "place the explosive charges on the target and get out of there completely undetected."

Even though Hal Brognola had the President's permission to let an outsider into a SOG operation, the man still hadn't been told exactly what his company's products were going up against. He had a high-level clearance, but not quite that high.

As Phoenix Force's resident ex-SEAL, Calvin James had the most experience with underwater warfare. Regardless of the company rep's cheery enthusiasm for his product, he wasn't so sure about using these experimental two-man underwater sleds. Making a HALO drop and going on in with scuba gear and fins was more to his liking, but that plan had been ruled out as being too risky.

"What's the range of those things at full load and full power?" James asked.

"We've never actually run the MS-3s at full power for an extended period of time," the rep admitted, "but the specs say that they're good for two and a half hours."

"You mean *should* be good for two and a half hours, don't you?"

"Ah..." The factory man stumbled. He didn't know exactly who these guys were, but they were sure a hell of a lot more difficult to brief than the run-of-the-mill military types he had talked to before. "I guess you could put it that way if you want."

"I do want."

"I'll get back to the engineering department on that right away," the man answered, "and tell you what they say."

"You do that."

There was a long moment of silence as James went over the spec sheet one more time. "What's the on-board oxygen capacity?" he asked.

"They carry two hours of air, but you'll have your rebreathing gear for a backup."

"Is that two hours for both men?"

"Ah...yes, sir," the rep replied, frantically thumbing through his files. "I think so."

"'I think so' isn't going to cut it," James snapped. "You'd better find out for sure."

"Yes, sir."

Bolan smiled to himself at James's grilling of the Conger representative. Calvin was thorough, and he knew what counted in the down-and-dirty reality of combat. You either knew what you were doing down to the last detail, and knew what your hardware could do as well, or your butt was hanging in the wind.

This mission had no slack in it for anything other than perfection, and the minisubs were turning out to be the weak point. The problem was that with the President's deadline to take out the pirate sub, there was no time to rethink the mission. They would have to do the best they could with what they had on hand.

"I'M GOING IN WITH YOU again," Viktor Solikov said when he caught up with Bolan and Katzenelenbogen after the briefing. "And I want you to listen to me before you say I can't go."

"I'm listening," Bolan replied.

"You're going to need another demo man, an expert who knows where to put those charges on that boat. It's stupid to go all the way into the harbor and not put the explosives in the right place. If that sub gets to sea again, there's no telling what she might do next.

"Plus," he added, "I am also scuba trained. It was part of the naval commando school I told you about."

"He's right, Striker," Katz said when Bolan hesitated. "Let's take him with us."

"You get a release from your government saying that you can go into combat, and I'll let you suit up."

Solikov reached into his breast pocket and pulled out a folded hard copy. "This is a release for me to do anything necessary to assist in the destruction of that sub, to include going into combat bare-ass naked. It's signed by President Boris Yeltsin.''

Bolan smiled. "I guess that's good enough for me. Welcome to the party.''

"Thanks, I think.''

MISSION PREP THIS TIME was more complicated than merely going over the strike force's weapons and ammunition. Fitting the wet suits and scuba rebreathing gear for each man took some time. Calvin James had the *Puller*'s SEALs to help him, though, and the outfitting went as quickly as possible. After each man had been outfitted, the SEALs took them for a test dive off the stern of the ship to make sure they knew how to use the rebreathing gear.

While this was going on, the Conger representative was busy getting the minisubs operational and ready to be launched. The man was more than willing to get his own hands dirty. That turned out to be more trouble than had been expected. In fact, of the four minisubs that had been flown in, only three checked out well enough to be used. The fourth machine went down with a gyro failure that couldn't be repaired except back at the factory.

"Can we go with just the three?" Katzenelenbogen asked when Bolan told him about the deadlined minisub.

The Executioner nodded. "We'll just split up the explosive charges and have each man carry some of them instead of transporting them on the fourth sub as we had planned."

Brindisi, Italy

"DON'T YOU THINK we could use Mario's last name?" Schwarz asked after the third man in a row told Blancanales that he didn't know anything about anyone named Mario in either the south or the north dock area.

"It would probably help, but we don't have it, so we'll just have to keep on trying to find someone who knows this guy. I am surprised, though. I would have thought that old Emilio would have known what he was doing when he told us to come down here."

"Let's just get on with it," Lyons said. "If we can't find this guy before the day's out, we'll have to find another pilot or just steal a boat."

After the tenth sailor didn't know anyone named Mario, they were about ready to give it up when a street kid about twelve years old walked up to them with a shoe-shine box in his hand.

"Hey, you, DEA man," the boy said. "You want to talk to Mario, no?"

"Yes, I do," Blancanales answered. "I have a message for him from his cousin in Rome."

"You wait here," the boy said. "I go see if Mario wants to talk to you."

"Smart ass," Schwarz muttered as the boy ran out of sight around the corner.

"It's pretty obvious that we're being watched here as well," Blancanales observed.

"So much for keeping this thing quiet." Schwarz looked around. "We might as well hire a marching band and have a banner leading the parade saying that we're Feds. No wonder no one will talk to us."

The boy was back in a few minutes. "You follow me," he said. "I take you to Mario."

Lyons opened his coat to clear his access to the Colt Python in his shoulder holster. He might be in Italy where gun ownership was illegal, but there was no way that he was going to walk into an ambush.

Alert for any signs that they were being set up, the trio followed the boy into a cluttered alley between two ramshackle apartment buildings. If they were being set up, this was a good place for it. Schwarz and Blancanales cleared their leather, too, just in case.

"Mario here," the boy said, stopping and jerking a thumb at a wooden door covered with three colors of faded and chipped paint.

"You go first," Lyons said, his hand going for the butt of his Colt.

The boy shrugged and opened the door. When he wasn't immediately blown away, Lyons followed him into the dimly lit hallway, his Colt in his hand, Schwarz and Blancanales behind him.

The youngster knocked on a door at the end of the hall and stepped aside when it opened to reveal a man in his early forties with a jaunty mustache. "My American friends," the man greeted them, ignoring their weapons. "Please come in."

"You're Mario?" Lyons asked.

"That is right. I am Mario Gambelli, at your service."

"A mutual friend told us that you will help us," the Able Team leader stated as he holstered his Python.

"Emilio," Mario said. "He told me that you were his great friends and that I should do anything you ask as a favor to him. So, what can I do for you?"

"We need a fast boat and a pilot who can take us into Split."

"My friends!" Mario smiled even wider and spread his arms. "And I thought that you were going to ask something difficult of me. There is no problem. I have a fast boat, and I go into Split all the time."

The men of Able Team looked at one another in amazement. If this was so simple, why had they been put to all that trouble just to meet this guy?

"You go into Split all the time, you say?"

Mario grinned. "But of course. There is money to be made in the new Serbia and I am a man who likes money."

"What about the naval blockade?" Blancanales asked. "How do you get past the ships?"

Mario dropped the grin for a moment. "It is sometimes difficult, but I have a fast boat and it is made of wood so it is hard to see on the radar. Also, it is low to the water, which makes it even harder to see."

"And you talked about liking money," Lyons said, getting to the point. "How much money will you need for us to rent you and your boat for the next few days?"

"For you, my friends, it is, how do you say, on the house, no?"

"Why is that?" Lyons asked suspiciously. If there was anything he didn't trust, it was a crook who was willing to do something for nothing. It usually meant that you were being set up for a double cross or worse.

Mario looked a little embarrassed. "Let us just say that you have a friend who is also my friend. He says

I am to help you—'' he shrugged ''—so I will help you.''

Lyons smiled. The godfather connection was proving to be worth its weight in gold. ''Okay, then, here's the story. Like I said, we need to use your boat. I'd like you to get it ready right away and stand by until I get back in touch with you this evening.''

He nodded at Blancanales. ''One of my men will go with you in case you need to buy anything for the trip.''

''But that will not be necessary. As I said, this is all on the house.''

''He goes with you anyway.''

Mario shrugged. ''I understand.''

''Where can I find this boat of yours?''

''Just ask at the south docks. Everyone knows me.''

AFTER MAKING CONTACT with Mario, Lyons checked in with Aaron Kurtzman at Stony Man Farm to report that his end of the plan was finally coming together.

''About time,'' Kurtzman said and proceeded to brief him on the plan to raid Split harbor with the minisubs. ''I want you standing by at sea, just in case. If something goes wrong, you'll have to go in and try to pull them out. With the Serbian threat, the President doesn't want to risk further confrontation at this time by using a Navy ship or helicopter if a rescue is needed. We figure that another smuggler's boat will escape notice.''

"Who's going to rescue us if we step in it?"

"Just make sure you don't.''

CHAPTER TWENTY-SIX

In the Adriatic

The USS *Lewis B. Puller* reduced her speed in the calm, dark sea to twelve knots before launching the Stony Man team's raid on the stealth sub. Her American destroyer escort slowed as well, so as not to leave the assault transport unprotected in hostile waters. The launch point had been chosen more with the protection of the *Puller* and her crew in mind than its being the best point to release the minisubs.

The Serbian coastline was a mere twenty miles away, right over the curve of the horizon. Even though the ship was sailing through the night blacked out, radar didn't need the light of day to see—neither did radar-directed antishipping missiles.

The six scuba-equipped men waited in their three Conger MS-3 minisubs for the signal to launch. The hull-busting demolition packages had been broken down into three-man pack loads carried by McCarter, Encizo and Solikov. They would team up with James, Bolan and Katzenelenbogen for security while they placed the charges on the sub, set the timers and escaped. If all went as planned, they would be in Spilt harbor in only a little more than half an hour.

When the Navy officer wearing the comm headset linked to the bridge gave the signal, the minisubs slid off the *Puller*'s rear ramp deck one by one and immediately sank beneath the waves.

As soon as the raiders were on their way, the *Puller* and her escort turned their bows to the west to rejoin the rest of the NATO blockade fleet off the Yugoslavian coast. The assault transport would remain in the area, however, to recover the minisubs as soon as they completed their mission.

As soon as the *Puller* and her escort were clear, the minisubs set out for Split harbor more than twenty miles away. As the team's best underwater navigator, Calvin James led Bolan and Katz in a simple follow-the-leader formation. This was no time to be losing someone in the dark. To conserve the minisub's battery power, the approach run was being made at half power. The Conger rep hadn't been able to answer James's question about the machine's endurance, and he was taking no chances on exhausting the batteries.

Unlike so much of the Mediterranean, the Yugoslavian side of the Adriatic was fairly clear and unsullied from industrial pollution. The vicious ethnic wars had halted what little heavy industry there had been in the region to the ultimate benefit of the coastal marine life. This made it easy for James to navigate on the run into the harbor. It would also make it easy for them to see their target in the reflected lights of the port.

At half throttle, it took almost an hour for the minisubs to reach the mouth of the harbor. When James's navigational chart showed that they were inside the protected waters, he reduced his speed even more for the final approach in to the target, now only a thousand yards away.

They all heard the Serbian hydrofoil patrol boats approach at the same time. The whine of their turbines, the beating pulse of their high-speed props and the hiss of their hydrofoils cutting through the water sounded loud over the whine of the minisub's motors. The problem was that they didn't know how far away the patrol boats were. Sound travels five times as fast in water as it does in the air, and it sounded like they were coming on fast.

Jerking his thumb toward the sea bottom, James put his underwater sled into a steep dive. If the Serbs were towing sonar arrays, their best defense was to hide in the clutter of the bottom returns. And if the boats were trailing acoustical detection gear, they would have to shut down the minisubs immediately so the sounds of their power packs wouldn't be detected.

Following like a school of fish, the other two minisubs trailed James to the muddy bottom. At his signal, they cut the power to their packs and waited for the hydrofoils and the high-speed screws of the patrol boats to cut through the water fifty feet above their heads. They were close enough to the harbor that the light reflecting off their churning wakes looked phosphorescent against the dark sea. In a second, the boats were past, and as the beating of the props faded in the distance, James gave the signal to move out again.

Keeping close to the seaweed and debris littering the muddy bottom of the harbor, the three minisubs continued on to their target.

TWENTY MILES off the Yugoslavian coastline, Carl Lyons, Rosario Blancanales and Hermann Schwarz were drifting on the current in Mario Gambelli's cigarette boat. In the middle of the sleek wooden craft, a five-hundred-horsepower Lamborghini V-12 marine engine bubbled at an idle, waiting for the lightest touch of Mario's hand on the throttle to roar into full life. As the smuggler had proudly demonstrated on their way over from Italy, the big Lambo could push the sleek craft to speeds of more than eighty knots.

"They should have launched by now," Lyons said as he glanced at his watch, "and be almost to the harbor."

"Since we have to wait, my friends," Mario said, pulling a large wicker basket from the forward hold, "I have brought a lunch for us to enjoy. The white cheese is a local specialty. The bread and cold chicken was made by my wife. And the wine—" he brought the tips of his fingers to his lips "—it must be tasted to be believed."

"You sound like a maître d'," Blancanales stated.

"But I am," Mario said with a grin. "When I am not making the run to Serbia and Croatia, I run my family's little restaurant. My wife and my mother are the cooks, and my father sees to the wine."

As soon as the basket was opened, Schwarz reached for the loaf of bread and broke off a piece. "Thanks, Mario, this looks great."

"Have a few of the olives," the smuggler offered. "They come from my family's estate and they go well with the chicken."

MAJOR RASHID HADN'T BEEN content to depend on the Serbian and Ukrainian threat of retaliation to protect the *Petlyura* from American attack while it was tied up to the dock. The Yankees might not risk a full-scale military assault, but that didn't mean that the submarine was safe. As he knew full well, they had more than one way to deal with a sub moored out in the open.

For a desert nomad, Rashid had picked up on the details of underwater warfare rather quickly. One of the first things he had requested from the Serbian command in Split were scuba divers to protect the *Petlyura* as long as she remained tied up to the dock. He had also laid in a stock of Russian concussion grenades. There was nothing that would put a diver out of action quicker than an underwater explosion close to him.

The Libyan was in the control room watching the two Serbian electricians hook up the last of the wiring for the new missile-firing control system when the landline from the harbor patrol headquarters rang. "Rashid here," he answered in Russian.

A second later, he slammed the phone down. "Get our divers in the water immediately!" he shouted in Arabic. "The Serbian patrol boats have picked up sounds of enemy divers approaching."

Grabbing up an AK-47 and a bag of grenades, Rashid ran for the ladder to the hatch leading outside the submarine. "Follow me!" he shouted to the crew on the bridge. "We are being attacked!"

As CALVIN JAMES had hoped, the water in the harbor was clear enough that the reflection of the dockside lights alone was enough for them to see their target clearly. Two hundred yards ahead, the stealth sub lay tied up to the dock like a long, sleek steel whale resting half out of the water. Her oddly canted, triangular tail fins looked like a whale's flukes, enhancing the resemblance.

Signaling with his hands, James ordered the minisubs to the bottom of the harbor. They would leave them there and go the rest of the way in with their fins and tanks. The minisub's electrical motors were quiet, but if the stealth sub was running a passive sonar watch, they might pick up the faint whine.

The six men formed into three teams and started swimming toward the dock. Now, Bolan and Encizo took the lead as they were to attach their explosives at the far end of the sub. Following them with McCarter in his wake, James suddenly caught a reflection in the water in front of them. There was something moving in the long bottom shadow cast by the sub's hull.

The dock lights made it easier to see, but they also threw deep black shadows in the already dark water. Something in his peripheral vision made him snap his head to the side, and he saw enemy frogmen swimming toward them out of the shadow of the sub's sharply pointed bow.

Spinning in the water, he signaled to the three men swimming behind him and the battle was joined.

MAJOR RASHID CLAMBERED out of the forward hatch and raced across the deck toward the sloping bow of the stealth sub. Reaching into his bag, he snatched a hand grenade, pulled the pin and threw the bomb as far out into the harbor as he could. Three seconds later, a muted crump and a geyser of water leaping into the air showed where it had detonated. He quickly armed another grenade and tossed it off to the other side of the *Petlyura*.

The underwater explosions would be as dangerous to the Serbian divers as they would be to the Americans, but he didn't care. The submarine had to be protected at all costs. If some of the Serbians died in the underwater battle, it would be their nation's contribution to the people's fight against Western imperialism.

BOLAN AND ENCIZO had spotted the enemy divers as well and were closing in on the sub when an explosion erupted in the water beside them. The detonation hit them with the force of a hydraulic hammer, smashing them into unconsciousness.

At first, James thought that Encizo's demolition charges had accidentally exploded. But when the water cleared, he saw that the men were in one piece, but hanging limp in the water with Serbian divers swarming around them. A second explosion a few yards off made him realize that someone was throwing hand grenades from the sub. That brought a new danger to the underwater fight. But even worse was that there was no way to get to Bolan and Encizo because the four remaining Stony Man warriors were fighting for their lives.

There were a dozen or more enemy frogmen in the water, and whoever was throwing the grenades was causing more damage to them than he was to the assault team. Nonetheless, they were badly outnumbered. But as James knew full well, even in underwater warfare, the best defense was a strong offense.

Swimming ahead of the others, he speared the Serbian point man and then lashed out with his diver's knife to slash the belly of his buddy. Stopping the two lead enemy swimmers didn't slow the rest of them, though. James soon had his hands full.

Even with the prosthesis, Katzenelenbogen was handling himself in the water like a real pro. This wasn't the first time he had fought as a frogman. Reloading the CO_2-powered spear gun gave some trouble, however, as he had to transfer it to his artificial arm to shove a new spear into the launching chamber.

He was holding his spear gun in his hook when a Serbian swam toward him, a spear gun at the ready. The Israeli jammed a spear into his weapon and twisted out of the way when the Serbian fired. The enemy's barbed point missed him by mere inches. Not bothering to transfer his gun back to his good hand, he just reached out and triggered it. The spear took his opponent in the belly, and the Serbian folded up like a gaffed fish.

When James found himself without an opponent, he looked around and saw that Solikov was handling himself rather well. At least he wasn't making the mistakes that most novice underwater fighters made. With his breathing gear and weight belt bringing him to neutral buoyancy in the water, it would have been all too easy for him to overreact. But he was timing his movements like a pro.

James swam up beside him and gave him a hand, then backed off to assess the situation. Even though the Stony Man team members were holding their own, there were simply too many of the Serbians. There was no way they were going to get close enough to place their charges on the sub or try to rescue Bolan and Encizo. Their only option was to back off for now and try it again later.

Reaching around to the air tanks on his back, James hammered on them with the butt of his diver's knife. Three sharp blows followed by a pause, then three more was the signal for them to retreat.

James remained where he was when the other three men disengaged and fled north as fast as they could. He would fight a rearguard action while they got a bit of a head start. He could swim faster than they could and would have no trouble catching up with them.

Even though he was alone, the Serbian divers were in no mood to give him any more trouble. Between their own people's grenades and the opposition's spear guns, they had had more than enough for one day.

When James glanced over his shoulder and saw that the other three men were disappearing into the dark water, he spun and took off after them. He wasn't pursued, and strong kicks of his powerful legs quickly closed the gap. Taking the lead again, he turned north.

CHAPTER TWENTY-SEVEN

Split Harbor

Calvin James was the first of the assault team survivors to surface at the end of the bay a few miles north of Split harbor. Rising only high enough to allow the top of his face mask to clear the water, he slowly scanned the rocky beach, the graveled road running along the shore and the wooded area on the other side of the road.

Seeing that they had the beach to themselves, he dropped his tanks, weight belt and fins before standing up. Retrieving the waterproof flashlight from his diver's belt, he stuck the lens underwater and signaled one long and two shorts to let the other swimmers know that it was safe for them to get out of the water.

James's legs were shaky when he walked up onto the beach. It had been a long time since he had swum that far and he was feeling it. And if he was that tired, the others would be exhausted.

Katzenelenbogen painfully pulled himself from the water and up onto the beach. James helped him strip off his diving gear and carried it back down to the surf for him. Their tanks and fins would probably be discovered sooner or later, but there was no point in making it too obvious where they had come ashore.

McCarter and Solikov surfaced together and helped each other shed their gear. As soon as it had all been carried back into the water, the four took cover on the other side of the road.

"Now what do we do?" James asked when the four were safely in the woods.

Katzenelenbogen's face was grim. With Bolan out of the picture for the moment, he was the team leader. He knew that he could call for Lyons to come in and pick them up and no one would fault him for the decision. He also had never abandoned a mission before, and he wasn't about to start now.

"The mission remains the same," the Israeli said. "We still have to kill the sub."

"How do you propose that we do that?" Solikov asked. "It looks to me like we're a little short on weaponry and demolition material right now."

"We still have our knives and there is no shortage of weapons in Serbia. All we have to do is take them from their present owners."

"Then what?"

"As long as the submarine's tied up to that dock," Katzenelenbogen said, "we can get at her one way or the other. As soon as we're outfitted, we'll go into town and recon that base."

"How do we go about getting Striker and Rafe back?" McCarter asked the main question on everyone's mind.

"We sink the sub," Katz said, "then we'll try to get them back."

No one mentioned the obvious fact that if their teammates were being held on the sub and they sank it, they would go to the bottom along with it.

The Israeli reached into the pocket sewn into the leg of his wet suit for the small satellite link radio. "First," he said, "I'd better let Barbara and Aaron know what has happened."

WHEN MACK BOLAN REGAINED consciousness, there were a dozen AK muzzles sticking in his face, ensuring that he would do exactly what his captors wanted him to. Though he was still reeling from the concussion of the grenade, he stood stock-still while his scuba gear was unbuckled and carried away. Rough hands searched him, stripping the knife from his leg sheath and making sure he didn't have anything else stowed on his body.

Another group of Serbian divers brought Encizo in a few moments later and stripped his gear from him, as well. He didn't look too much the worse for having been blasted into unconsciousness, but this was no time to compare notes. Some of their captors might understand English.

When both of the divers were completely clean, their guards motioned for them to stand against the bulkhead with their hands up over their heads. A minute later, a tall Arab dressed in a desert camouflage uniform walked into the compartment. When the guards stiffened to attention, Bolan knew that this had to be the honcho

"I am Major Omar Rashid of the Libyan People's Army, and you will be tried and convicted as enemies of Islam."

"I'm not an enemy of Islam," Bolan stated. "I'm only an enemy of terrorists."

"What you call terrorists," Rashid snapped, "I call soldiers of God in the holy struggle against the decadent West."

"Soldiers don't attack peaceful merchant ships as you have done," Bolan replied, "then kill their crews and steal their cargo."

"Soldiers do whatever is necessary to ensure victory for their cause." The Libyan shrugged. "Those cargoes were needed, so I captured them."

"In my book," the Executioner answered, "soldiers fight other soldiers, not civilians."

"There are no noncombatants in this war," Rashid said. "Anyone who is not fighting for the cause is an enemy and will be destroyed."

"Hasn't your leader learned that killing noncombatants only angers the Western governments and invites retaliation? If I remember correctly, the colonel has lost every time he has challenged the West directly."

"You have won some of the battles, American," Rashid admitted, "but even you must realize that you cannot win the war. This is the last century of Western domination over the struggling peoples of the rest of the world. The next century will be the century of a resurgent Islam and freedom for the millions living under the imperialism of the West.

"And," he said, leaning closer to Bolan, "it is fitting that you will be a witness to the beginning of the end for the West. In a few days, the outlaw state of Israel will cease to exist as will the cowardly Arabic nations that foolishly have made peace with the Zionists."

That threat confirmed that the sub still had the nuclear missiles in their launchers. And since they were on board, Bolan had to bide his time and see if an opportunity presented itself to take them out.

"What is wrong with wanting to find a peaceful solution in the Middle East?" Bolan asked. "Hasn't there been more than enough killing in the past fifty years?''

"There can never be peace," Rashid snorted, "as long as even a single Jew is polluting the land that a merciful God gave to his faithful."

"That sounds a lot like what the hard-line Zionists say about you Arabs."

"They can say anything they like, but everyone knows that they speak lies. Only you foolish Americans believe what they say, and that is because your country is secretly run by Jews, too. But in a few days, it won't matter what they say and it never will again."

The Libyan turned to go. "Keep them under close guard until we get under way again," he ordered in Arabic.

"As you command."

Encizo waited until Rashid disappeared down the passageway. "Now what do we do?" he asked.

"We wait," the Executioner answered.

"I'M SURPRISED that the President was willing to give us another twenty-four hours to try to get our people out," Price stated with undisguised sarcasm. "I thought that he considered this mission all important."

"Barbara," Brognola replied, "you know that the President values our men highly. Outside of this room, there is no one who knows more what the nation owes them than he does.''

"Which is why he sent them on this operation in the first place.''

"Katz is there,'' the big Fed said gently, "and you know he won't abandon them.''

"If they're still alive,'' she sharply reminded him.

Katzenelenbogen's curt message had said only that he thought Bolan and Encizo had been captured in the underwater fight. He didn't have proof that they had been alive when they were dragged out of the water. And since the others had been forced to flee, he had no idea where the captives were being held.

"I have alerted Lyons,'' Kurtzman broke in. "They're going to move in closer so they'll be ready when Katz calls for the extraction.''

"Do they have enough fuel to wait around that long?'' Price asked.

Kurtzman nodded. "Ironman says that they can stay on station about twelve hours—that's till tomorrow afternoon their time.''

"And the bombers go in right after that.''

"The President said that the strike is scheduled for midnight,'' Brognola confirmed. "I need to tell the President what our plans are.''

"Then let's get down to business,'' Price stated.

OBTAINING WEAPONS in a warring Serbia turned out to be as simple as Yakov Katzenelenbogen had predicted it would be. The first two came early that morning from a pair of Serbian infantrymen who wandered down the road with their AKMs slung over their shoulders. Even at that early hour, they had obviously been drinking while they shared a loaf of fresh bread and some sausages they carried in a string bag. They stopped stock-still when James walked out into the road in front of them.

A black man was the absolutely last thing they expected to see. In fact, neither of them had ever seen a black before except on television. Their amazement cost them their weapons and uniforms. As the Serbians gawked at James, McCarter and Solikov slipped up behind them and knocked them unconscious.

Along with their assault rifles and ammunition, the two Serbians provided boots and uniforms to wear in place of the wet suits. McCarter was able to fit into the smaller Serb's uniform while Katzenelenbogen put on the other one. It wasn't a good fit, but was a lot less obvious than a black diver's wet suit. Plus having boots made walking the rough paved road much easier.

After tying up the soldiers, McCarter picked up the fallen string bag, removed a sausage and bit into it. "Not bad," he said, holding out the remainder for anyone else who might be hungry after their long swim to shore and a cold night spent in the woods. "Anyone else for a spot of breakfast?"

Dividing up the food, the four ate on the march toward Split. McCarter and Katzenelenbogen took the point since they wore uniforms while Solikov and James hung back fifty yards or so.

A little more than an hour later in the hills overlooking the town, they came across a group of three Serbian troopers. Each was knocked unconscious, and they, too, were quickly stripped of their uniforms, boots and assault harnesses before being dragged out of sight in the woods.

Both James and Solikov found perfect fits in both uniforms and boots, and Katzenelenbogen traded his earlier uniform jacket for one that fit him a little better. After putting on his new uniform, he tore strips from one of the Serbians' shirts and wound the cloth around the part of his prosthesis sticking out of his sleeve so it would look as though he had a bandaged hand. There were lots of wounded in Serbia right now, so he wouldn't stand out.

"I don't speak Serbian," the Russian said as he buttoned up his borrowed Serbian uniform blouse and buckled the assault harness and ammo pouches over it. "But most of them speak at least a little

Russian. If we're stopped, I can tell them that we're a unit of foreign volunteers fighting for the new republic.''

"A black volunteer?" James raised the one issue that would stop short Solikov's planned masquerade. "Do you really think they're going to buy that one?"

"Do you speak Spanish?"

"A little."

"Good. That makes you a black Cuban freedom fighter, a mercenary. The Cubans are well-known as hired guns around here. Quite a few of them are fighting for both the Serbian and the Croatian armies. The Bosnians won't use them because they're not Muslims, or they'd be fighting there as well."

Solikov clapped the ex-SEAL on the shoulder. "You'll do fine, Calvin. Just remember to speak Spanish. I understand a little of it, and look to me for directions."

Looking over his impromptu command, Solikov slung his AK over his shoulder. "Shall we go, gentlemen?"

CHAPTER TWENTY-EIGHT

Split Harbor

When the Stony Man commandos reached the outskirts of Split, they started running into troops on almost every street corner. As James had predicted, many of the Serbians took note of his black skin, but no one did anything beyond watching the four of them walk pass. There were a few checkpoints where soldiers were checking identification papers, but they were able to bypass them on their way down to the seawall and the harbor.

For a town at war, the harbor was lively. The small shops and eateries were doing a brisk business, and Viktor Solikov led the four through the crowds without attracting much notice. The old Soviet naval base where the stealth submarine was supposed to be moored was at the south end of the harbor. Barbed-wire fences, checkpoints and pillboxes surrounded it. As they got closer, they saw that the farthest of the three concrete piers had a sub tied up alongside. And from the unusual shape of its sail and tail fin, it had to be their target.

"It doesn't look like we're going to get anywhere near that dock," James said. "It's too well guarded."

Katzenelenbogen was forced to agree. There were too few of them to fight their way through the perimeter around the base and then onto the dock. And even if they did, they didn't have anything they could use to destroy the sub. At the very least, they had to come up with an RPG antitank grenade launcher or enough explosives to make up a satchel charge before they tried anything like that. And, when they did, it would be a suicide run with no chance of survival.

But in a city as militarized as Split, there had to be something they could commandeer to use to destroy that sub. Katz had just started to look around when he found exactly what he was looking for. A Russian-made T-62 tank wearing a crudely painted Serbian flag and the number 39 on the turret was parked on the far end of what remained of the prewar seaside esplanade. The barrel of its 115 mm gun was aimed in the general direction of the harbor and the submarine tied up to the pier.

"I think I've found the solution to our problem, gentlemen."

James followed his glance. "You're kidding!"

Katz smiled a rare smile and shrugged. "Why not? Who says you can't sink a sub with a tank? If that gun can penetrate main battle tank armor, it can punch through a submarine's hull."

McCarter shifted the AK slung over his shoulder. "It beats the hell out of our other options. I say let's borrow that tank."

Though Solikov wasn't a real member of the team, and was a novice to ground warfare, he nodded his assent. If he survived this, he would have enough war stories to last him the rest of his life. And, if he got back to Mother Russia in one piece, he was never going to leave again.

Katzenelenbogen hitched his AK around so the pistol grip was by his good hand. "Let's do it."

TWO OF THE THREE-MAN CREW of the T-62 tank were standing outside watching the hydrofoil patrol boats zip around outside the harbor. Only the driver was inside the Russian machine as he tried to keep the balky diesel engine running. The injectors were so fouled from contaminated fuel and lack of proper maintenance that if he shut the engine off, he wouldn't be able to start it again until it cooled down completely.

The Serbian forces were well armed with Soviet-supplied leftovers from the old Yugoslavian army.

But they weren't well supplied with the technicians needed to keep their weapons working properly. The main problem that third world nations always had with using Russian-designed military equipment was that it was all throwaway stuff. The T-62's engine was designed to be replaced when something went wrong with it, not repaired. The Serbs were so short on spares that they were forced to use the engines long past their scheduled service life.

With the engine running there was no way that the tank crew could hear the Stony Man warriors approach. After making sure that there were no other Serbian soldiers in the vicinity, Katzenelenbogen found a place to cover the tank. McCarter and Solikov peeled off to take out the two men on the ground, and James went for the driver.

McCarter took his man out with a simple hand over the mouth, a knife thrust to the kidney and a savage twist of the broad blade. He held the struggling Serbian upright while the life drained out of him.

Solikov had never killed with a knife before and had a bit more trouble taking out his man. He had tried for a kidney shot as well, but missed. The Serbian jerked around, tearing the knife hilt out of the Russian's hand. Solikov backed up and was trying to bring his AK into target acquisition when McCarter stepped up behind the Serbian and finished the job.

James used his skin color again to make his kill. He walked around the side of the tank and climbed up onto the track skirts behind the driver. When he tapped the man on the shoulder, he turned around to see a black face staring at him. While the surprised man tried to react, James reached down and, placing his hands on each side of the driver's helmet, gave a savage twist combined with a jerk to the rear.

The driver's neck snapped with an audible pop, and he went limp. Grabbing his uniform epaulets, James dragged the man clear of the hatch.

"Get the bloody throttle!" McCarter yelled at James as he scrambled up over the sloped side of the turret. "The engine's dying!"

James dropped into the driver's hatch, his feet automatically going for the foot pedals. As he slammed down on the throttle, the tank engine belched a cloud of black smoke and coughed several times before smoothing out.

When he reached the top of the turret, McCarter dropped through the open loader's hatch and took a look around inside the crowded turret. It had been a long time since he had been in a tank, much less a Russian tank. Guns, however, were guns, even a 115 mm smoothbore tank gun. All he had to do was locate the sights, load a round, aim the thing and fire. Piece of cake.

Subs were armored against the crushing pressure of water at their diving depth, but they weren't armored against armor-piercing tank gun shells. A single antipersonnel round in the right place should put an end to the sub once and for all.

"You figured that thing out yet?" James yelled from the driver's position.

"Hold your water! I'm working on it."

"You'd better get your ass in gear, man. The sub's pulling away from the dock."

Tripping a lever caused the breech of the cannon to open. Reaching behind him, he grabbed the first round he found in the ready racks and manhandled it into the feed tray behind the breech. An automatic trip rammed the round into the breech and he swung the lever to slam the breechblock closed behind it.

"I've got it loaded!" he called out.

Sliding into the gunner's seat, McCarter located the traverse and elevation controls for the gun. Pressing his eyes to the optical sight, he saw that the sub was to the right and below the lay of the gun. Twisting the traverse handle to the right swung the gun over, and half a crank on the elevating wheel brought the muzzle up. When the juncture of the sub's sail and the outer pressure hull filled his gun sights, McCarter pressed the electric firing switch on the traverse grip.

The muzzle of the 115 mm gun belched flame, and the recoil rocked the tank back on its suspension. Through the sights, McCarter saw the round impact on target. He hadn't known what kind of round he had fed into the gun. But from the way it punched through the sub's sail without exploding, it had to have been a solid-shot armor-piercing warhead.

Sliding out of the gunner's seat, he reached around behind him and levered another bulky 115 mm round into the cannon's feed tray. As soon as the round was up, he went back to the gunner's seat and put his eyes back on the sight reticles. Bringing the aim back up to the same spot he had hit the first time, he triggered the main gun again.

This time, he had loaded an HE round. A gout of flame and dirty brown smoke told him that he had made a direct hit again. The sub rocked from the blast, but continued on her way toward the harbor mouth. Apparently hitting the sail wasn't doing enough damage to even slow her down.

This time, McCarter looked for the characteristically shaped head of another AP shot round. When he found one, he loaded it into the gun breech, got back to the gunner's controls and reached for the traverse and elevation controls again. When he aimed this time, he lowered his sights to the waterline before tripping the firing trigger.

Even eight hundred yards away, he heard the clang of the tungsten carbide AP round hitting the sub's titanium hull at several thousand feet per second. Through the fountain of water thrown up by the impact, he caught a glimpse of the jagged hole left by the round punching through the plate.

That should do it. The submarine would be going to the bottom for good now. "Let's get out of here," he yelled to James.

"I'm gone, man."

BOLAN AND ENCIZO HEARD the strike of the first tank gun shell hitting the hull. It sounded as if they were inside a giant bell. One of the Libyan guards clapped his hands to his ears and screamed in pain.

A thin smile crossed Bolan's face. The others were alive. "It sounds like our man Katz is at it again."

"But we're in here, too," Encizo reminded him. "If this thing sinks, we'll sink along with it."

"We won't be here for long."

When the second tank shell hit, the guard with the sensitive ears ran from the compartment. Shouting for him to come back, one of his comrades ran after him. When the two didn't immediately return, the four remaining guards looked at one another for a few seconds, then looked up at the curve of the steel cylinder they were inside.

It took guts for desert nomads to man a submarine at the best of times. The thought of all that water pressing against a thin titanium hull was totally alien to their way of thinking. So far, their greater fear of Rashid had overcome their fear of the water. But now that the hull was being bombarded, they were reminded of the circumstances they were in. As one man, they, too, spun around and raced down the passageway.

The third round hit an instant later. The concussive blast of heated air slammed into the compartment, and the two men automatically dropped to the deck plates. "We'd better get out of here," Encizo said. "I think this thing's going to sink."

Bolan noted the slight tilt to the deck that hadn't been there a moment before. "I think you're right."

The Cuban looked around their compartment. "Did you see where they took the rest of our tanks and gear?"

"There's no time for that. We'll swim for it if we can get out."

GUNFIRE from assault rifles suddenly sounded from the buildings closest to the Serbian tank. Rounds splashed off the armor, and James hunched farther in the driver's hatch. "Hurry up!" James shouted back into the turret behind him. "Get your ass out of there!"

"Bail out," McCarter replied. "I'll try to slow them down a little first."

Looking up through the open loader's hatch, he saw that the 12.7 mm antiaircraft machine gun on the top of the turret had an ammunition belt fed into the breech. Even though it was in an exposed position, the heavy gun would do more damage than the smaller 7.62 mm weapon that was mounted coaxially with the main gun.

AK rounds sang past his head as he scrambled up behind it and hauled back on the charging handle to ensure that a round was in the chamber. Taking aim at the Serbs running toward them, he pressed down on the trigger bar. The 12.7 mm weapon stuttered, and the heavy rounds cut through the charging Serbs like a scythe. The survivors ducked for cover anywhere they could find it. One of them tried to rush the tank, but McCarter depressed the muzzle of the 12.7 mm gun and cut him in two.

When a Serbian armored personnel carrier poked its nose around the corner of the building and leveled its 37 mm autocannon, McCarter was on it in a flash. The big gun couldn't penetrate the T-62's armor, but it could sure as hell keep him inside while the infantry took him out with a Molotov cocktail or a grenade down the hatch.

Dropping back down into the turret, the Briton slammed a shell into the breech of the main gun and took his place on the gunner's seat again. Swinging the turret over to the side, he lined up the sights on the armored vehicle and sent an HE round after it.

The 115 mm high-explosive package hit on the front slope armor and detonated with a flash. The force of the explosion ripped the 37 mm gun turret off and hurled it crashing into the side of the building. A second later, the fuel tanks went up, sending a boiling dirty black cloud up into the sky. Men screamed and tried to wipe the flaming fuel from their uniforms. For a moment all was chaos.

Now it was time for McCarter to get out.

Pulling himself up through the loader's hatch, the Briton slid down the rear slope of the turret, jumped off the track skirts and hit the ground running right after James. Scattered shots followed them, but they went wild.

"Over here!" Katz yelled from behind a low stone wall at the end of the esplanade. "Run for it!"

Under the cover of Katz and Solikov's blazing cover fire, McCarter and James dashed the twenty yards to safety.

CHAPTER TWENTY-NINE

Split Harbor

The ex-Russian prototype stealth submarine *Petlyura* was rapidly flooding. McCarter's last shot had holed her below the waterline, and she was doomed.

Major Rashid fought his way through the panicked crew crowding the escape hatches. Let those frightened children run for their lives if they wanted. He was going to personally kill the American and his companion before the swiftly rising water of the Adriatic did it for him. He didn't know exactly how, but he knew that the American was responsible for this disaster.

Mack Bolan and Rafael Encizo were still in their compartment, stripping their diving gear for weapons. Both of them had their diver's knives, but only one of their CO_2-powered spear guns had been recovered. Encizo was loading a spear into it when Rashid burst into the room, his 9 mm Makarov in his hand.

Catching the movement out of the corner of his eye, Encizo spun and fired the spear gun with one smooth movement. The barbed spear caught the Libyan officer in the throat and tore through his neck.

Rashid staggered back, the pistol falling to the deck. His hands clawed at his throat, vainly trying to stanch the flow of blood pouring from his neck.

"You!" he gurgled as he lunged for Bolan, his bloody hands outstretched.

The warrior sidestepped and let Rashid's body fall to the flooded deck plates. Reaching down, he scooped up the Makarov pistol and checked to make sure there was a round in the chamber. Peering around the watertight door to make sure that the Libyan had been alone, he saw that seawater was covering the deck plates in the passageway.

He motioned for Encizo to follow him. "Let's go."

BY NOW, the entire harbor front was alive with gunfire. Another Serbian tank had moved into position on the seawall and was firing at the hydrofoil patrol boats in the harbor. To their credit, the crews of the hydrofoils weren't shooting back. Instead, they were screaming over the radio while they raced for the safety of the open sea, out of range of the tank's gun.

Katzenelenbogen, Solikov, McCarter and James were making their way toward a small fishing jetty to the south of the naval base. Katz figured that they could keep a watch from there to see if two men in black wet suits made it out of the sinking submarine. It was also a safer place to bring Lyons's boat in for the pickup.

He vowed, though, that he wouldn't leave until he had seen every one of the submarine's survivors. He wasn't going to leave Bolan and Encizo behind this time.

THE LIBYANS STRUGGLING in the water paid no attention to Bolan and Encizo when they swam past. Being a desert people, most of them had never learned how to swim. Since the breach in the sub's hull was small, no debris had floated up from the wreckage for them to hold on to. Though it was only a little more than five hundred yards back to the dock, few of them would make it.

When Bolan and Encizo reached the end of the dock, they pulled themselves out of the water and climbed up the fender ropes. When they reached eye level with the top of the pier, they saw a mob of armed Serbians running down the dock toward them.

"Back into the water," Bolan said, putting Rashid's Makarov back inside his wet suit. "We need to swim out of this base area."

"Which way?"

There was a fishing jetty with small boats tied up to it three hundred yards or so to the south. "Let's try for that jetty."

"HERE'S WHERE YOU EARN your pay, Mario," Lyons said. "There is a fishing jetty south of the harbor. Do you know where it is?"

The Italian nodded.

"Our friends are waiting for pickup there."

The smuggler hastily crossed himself. "Maria!" he muttered.

Grabbing the throttle lever, he slammed it forward against the stop. The sleek cigarette boat almost jumped out of the water as the 500-horse V-12 engine howled its way up to its 10,000 rpm redline. In seconds, they were running at top speed, the wooden hull almost skipping from wave top to wave top.

Mario hunched behind the windscreen, ducking more from the bullets he was sure were coming his way than from the salt spray flung up by the pounding bow. He prayed to Saint Dismas and the Blessed Virgin as he whipped the boat's wheel from side to side every few seconds to make himself a more difficult target. He also cursed Emilio Zappa for ever getting him involved with these crazed Americans.

The Able Team warriors were holding on for the wild ride into the mouth of the harbor. "There they are," Lyons said as he pointed to the south.

Mario heeled the boat over and headed for the jetty. Now that the hydrofoils were out of range, the tank spotted the zigzagging cigarette boat and decided to send a couple of rounds in its direction. Columns of water leaped into the air with each round, but the boat was moving too fast for a tank gun to track.

BOLAN AND ENCIZO WERE a hundred yards from the jetty when they spotted the four men wearing Serbian uniforms standing on the end of the dock. "We've got to try it anyway, I'm too tired to swim much farther," Encizo said.

The Executioner stopped for a moment and trod water. "If you look closely, one of those Serbians is black and another one has a steel arm. I don't know how, but Katz has done it again. They're waiting for us."

"Son of a bitch," Encizo said as he struck out again for the jetty.

"Here they come." James nudged Katzenelenbogen, nodding but not wanting to point at the two black-clad swimmers in the water.

After spotting them, Katz turned back to watch the group of a dozen or so Serbians hanging around the other end of the dock. The shooting along the seawall had attracted every soldier in town, and this bunch had walked over to the jetty to get a better look at whatever was going on. Thinking that the four men on the end of the dock had a better view, they were coming to share it. Only about half of them were armed, but that was still too many.

Bolan and Encizo were only twenty yards away now, and their wet suits were sure to attract unwanted questions that no one would be able to answer, at least not in Serbian. James was in radio contact with the cigarette boat, but it was still ten long minutes away.

"Try to keep them back," James whispered to Solikov.

The Russian clicked the selector switch of his AK down to full-auto, slung the assault rifle over his right shoulder with the pistol grip close to hand and stepped forward to meet the Serbians. Katzenelenbogen and McCarter hung a few feet behind him on either side for backup if it got dirty.

To keep his face out of view, James went to meet Bolan and Encizo as they swam up to the end of the pier. Leaning over, he motioned for them to keep quiet and to stay under cover. The Executioner drew the Makarov from his wet suit and thumbed off the safety.

Just then, Mario's boat appeared around the end of the nearest navy pier. The smuggler was coming on fast, the V-12 engine screaming. At the last possible moment, Mario cut his throttle, and the engine's roar fell to a low burble. Cranking the wheel hard over, he sent the boat skidding to a halt against a fender hanging from the pier. The wave from the boat's wake rocked it as hands reached out to haul Bolan and Encizo on board.

After glancing behind him, Solikov said something to one of the Serbians, then raised his hand in farewell. Turning around, he calmly walked to the end of the pier and Mario's boat. Katz and McCarter matched their pace with his, but expected to feel shots in the back at any moment. Solikov stood aside and let the other two men board first, before waving one more time and stepping on board himself.

As soon as the Russian had both feet in the boat, Mario slammed the throttle forward and sharply cut the wheel to the side. The cigarette boat almost stood on her beam end as the high-speed prop churned the water. With all of the engine's five hundred horses bellowing, the boat fishtailed and streaked for the harbor mouth.

"What the hell did you tell them?" Katzenelenbogen asked Solikov as the jetty fell behind them.

The Russian grinned. "I told them that we were going after the Croatian traitors on the patrol boats who sank the submarine."

Katz just shook his head.

MARIO'S BOAT WAS CROWDED, but the men of Stony Man didn't mind. They were with close friends. The odd man out was the Russian.

Now that the mission was over, Viktor Solikov was quiet while the old friends congratulated one another and compared notes. The word from the States was that Gary Manning was already up and around, his leg healing nicely. Even better news was that the situation board at Stony Man Farm was clear for a change, and they would be able to rest up before they were called out again.

Solikov, however, would go back to Russia alone and try to do what he could to help his confused country make its way in the modern world. While he loved Mother Russia, he wished that there was some way that he could continue working with these men. He knew, however, that he would always be able to call upon the men of Stony Man Farm if he was ever in serious trouble. It was a good thing to know in today's uncertain world.

"You wouldn't happen to have a bit of a nosh around, would you, Gadgets?" McCarter asked. "We've been on short rations lately."

"There may be some bread and cheese left." Schwarz opened up Mario's picnic basket.

James reached past the Briton's hand and grabbed the half loaf of bread inside. "You snooze, you lose, partner," he said with a grin.

"But you missed the cheese, Cal," McCarter said, waving his prize. "You can't have a proper nosh without a bit of cheese."

Encizo spotted a leftover chicken leg and dived for it. "If you two are done trying to get the better of each other," he said, "I could use some bread to go with my chicken."

In the front of the boat, Bolan handed the radio back to Katzenelenbogen. "The *Puller* will meet us at the twenty-mile mark."

"And then home to the Farm?"

Bolan nodded. "For a while at least."

Both men knew that they wouldn't stay "home" for very long. This threat had been ended, true. The Russians would come in and recover the stolen missiles from the sunken sub, but there would always be the next threat and the next after that.

As long as there was a new threat on the horizon, they would never be able to stand down for long.

Gold Eagle presents a special three-book in-line continuity

Beginning in March 1995, Gold Eagle brings you another action-packed three-book in-line continuity, THE ARMS TRILOGY.

In THE ARMS TRILOGY, the men of Stony Man Farm target Hayden Thone, powerful head of an illicit weapons empire. Thone, CEO of Fortress Arms, is orchestrating illegal arms deals and secretly directing the worldwide activities of terrorist groups for his own purposes.

Be sure to catch all the action featuring the ever-popular THE EXECUTIONER starting in March, continuing through to May.

Available at your favorite retail outlet, or order your copy now:

Book I:	March	SELECT FIRE	$3.50 U.S. ☐
		(The Executioner #195)	$3.99 CAN. ☐
Book II:	April	TRIBURST	$3.50 U.S. ☐
		(The Executioner #196)	$3.99 CAN. ☐
Book III:	May	ARMED FORCE	$3.50 U.S. ☐
		(The Executioner #197)	$3.99 CAN. ☐

Total amount $_____
Plus 75¢ postage ($1.00 in Canada) $_____
Canadian residents add applicable
federal and provincial taxes
Total payable $_____

To order, please send this form, along with your name, address, zip or postal code, and a check or money order for the total above, payable to Gold Eagle Books, to:

In the U.S.
Gold Eagle Books
3010 Walden Avenue
P. O. Box 9077
Buffalo, NY 14269-9077

In Canada
Gold Eagle Books
P. O. Box 636
Fort Erie, Ontario
L2A 5X3

AT95-2

**Bolan draws fire from
ruthless warlords**

**Adventure and suspense in the
midst of the new reality**

JAMES AXLER

Shadowfall

The nuclear conflagration that had nearly consumed the world
generations ago stripped away most of its bounty. Amid the ruins
of the Sunshine State, Ryan Cawdor comes to an agonizing
crossroads, torn by a debt to the past and loyalty to the present.

Hope died in the Deathlands, but the will to live goes on.

Remo and Chiun come face-to-face with the
most deadly challenge of their career

THE Destroyer

Last Rites
Created by
WARREN MURPHY
and RICHARD SAPIR

The Sinanju Rite of Attainment sounds like a back-to-school
nightmare for Remo Williams. But as the disciple of the last
Korean Master, he can't exactly play hooky. Join Remo in
LAST RITES as Remo's warrior skills are tested to the limit!

Don't miss the 100th edition of one of the biggest and
longest-running action adventure series!

SURE TO BECOME A COLLECTOR'S ITEM!

Look for it in August, wherever Gold Eagle books are sold.